THE
J. ALFRED PRUFROCK
MURDERS

THE
J. ALFRED PRUFROCK
MURDERS

BY

CORINNE HOLT SAWYER

DONALD I. FINE, INC.
New York

Manufactured in the United States of America
10 9 8 7 6 5 4 3

Library of Congress Cataloging-in-Publication Data

Sawyer, Corinne Holt.
The J. Alfred Prufrock murders.

I. Title.

PS3569.A864J2   1988   813'.54   87-46265
ISBN 1-55611-081-2

To two wonderful women:
my mother, Grace Ueland Holt
and
my sister, Madeline Holt Campillo

"I grow old . . . I grow old . . .
I shall wear the bottoms of my trousers rolled.
Shall I part my hair behind? Do I dare to eat a peach?
I shall wear white flannel trousers, and walk upon the beach . . ."

"The Love Song of J. Alfred Prufrock"
by T. S. Eliot

T HE SEA spray met the mist, mating with it in a gray haze
that made the early morning air heavy and wet against the
skin. The call of sea birds was lonely and far away as they
wheeled over the shallows looking, bright-eyed, for a breakfast of
minnows or small shellfish.

If you stood at the top of the bluff facing outward toward the
sea, you could imagine you were alone, far from civilization. But
there is hardly a spot left in all of Southern California where such
aloneness is possible. Off to the right sat the Sunny Daze Motel—
squat and brown and looking like a design that Frank Lloyd
Wright had discarded. To the left a straggling line of meanly
crowded little rental cottages stretched to the estuary, where more
sea birds wheeled and called out. If you turned and faced behind
you, you saw a garden bright with flowers—tiny specks of random
color, like confetti scattered among the shrubs—with a line of
small bungalows on either side leading up to a huge, two-story
stucco building with a red-tiled roof.

If you looked back down the hill again, toward the sea, casting
your gaze past the brick pillars that held a wrought-iron gate with
a hand-lettered sign that said PRIVATE, STAY OUT, THIS MEANS YOU!,

you saw the most significant thing about the view on that October day.

A body lay crumpled at the foot of the steps that led down to the sea, passing through the swollen-looking leaves of ice plant that covered the hillside and serving to hold back the sandy soil so it might not slide down to join the sand of the beach. The steps were old railway ties worn slick—and they were slippery with sea spray. A passerby might suppose that the person who now lay face down near the last step had been hurrying for an early dip, or a run on a beach made firm by retreating tide, but had slipped and would immediately sit up, cursing, and brush the loose sand off the dark garment. But of course that could never happen. Never again for that one.

CHAPTER 1

TO EVERYONE who met her for the first time, Mrs. Angela Benbow, the admiral's widow, was adorable—and she knew it. Absolutely barrel-shaped, barely five feet tall in her support hose, with a wealth of carefully waved, snow-white hair generally worn in a gigantic chignon, and with no more wrinkles than most old ladies of seventy-eight have, Mrs. Benbow had been told all her life that she was as cute as a button—a little doll—and her own picture of herself as being pretty, clever, amusingly outspoken, and in all ways superior, was firmly set by the time she was ten. It never changed.

The silvering of her red-gold hair, the gradual thickening and final disappearance of her waist line, the addition of glasses, the appearance of liver spots on the backs of her dainty hands, and the deepening of her silvery, little-girl voice—all of these had no effect whatsoever on Mrs. Benbow's self image.

Her husband completed the process that her mother and father had started—spoiling her rotten. For instance, the admiral had merely laughed indulgently when she insulted the wives of other high-ranking officers in her tart-sweet little voice, giving two-edged compliments or asking the sort of probing questions that opened wounds. The admiral would not have tolerated rudeness to a subordinate, but he had the instincts of a hunter when it

3

came to fair game, and he genuinely thought it amusing and thoroughly charming of her to speak her mind about any and everything. "Feisty little dickens," he would say of her, indulgently.

The things she said were, in fact, not meant maliciously. She only meant to tell the truth (as she saw it)—and sometimes to have a little fun. The disastrous outcome that often resulted was quite beyond her ability to foresee. She moved through life as blissfully unconscious of the havoc she wrought in others as is a hurricane: it certainly doesn't mean to do you harm, and it never knows the difference when it uproots your trees and smashes them through your roof.

"Why do you always wear that funny-looking wig?" she had asked Madame Rochaud, the French ambassador's wife, who was dressed in her magnificent best for a Washington embassy reception. Madame Rochaud, who had never worn a wig, was devastated, and the ambassador's life was made miserable for the next week while his increasingly irritable wife searched the city for a superior hairdresser.

The ambassador got short-tempered himself and, blowing up over some minor error in punctuation in a report on American grain production, bit off the head of an undersecretary. The undersecretary was a sensitive young man with a first cousin who was not only a sympathetic listener on the long distance phone— he was also an aide to the then-President of France. Some six weeks later the ambassador was brought home to take a perma- nent desk position on the Paris Sewer Commission. Mrs. Benbow liked the new ambassador and his wife very much.

Mrs. Benbow had reduced Dr. Hyman Trudger, a prominent theoretical mathematician, to gibbering frustration. Their conver- sation took place one snowy evening during a small wine-and- cheese gathering at the home of an American University professor of English. Mrs. Benbow wasn't trying to be difficult—she was just bored; this was not her idea of a pleasant evening but the admiral had insisted, for the sake of the host, who had once served on the admiral's staff.

So Mrs. Benbow smiled sweetly at Dr. Trudger and asked him, "Why on earth do you mathematics people always teach square roots to children? What do you suppose they're going to use them for? I have racked my brain and I cannot think of a single time when the ability to calculate a square root was of use to me."

In his still-heavy Viennese accent, Dr. Trudger tried to discuss mathematics on a high plane: the kind of calculations that could send a man into space, the kind that could determine that energy equaled MC-squared. "There you are, Mrs. Benbow. There is the use of a square," Dr. Trudger said brightly.

"But what about the use of a square *root*," Angela persisted.

"Well," he said, "let us suppose that you wish to find the dimensions of a right triangle. Any schoolboy knows that the square of the hypotenuse is equal to the sum of—"

"But not the square *root*," she said, still smiling sweetly. "That really is quite beside the point."

"Well then, let us suppose"—Trudger mopped his brow—"that you wish to calculate the length of a wall in a perfectly square room. And suppose that you already know the square footage—"

"How silly. I'd get out a yardstick, of course, and simply measure it. I certainly wouldn't fool around doing square roots with a pencil and paper."

It was at that moment that Dr. Trudger correctly concluded that he was being baited. He choked slightly, jumped to his feet, bowed choppily to Mrs. Benbow and the other guests, and blundered out of the room. So preoccupied was he with controlling his emotions that he did not see the film of ice that had formed over the professor's front steps—five narrow steps leading down to the sidewalk. As he descended the steps, far too fast for caution, his feet suddenly kicked off in opposite directions. He performed a graceful pirouette, grasped futilely at the equally icy iron railing, slid bumpily down to the public walk using his own knees as a sled, and consequently broke one leg in three places. Mrs. Benbow remarked later that it was a pity a man otherwise so intelligent should be so incredibly careless.

Angela Benbow was also the terror of every chef in the nation's capital, because she herself was a superb cook and her standards were as rigid for others as they were for herself. "What's the point of eating out at all," she would say, nodding sweetly to her husband, who simply smiled indulgently back at her, "if it isn't at least as good as eating at home?"

She regularly returned her plate to the chef, saying such things as, "If you must use paprika, it should at least be *fresh*. Now this dreadful brown stuff you've sprinkled around this plate suggests to me the rest of the dinner will surely be off, as well. Take this back to the kitchen, if you please, and bring me something more suitable."

On more than one occasion, a usually obsequious headwaiter had used his hands to make shushing motions toward Mrs. Benbow while looking nervously over his shoulder at the other diners. Mrs. Benbow, of course, never shushed.

As we grow older, our characteristics exaggerate themselves. A beak-nosed man begins to look like a bald eagle. A man with heavy brows takes on the menacing look of a John L. Lewis. A heavy-bosomed woman turns into one of those caricatures of an opera singer in which a pouter pigeon is sketched standing by a piano in an evening gown.

And our mental and spiritual characteristics grow and set themselves in cement as well. The willowy blonde's appealing languor as a twenty-year-old beauty turns to the lazy shiftlessness of the fifty-ish slattern. The little boy who plays with his food becomes the table-dawdler whose dinner congeals while he delays. The curious child becomes the aging busybody, the bully becomes the wife-beater, the flirt becomes the adulterer.

In fact, it takes great strength of character to avoid becoming, as one ages, a one-dimensional caricature of one's youthful self.

Mrs. Benbow was no exception to that rule. She certainly had the strength of character to avoid it, but because of the admiral's habitual tolerance of her self-indulgence and self-delusion, she did not see herself becoming sometimes objectionable, often wickedly malicious. Until the day he suffered his massive and quickly fatal heart attack, Douglas Benbow had assured her she was lovely, quick-witted, amusing and wonderfully honest—and she chose to believe him.

When the admiral went to his final rest in Arlington, Mrs. Benbow tried to stay on alone in their splendid Georgetown house. But she discovered a sad truth most aging widows discover, and that in Mrs. Benbow's case was an inevitability: the friends her husband had made in his work were not her friends; they were merely nodding acquaintances. And the friends she and her husband had made together sought other couples, behaving as if she like the widow of some ancient Indian rajah, had thrown herself living onto her husband's funeral pyre. "They knew what they were doing, those Indian women," she thought, in a wave of self pity.

For a time the woman who had been Mrs. Douglas Benbow and who was now Mrs. Angela Benbow moped her way around the house, calling old friends to join her for cocktails, redecorating the study, spending hours shopping for the tiny antique boxes she loved and with which she had already filled a display case in her parlor, and—occasionally—tagging along with some kindly couple to a concert or a play. . . . But people seldom called her. She usually did the calling, which she hated—so most of her time she spent alone, a state she had not learned to enjoy.

She concluded at last that it was Washington: Washington was a cold town, Washington didn't care if your heart was broken, Washington was a "couples town."

She packed up and moved to Southern California, where she and the admiral had lived for several happy years while he was assigned to the Pacific fleet.

After a couple of rather lonely, uninteresting years in a high-priced apartment in San Diego, Mrs. Benbow concluded that California was a young person's paradise—surfing, sunbathing, beach volley ball, open-air rock concerts—but not really suited to a mature person like herself. There was literally nothing for her to do. She knew a few people, but she had made no real friends, and the antique shopping was dreadful. Things they called "antiques" out in Southern California generally dated from no earlier than the 1920s, or else they were heavy "pioneer primitives": rusted plows and rakes, worn wagon wheels, crusted black iron skillets and old handcuffs. Not the sort of thing she cared about at all. She used up a month's worth of disdainful sniffs each time she pursued what had once been her favorite hobby.

And then luck took a hand. She met Mrs. Wingate, also the widow of an admiral and an extremely impressive woman, even to Mrs. Benbow.

Mrs. Wingate lived about twenty miles up the coast in a converted hotel that had been turned into a retirement center—a gracious, Spanish-style building with a red-tiled roof, a charming rose garden and a tiny stretch of beach all its own.

"Camden-sur-Mer" was once the showplace of the tiny town of Camden. In the days of movie stars and open roadsters, it had been a favorite watering hole of Doug Fairbanks and Charlie Chaplin and Gloria Swanson, as they motored to or from Mexico and the bull fights. When Del Mar Race Track opened, another generation of movie stars adopted the aging, cream stucco castle on the coast. . . . Tyrone Power stopped by for a drink at the circular bar, Joan Crawford danced to a small orchestra there on New Year's Eve, and Nelson Eddy once held an impromptu concert at the giant grand piano which stood among the potted palms in the cool, marble-floored lobby.

But the glory days passed. World War II curtailed automobile travel: government bulletins urged people to drive as little as possible, and with a few exceptions, Californians cooperated. Then after the war, things were never the same; the habit of stopping in Camden had been broken, and when the rich and famous motored down the coast highway from L.A., they drove straight through. The hotel struggled, but the completion of the freeway was its death knell, and it closed its doors forever—as a hotel.

Paint peeled and stucco eroded; beach sand blew into broken windows; derelicts sometimes eluded the watchmen and camped out, leaving behind their ragged mementos—a torn newspaper, a tattered shoe without a mate, empty cans that once held baked beans.

Then after ten decaying years, an Eastern businessman surprised the real estate company that held the hotel's title by negotiating a good price for the building. The efficient Easterner represented a dogfood company that had diversified; they owned a steel plant in Alabama, a kaolin operation in Georgia, pulpwood forests in Washington and Idaho, two cosmetics manufacturing plants near Chicago, a national chain of fried fish restaurants, a paper bag factory in Wichita, a mobile diaper service in Toledo, and they wanted the hotel to join their seven other "old folks' homes" in Southern California.

The company was reputed to be a money laundering operation for the Mafia, and that may have been the truth. But whatever the truth about its parentage, the company had a policy of hiring excellent managers, who in turn hired superior staff, and everything the company owned met with success. If its owners were really Mafia, they could afford to go straight, so lucrative were these legitimate enterprises.

So it was with an air of optimism that the process of renovation began on the old building to make it suitable for people who were even more elderly, but for whom no renovation was possible.

The hotel's rooms were pleasantly large, but each had a barely adequate little bathroom and a tiny closet suitable only for transients. As a first step, the closets were enlarged, because the elderly treasure the mementos of their pasts, and storage space becomes a prime consideration for them, a fact almost no retirement home builders seem to realize.

Next, bathrooms were modernized with infrared heating lamps set into lowered ceilings, and large storage cabinets built around the little sinks—not only to hide the bare plumbing, but to accommodate odds and ends the elderly use that the young do not: hot water bottles, enema bags, containers of epsom salts, foot baths with built-in electric massagers, heating pads, trusses, spare arch supports and denture cups. Each tub got a sit-down stool inside it, chrome-plated "crash bars" on each adjacent wall, and "telephone style" hand-held shower units. Heated towel racks were installed as well.

Doorways were enlarged to accommodate walkers, and one wing of the U-shaped building was set aside for those whose legs would no longer support them: because what was once servants' quarters already had wide halls and doorways suitable for delivering boxes and crates, it became the wheelchair-bound residents' section. The old bar room became a theatre and/or chapel. The old flower and gift shop became a nurses' office, and a new sundries shop with a tiny soda fountain was carved out of the old bellboys' station and luggage closet.

Each room was freshly painted a neutral cream color, and as residents moved in, they chose carpeting and drapes from a set of samples furnished by the office—so they were able to blend the decor with whatever furniture they brought with them. In short— a cozy and acceptable, though tiny, apartment was created in each room—except that there were no cooking facilities, old people not being entirely trustworthy when it came to turning off electricity or (God forbid) a gas flame. The residents ate their meals together in the old hotel dining room; the portions were tiny, designed by the dietician to satisfy the reduced caloric demand of the elderly, but the food was surprisingly good.

Camden-sur-Mer charged a high entrance fee and stiff monthly rental costs—it was not meant for the indigent. But during its first month of existence, it took in the penniless and ailing mother and father of a middle-aged Swiss woman, herself a widow. In return for a drastically reduced rent for her parents, this Mrs. Schmitt signed a long-term contract as Camden's cook. Her mother was still alive and happy there, though bedridden and resident in the little "health care facility" (Camden's euphemism for its own nursing home), and Mrs. Schmitt still ran the kitchen with her inspired hands.

She in turn hired an alcoholic baker who loved his work, but who was looking for an easy job that would pay for vodka-blurred weekends; since he got Saturday and Sunday off and a free room in the basement, he took the job and stayed.

When the main building was filled up, which happened within the first six months, the management built additional facilities—a line of one-story apartment buildings, each containing four or five units, extending from each of the ends of the original U-shaped building, down the edges of the garden toward the sea. The cottages, as the residents called them, were very popular with couples who came in, because most units had two rooms and a tiny kitchen. Of course they were much more expensive than the apartments in the main building, the majority of which had only one room and none of which had a kitchenette.

In time the retirement center sold off its beachfront property to help pay for improvements to the building, retaining only a narrow one hundred fifty-foot strip of beach as its own—exactly as wide as the hotel gardens. The residents didn't mind as much as younger people might have; after all, only a few still went swimming or gathered shells—or even went down the steep steps to the beach at all. Most of those who still took daily walks were well pleased with the easier footing of the town's streets, as long as there were no hills to climb.

With her concern for meticulous service, her demanding attitude about food, her sense of complete superiority to everyone else, and her image of herself as young and clever and lovely, unchanged by the years, Mrs. Benbow was the last person in the world you might imagine would become a resident at Camden. But she met Mrs. Wingate, and one of Mrs. Benbow's other characteristics temporarily took command: her snobbery.

Caledonia Wingate was as large and physically overwhelming as Mrs. Benbow was tiny; she too was the widow of an admiral, so that her social station was equal to that of Mrs. Benbow's, and she was wonderfully wealthy. It showed in the elegant silk brocades she wore to clothe her enormous body—vaguely Arabian garments that used enough material to cover a king-size bed twice over. It showed in the rope of exquisite, very large, very real pearls she wore so carelessly—and so habitually. It showed in the diamonds that winked on four of her ten fingers and in both her pierced ear lobes. And it showed in the chauffeured limousine in which she appeared at several important social functions in San Diego.

"I'm at the Loma Lita Apartments," Angela told Caledonia Wingate. "I can't say I think much of them—and the neighbors . . . Nobody I have any interest in, you know?" Angela shrugged her little shoulders till they almost touched her snowy chignon. "Do you live here in San Diego?"

"No," Caledonia said. "I've taken a cottage at Camden-sur-Mer."

"An apartment?"

"Ah, well, not exactly. That is, there's an apartment building and these individual cottages, each with little apartments like the one I have. It's a retirement center. You know—designed for old biddies like you and me."

Angela was about to rebut but restrained herself. "Oh, really," she managed to say with a smile. "Old?"

"Well," said Caledonia, "what on earth would you call sixty-five years and seventy years? At least, I assume you're about sixty-five. Right? And I know I'm seventy."

Angela, who was in fact seventy herself, kept the sweet smile on her face and said, "I really don't think of myself as old, you know."

Caledonia smiled. "Well, of course not, dear. If you did, you'd be in a rocker knitting for your grandchildren. I don't *think* old, myself, In fact, I don't think of age at all, if I can help it. What on earth does it matter, anyhow? Listen, there's an opening at Camden at the moment. Poor old Clarice popped off last week. Heart. Gets us all, if something else doesn't first. If you're not happy where you are, think about it. I belong to a nice bridge group you could join . . . Good at needlework?"

"I don't really think . . ."

"What do you do? Do you sew?" Caledonia gestured toward Angela's chic suit. "Make your own clothes?"

Angela choked a little, thinking of the three hundred fifty dollars she had laid out for this charcoal shantung, not just because of the designer's name, but because it very nearly gave her a waistline again. "Well, I do sew extremely well," she managed.

"Good," said Mrs. Wingate. "Good for you. There's a quilting group—and one that does baby clothes for the orphanage in town." Angela closed her eyes. "Then there's the one I like the best, the ladies who sew for the bazaar. We each do some sort of craft thing—quilts, dolls, aprons, bun-warmers, fancy note card designs . . . Not much pottery or stained glass—nobody has room. But we sell 'em once or twice a year and buy things for our facility with the proceeds.

"Like—oh, we bought some fancy wheelchairs for the nursing home section one time. Another time we refurbished the spa at the old place . . . and made it useable again. You know what I mean by 'spa'? Like a hot tub with crash bars? It's wonderful when your joints are aching to sit and let that warm water massage you . . . Listen, you'd love it. A safe, sheltered place to live—good food—built-in friends—something to do all day, every day, if you like . . . Of course most of us there are women. Men don't seem durable enough to last past the seventies, for the most part."

"Yes. Well, we'll see," Angela said, as coolly as she could without sounding rude. This was one woman worth cultivating, despite her strange enthusiasm for the sewing circle and that wretched institution she lived in.

The following week there was a mugging down the block from Angela's apartment, a shooting about a half mile down the street, and a robbery on the third floor of her building.

When Angela Benbow moved into Camden-sur-Mer, she was invited to join a number of the bridge groups and sewing circles the other retirees had established for their own amusement through their declining days—as the active life grew less active, the husbands died away, and the light dimmed slowly in the approaching sunset.

She was a favorite bridge partner, at first, because she played extremely well, in contrast to a number of the other residents who were getting forgetful—unable to remember to count trump, constantly asking who took the last trick. She was invited to someone's apartment to play bridge almost every afternoon in the week, at first. But she soon made it clear that she wasn't interested in partnering anyone who wasn't a really good player; for that matter, she could barely tolerate weak players even as opponents, laughing aloud in real delight when they would make a clumsy lead or fail to bid to slam. If she was a sore loser, she was an even nastier winner; she pouted when she lost, gloated when she won, and always played the teacher, pointing out mistakes with exaggerated (and entirely phony) patience.

In time she was asked to fill in only when a substitute was needed—and not even then if anyone else was available. Eventually, she made it a point to ask each new resident to join her for an afternoon of bridge, and from these newcomers she selected the best for her own group. But eventually either she tired of them or they of her, and that group too would dwindle away. She would start another group, and then another, and each in time would also founder on the rough rocks of her inflexibility.

At first she had also been everybody's choice as a sewing companion, because she was so clever with a needle and a stray piece of cloth. She was invited to every quilting bee, every "sewing morning."

"Why, that would make a darling breakfast tablecloth," she'd say, holding up an off-shape piece of bright cotton. "All you'd need would be a ruffled edging to bring it up to cardtable size and pick up the colors . . . Look, does anybody have some yellow print cotton? Here we are . . . Now, let me try." And within an hour— there was a frilly breakfast cloth.

Of course after that she lost interest—someone else could make the matching napkins; someone else could find the right sized box; someone else could store it away till the bazaar, carry it to the sale table, price it, sell it, put the proceeds into a TV for the nurses in the infirmary section, or into a whirlpool bath for the arthritis patients. She had done all she was going to do.

And when someone brought her a piece of their work . . .

"How do you like this sofa cushion?" Mrs. Armstrong had bubbled. A dear little fuzzy-headed woman, Tootsie Armstrong, but her eyes were no longer very good. The little pillow she had held out was an ugly, Early American primitive, with unbleached muslin and figured cotton stitched clumsily together in an ill-cut "double wedding ring" pattern.

"That's awful," Angela had said sweetly. "I don't even think we can fix that up by redoing it. And it won't sell. Why not just throw that away, dear, and let us do the dainty work?"

Mrs. Armstrong had looked stunned. "B-b-b-but . . . I only . . . I mean, I thought it was nice."

"Well, don't feel left out, Tootsie," Angela had said, noticing her dismay. "You can do something useful. Why not clean up the sewing room when we're done today?"

In time, they decided to forego Angela's presence at the sewing circles.

It was remarkable that through this all, Caledonia Wingate

continued to tolerate Angela, to include her in all activities and plans, to invite her to stop by the cottage for tea. Perhaps the spirit of the late Admiral Benbow had whispered in her large ear. For whatever reason, to the amusement and sometimes to the exasperation of her other friends, Caledonia continued to treat Angela as one of her circle.

Angela could count only two others as genuine friends. The first was a chubby, cheerful woman with a dimpled smile and an incredibly ample bosom, who simply paid no attention when Angela was unpleasant, who scolded her when she bullied another resident, who enjoyed Angela's *bon mots,* who teased her unmercifully, and who to the amazement of the other residents, appeared to like Angela. This was Nancy (nobody ever called her anything but "Nan") Church, who was also a particular favorite of Caledonia's.

The second was Stella Austin—as fine-boned as Caledonia was solid, as slim as Nan was chubby. With her automatic snobbery, Angela had taken note of Stella's genteel manners and New York chic the first time she saw her. Others might laugh at Stella's stylish "dress for success" suits and silk blouses; Angela found them delightful, California fashions being, to her mind, suitable only for picnics and camping trips. When Stella's hands were not forced to lie at rest in her lap, they were usually occupied with knitting, "In my family, that was considered a lady's occupation," she confided to Angela. Her knit-purl-knit-purl marked time in the conversation of others, while she silently listened, and behind her back the other residents called her "Madam de Hush" (for Madam Defarge, who knit and counted her stitches by the falling heads of aristocrats in the French Revolution).

Caledonia called Stella "Beanie"—insisting that Stella came from true Boston blue bloods, despite Stella's good-natured reminders that her family was from New York State. "Doesn't matter," Caledonia would say. "They outdo the Cabots and Lodges for baked-bean, lace-curtain, uppity snootiness. If they aren't from Boston they should have been. Isn't that so, Angela?" Stella would let her amusement crinkle the corners of her mouth, but she would never object. And that was part of what Angela enjoyed about Stella—that eternally calm demeanor (which allowed Angela to stage all the fireworks) and habitual silence (which allowed Angela free rein of tongue and wit). Good listeners are hard to come by, among the elderly.

So together these four—the gigantic Caledonia, big in every dimension and with a booming voice and hearty laugh to match her size; the rotund, jiggly, giggly, good-humored Nan; the silent, slim, gently smiling Stella; and the diminutive, sharp-tongued Angela—made a constant group.

Life and energy are like magnets. In spite of themselves, other residents found they were drawn to the four, though as Tootsie Armstrong once whispered to a friend, it didn't pay to turn your back on Angela.

CHAPTER 2

I F IT had been Angela Benbow lying dead at the foot of Camden's walk to the beach, everybody would have assumed that she had been murdered, and they would not have been in the least surprised. If Angela had been found smeared with honey and staked for the ants, only a few of her acquaintances would have expressed shock. But the body was that of Sweetie Gilfillan, one of the quietest and—one would have said—least offensive of all Camden-sur-Mer's residents.

The other residents naturally assumed that Sweetie had slipped on the stairs and been killed by the fall, though as Paulette Piper pointed out to a group of residents after breakfast, it seemed odd that Sweetie would have gone down to the beach because she hated the sand, especially hated getting it in her shoes. The group had just heard of Sweetie's death from Kathy, one of the youngest and newest waitresses, still green enough about retirement center work to be horrified by the death of someone she knew.

"Well, she's got sand all over her, now," Mr. Grogan said, pushing his way through the group of women that had formed by the dining room exit. "Damned silly old cows," he added audibly, a remark so typical of the irascible Mr. G. that none of the women even turned her head.

After further discussion the ladies did agree that Sweetie was just the type to fall accidentally. It wasn't that she was feeble, or even particularly clumsy—but her eyesight was not the best, and her mind was generally occupied with something other than her immediate surroundings, usually the book she inevitably carried and read as she walked along. If there was a gardener's rake left lying on the path, even though most of the residents could step over it or walk around it, Sweetie tripped over it. If there was a tiny rip in the hall carpeting, Sweetie's toe found it, caught in it, and stayed behind as her body moved on, propelling her to the floor.

Sweetie, an ex-librarian from Duluth, was constantly reading—books, magazines, newspapers, and letters, which she excerpted aloud to whomever was near her—and the habit didn't help her at all to keep her footing or to avoid bumping into things. Only last week at lunch, when the little silver chimes were rung to summon the residents to the dining room, Sweetie had been engrossed in a book on popular science. "Oh, listen to this, Mrs. Grant," she'd said, grabbing the arm of a pleasant-looking resident passing by. "It's possible that within this century man and the dolphins will be able to talk to each other. Isn't that just the most exciting thing?" Emma Grant, deaf as a post, nodded amiably, as she did to everything said in her general direction.

Sweetie, reading on about the dolphins, walked straight into the closed half of the dining room's double doors.

In the placid atmosphere of the retirement residence, conversation was usually confined to three topics: what the next day's menu would be; the state of one's own digestive processes, in endless and nauseating detail; and/or the other residents' comings and goings—except in death. Ordinarily, death was not discussed at any great length, certainly not much more than to say "Did you hear—" and "What a shame about—" Among people who were all old, death was neither an oddity nor a surprise, only an often-postponed visitor who at last could be put off no longer. Sometimes to the old, death was even a welcome friend.

When a young person dies, his acquaintances can think of little else for days, even for weeks; when the old die, there is a sense of fitness overlaying the sadness. Heart attack, stroke, and cancer were not really worth much comment at Camden. But Sweetie's passing was a little different—an accident, it seemed, and certainly unusual—and therefore worthy of comment.

"Well, if she'd watched where she was going, this wouldn't have happened," Angela Benbow said. "It's a wonder those joggers found her. She might have lain there for hours." She shivered as she stirred her coffee. "May I have more cream, Nan?"

Nan Church ignored the request. "I don't see how it would have mattered to Sweetie if she had lain there for hours," she said. "The dead can't get impatient, you know."

"But all that sand—and getting all wet . . . You used to go down there to swim, once in a while. I don't suppose you would mind the sand at all. But I would hate it." Angela shook her head slightly and reached out her hand. "Did you hear me, Nan? I want the cream, please."

"Bad for you," Nan said. "At your weight you should be taking only skimmed milk."

Stella Austin reached forward with her own slim, long-fingered hand, in the process displaying a diamond-studded watchband and sapphire-covered fingers, "Oh, Nan," she said softly, "let Angela be." She smiled and handed Angela the cream, then wrapped herself again in silence.

Caledonia Wingate was not prepared to let the matter lie. "Nan, that's the pot calling the kettle black. With your heart condition, you should watch what you eat more carefully. And at your size . . ."

Nan took another blueberry muffin and layered on the butter. "I wear a size twelve, Caledonia, just as I did when I was twenty years old. Which is more than Angela can say." She glanced at Angela Benbow's nonexistent waistline and shifted her own tightly strained silk blouse more comfortably across her meaty shoulders and her ponderous bosom.

"You may get into a size twelve," Angela said, "but only after you've opened all the seams. Now I wear a size fourteen—that's fourteen petite, of course. That is an eighteen you've got on now. I saw the tag when it was hanging out earlier. You really must be neater about your clothing, Nan, if you're going to buy off-the-rack frocks and lie about the size as well . . ."

Nan burst out laughing. "You bit! You did! You always do," she said. "I know I shouldn't be having fun with Sweetie just dead and all . . . but, you—you're so easy to tease. You ask for it, you know. Size twelve! *Imagine.* I haven't worn size twelve since I gave up my acting career. And even back then I had to fight to keep my weight down. Gosh—you are gullible."

Nan, Stella and Caledonia were the only three people at Camden-sur-Mer who could manage to sit comfortably through a meal with Angela. Most of the other residents changed tables and dinner companions every six months, drawing their places by lottery. But a few residents—those growing senile who troubled the others with repeated questions ("What time did you say it was?"), and those growing bad tempered and quarrelsome ("If you can't eat silently, get new dentures or go eat somewhere else!")—were left out of the drawing and were regularly assigned a place to sit and a dining companion who could tolerate or ignore them. One of the deafer residents, for instance. Angela was one of those assigned over and over to the same place. The other residents, one by one, had asked to be shifted away when they drew her table, and at last the management had given up. Angela had been at Camden-sur-Mer for a bit over eight years, and for most of that time she dined alone, or with one of the threesome that usually accompanied her.

Nan had been on the way to stardom, once, or so some residents said. "*I* never saw her in the movies," Angela had said doubtfully when she was told she was sharing her table with a genuine movie actress. But Caledonia replied, "She used a stage name, of course—don't know what—and she was younger then—not so heavy. I imagine we saw her a dozen times in bit parts and don't recognize her now, that's all."

Nan told anyone who asked that her last big picture had been in the early forties. Since then she had virtually retired, and lived quietly with her husband, a dentist; she had evidenced no desire at all to resume her career. In time they had come to Camden and taken a cottage, the closest to the main building. Nan still lived there, although her Dr. Church, grown helpless and childish, now lived across the street in the little hospital owned by the retirement center, where residents were transferred when they needed permanent nursing care.

Unlined because her layer of fat filled the skin that might otherwise sag, Nan looked like a roly-poly kewpie doll—except that her smartly bobbed hair was white. But she had the same mischievous expression in her little half-moon eyes, and the same dimple in her round, plump chin.

"You'll never learn when I'm kidding, will you?" she said to Angela now as Caledonia got up and left the dining room.

Angela shrugged. "I certainly knew you were having your little joke. Not a very clever one, of course. I just played along to humor you. And now if you'll excuse me"—she lifted her little nose a tiny bit higher—"I'm going down to Beach Lane to see if they've decided whether to close the stairs or not. They really should do something about them—nasty, worn, slippery things . . . Why, anybody might have fallen. Of course with Sweetie"—she waved her hand airily—"it was simply inevitable."

Nan just shook her head and watched Angela skitter down the garden path with her tiny, little-girl steps. "Isn't she a caution?"

she said good-naturedly to Stella. Stella smiled her agreement and nibbled on another bit of buttered toast with just a hint of marmalade spread lightly on it.

Stella's habitual silence led some people, meeting her for the first time, to guess that she was one of Camden's small cadre of residents who were growing a little vague. They functioned well in the sheltered environment, got to the dining room okay, undressed themselves, but you could tell from their placid, slightly puzzled air, that they were really not quite sure of the time and day—nor even, as their arteries clogged further or their brain cells shrank more drastically, who all these other people around them were. In time, when they were no longer sure who they were themselves, they were consigned to a wheelchair across the street at the health facility, also managed by Camden's board of governors.

But Stella certainly seemed to be—as were the decided majority of the residents—in full command of herself and her affairs. Her shrewd, faded blue eyes twinkled behind rimless glasses tinted slightly gray, her white hair was always carefully combed and curled (unlike the vague ones, whose hair tended to look wind-tossed), and it was apparent from her reactions that she understood everything around her—and reacted to it, usually with amusement.

Stella just didn't talk any more than she could help, that was all. Among the elderly the most common shared trait is not sickness or infirmity, but garrulity. So her silence made her a good companion to those who wanted to reminisce about their youth or comment on national politics or curse the income taxes that chewed up their fixed incomes like a beaver gnaws a birch. Thus, even if people considered Stella's aristocratic airs and silent demeanor a bit odd, they genuinely liked Stella as they liked bubbly Nan.

With Nan babbling along and Stella listening and nodding in companionable silence, the two ladies finished breakfast at a leisurely pace and pushed away from the table. Nan strolled down

the garden toward her residence and her invariable ritual—
another cup of coffee (instant this time) sipped while she watched
the last segment of "The Today Show"; Stella went to have her
hair done—her regular appointment. All seemed serene.

Of course, that was on the first day. By the second day at lunch,
they had all heard that Sweetie had been murdered, and even
Angela could not be indifferent and superior.

"Who on earth would murder Sarah Jane Gilfillan," Angela
said, using "Sweetie's" real given name. "Are you positive that's
what they said?"

"Well, let's ask the desk. They know everything," Marian suggested. Marian Littlebrook was one of those plain women who
have been plain all their lives—women who can make up, make
over, make out, and nothing changes the fact that they are plain.
But Mrs. Littlebrook's husband was the handsomest male resident
at Camden—a retired military man with upright posture, still tall
and slim, and with his own teeth and hair, a fact as remarkable as
his seemingly incongruous marriage with the woman Angela
Benbow called "The Mud Fence," though mercifully, for once,
only behind her victim's back. The incredibly handsome Len Littlebrook and his incredibly plain wife made for a constant point of
discussion among the other women, and Len Littlebrook's taut,
tanned skin and bright blue eyes made his wife a bit more acceptable to Angela.

"I doubt we'll get much information at the desk," tiny Mary
Moffet said. "Clara's putting up the mail and she hates us to
bother her then." Mary was the only woman at Camden shorter
than Angela, though not the only one daunted by Angela.
"Maybe we ought to wait—they'll tell us eventually."

Angela stared exasperatedly at Mary. "Don't be ridiculous," she
said. "The staff is here to serve us; it's not up to us to wait their
convenience." And she turned on her heel and marched directly
to the desk across the lobby from where their group had gathered
outside the dining room door, waiting for the lunchtime signal

chimes. "Clara," she called imperiously to the clerk. "Come here a moment . . ."

"Nothing for you yet, Miz Benbow," Clara said, "except one of those catalogues. Lillian Vernon, I think. Mail'll be ready after lunch, as usual." She continued her sorting.

"I don't want my mail yet," Angela said. "I want to know about Sweetie Gilfillan . . ."

Clara's eyes shone, and she interrupted the placing of the mail to come forward within whispering range.

"Stabbed," she said. "Stabbed over and over . . . little gashes that they couldn't see when they found her. Had to turn her over . . ."

Angela's hands went up and out in a pushing gesture, as though to shove the truth away.

Clara continued, "The blood soaked into the sand under her, there . . . They say she lost a gallon."

"My god . . ."

Clara leaned further across the desk. "She was in here talking to me yesterday . . . I said at the time to Rosella—you know, the new maid on the second floor—I said to her, 'Rosella, there's something funny about Miz Gilfillan.' She looked—you know—pale and distant. She was thinking of something else, because I had to tell her three times that the van had already left for the shopping center . . .

"She kept saying that it couldn't have gone—that she had to go to the bank to deposit a check. She was mad but there wasn't a thing she could do.

"And like I say, she wasn't really listening anyhow, because she kept saying, 'Are you sure? The driver knows he's supposed to wait for me.'

"Now she's down there in the morgue in one of those drawers like you see on TV—she's all cold and white and stiff and smelling of—"

Angela staggered backward a little, turned, and hurried to the waiting group across the lobby by the dining room doors, where she repeated Clara's words, with as much enthusiasm as Clara had shown, and with the same reception. Even Tootsie Armstrong, who lived in terror of a direct confrontation with Angela, toddled up on the little high-heeled pumps she wore, "because they make my legs look so nice," as she once confided to Mrs. Wingate.

"Blood everywhere," Angela was saying.

"Please, Angela," Stella murmured, putting up a delicate hand, as though to ward off the words themselves. "Not just before lunch."

"Oh, Stella," Mary Moffet said, "don't make her stop. You know we want to hear."

"It's so awful. Who would do such a thing?" Tootsie put in.

Stella shrugged slightly, as though to say, "Have it your way," and drifted a little way toward the door—out of earshot of the vivid retelling of Clara's version of the events.

It was the general opinion, voiced almost at once from several quarters, that some wild-eyed vagrant had done the deed, one of the "beach people" who came to surf and who occasionally stayed to sleep off Ripple or Thunderbird hangovers in the shelter of the seaward decking of the Sunny Daze Motel. There was no disagreement among the group on that point.

"It's a terrible world," Paulette Piper said. "Robbery and murder—hoodlums riding motor bikes on the street." She had a room on the street side of the building, and was one of the few residents with unimpaired hearing. As a result, she complained often of traffic noises none of the rest could hear; the motor bike remark was greeted by blank stares.

"There *are* some dreadful people in Camden these days," Mrs. Moffet pointed out. The other nodded, knowing she meant the town, and not their center. "Throwing old beer cans around everywhere, scattering broken glass on sidewalks, leaving newspapers every which way on the beach . . . I saw a sea gull last week with its beak caught in a metal pop-top ring . . . It was lying dead in the road." She shivered—too much talk of death and dying.

The Moffet cottage was the last in the line, farthest from the main building, right on Beach Lane, and every morning she had to clean trash out of the petunias the gardeners had planted along her walkway. She still had not fully recovered from finding one morning a brassiere, discarded among the flowers. But with her blank innocence, she could not imagine how it got there, and none of the other residents, almost universally more worldly, chose to enlighten her.

"Who's for a walk before lunch?" Mr. Brighton inquired cheerfully, as he limped painfully up to join the group. "Does your digestion good, you know. Twice around the building and back in time for the bell . . . I go slow with this bad hip . . ."

Only Paulette, wearing sensible low-heeled shoes and a sweater over her shoulders, agreed. "Oh, do be careful outside," Mrs. Moffet warned. "Dreadful people out there . . . dreadful."

"I have my cane, dear lady," said Mr. Brighton. "Fend 'em off with that." He offered his arm to Paulette and shuffled toward the door.

It was the second day after the murder before the residents realized that they—and the staff, of course—were under suspicion, and that no wine-sodden vagrant or vicious motorcycle gang member or drug-crazed surfer would be charged with the crime.

CHAPTER 3

ANGELA BENBOW looked at the young police lieutenant who sat across from her at a small table. They were in the second-floor sewing room, which the police had appropriated for interviews. The lieutenant's assistant sat in a corner, quietly taking notes.

"One of the residents? Don't be ridiculous," Angela said. "Do we look like murderers to you, Lieutenant?"

Lt. Martinez refrained from saying that his last murderer was a gray-haired, otherwise respectable matron who bore an incredible resemblance to his own dear mother, and who had brained her daughter-in-law with a wrought-iron poker, during an argument over which brand of English muffins to buy. "The staff is being questioned as well, Ma'am," he said.

"But why? Surely one of those dirty, unshaven people who come down here for the beach is to blame. A lot of them are . . . you know," she said conspiratorially.

"She wasn't robbed. She had her purse with her," Martinez said. "Nearly one hundred dollars in it. She was still wearing a diamond ring—big one. And no, I don't know about the beach people—what about them?"

Angela smiled the enchanting, dimpling smile that always used to melt the admiral. It was easy, she was thinking, to talk to someone who looked just like Gilbert Roland in his best years; the actor had still made her heart turn over when—in his sixties—he appeared on the Late Late Show. "You know—Mexicans," she said airily. "I realize they're your countrymen, but there's no denying—"

"My countrymen?" he interrupted, and to Angela's surprise, he closed his eyes.

"Is he upset about something?" she wondered to herself, but waited politely.

In a moment, the dark eyes opened and her Gilbert Roland look-alike was smiling calmly again, in complete control. "Mrs. Benbow," he said gently, "I'm an American. Fifth generation. It was my great-great-grandfather who came from Mexico. And his father came from Spain."

"Oh, I see!" Mrs. Benbow dimpled at him. "You're Spanish, then! That's tremendously interesting! An aristocratic background by any chance?"

This time her policeman smiled. "No, probably not. I'm sorry to disappoint you. It's just—well, I'm as American as you are. I just wanted to make the point."

Angela shrugged, without comprehension. "Oh. Yes. I'm sure. Well—" she could not see what point he thought he had been making. So she forged ahead. "What I was starting to say . . . would you repeat that bit about Sweetie's not being robbed?"

Lt. Martinez repeated his information. "She had money in her purse, and she was still wearing her diamond ring."

"That's crazy," Angela said.

"Crazy?"

"Yes. She hadn't any diamond ring. She was just a librarian. A librarian from"—she paused to let the import of her words sink in—"from Duluth." Obviously that was the frontier—the back of beyond, where women helped their husbands till the soil. What would someone from that dot in the Great Plains be doing with diamonds, was what Angela meant to imply.

"A gift from her husband, perhaps?"

"She was never married. Not her. Who could stand that nose-in-a-book all the time? Forever telling us some wonderful fact she'd just unearthed, forever researching the origins of the cuckoo clock or when the Nazis came to power or the medicinal value of blackstrap molasses—"

Martinez smiled in spite of himself. "Well, perhaps a relative then . . ."

"No. Definitely not. I remember her saying last Christmas how nice it would be to have some family, somewhere. She was envying all our bright cards and our gifts, and she said she never got anything because all her family were dead."

"But maybe someone had willed it to her . . . a long time ago . . ."

"Nonsense. Around here if we have diamonds, we wear them." Angela, of course, spoke for herself. But the truth was, she wasn't far wrong. Younger women could afford to put the stones into a safe deposit box and haul them out only on special occasions. For the elderly, there weren't too many special occasions left. So they wore their finest for everyday—or at least for the bridge afternoons and the silver teas and the visiting performers and the birthday dinners . . . "No, if she'd owned a diamond, we'd have seen it," Angela said confidently, and Martinez believed her.

"Well," he said, "then there's another mystery to add to the murder. Where did Miss Gilfillan get that diamond? It's a beauty—two carats plus, a good, blue-white color, a fine antique setting."

Angela raised her eyebrows. Really, the man was surprising. Imagine him knowing good stones.

There was a pause, while the assistant scribbled and Martinez looked at her, perhaps expecting more information. At last she asked, "Is that all?"

"No. No . . . Did you see or hear anything unusual during the night?"

"Well, no, but then my hearing is just a bit below average." That was the nearest Angela could bring herself to saying she was, like most of her fellow residents, slightly deaf.

"How about seeing anyone go down the garden toward the sea after dinner Tuesday evening?"

Angela smiled. "Obviously you don't know this place, Lieutenant Menendez?"

"Martinez."

She nodded. "Martinez. We have fifteen or sixteen cottage apartments in the four or five buildings that run down each side of the garden. Several married couples live in the garden apartments—we call them 'the cottages.' I'd say forty people live down there and would be strolling along the path after dinner.

"The staff comes and goes all evening long—nurses bringing trays to people who can't make it up to the main building for dinner, though some of them should be across the street in the hospital, if you ask me. Nurses bring shots, ear drops, pills . . . The physical therapist visits two ladies with arthritis, each evening . . . The hairdresser might come down to do a wash and set for someone who can't make it to the salon on her own during the day. Some evenings the gardeners work late—setting out poison for the snails, for instance. And those of us who have sat still most of the day sometimes take an evening walk before we turn in.

"Did I see anybody in the garden? Lieutenant, I saw *everybody* in the garden. If you hope to find a murderer by charting the trips the residents and the staff made, you might as well move in here with us. You'll be here a long time." And with that, Angela got up and marched out of the sewing room without waiting to be dismissed.

Martinez groaned. God help me, he thought, if they're all like her, she may be right. We'll be here forever. They do love to talk, don't they?

From the shadows of the corner, Martinez's cadaverous assistant unwound his length and stood to stretch. Charles "Shorty" Swanson stood nearly six-foot-seven, without his size thirteen shoes, and weighed hardly a hundred and sixty-five pounds; he had been the despair of his mother and the delight of his high school basketball coach. Now he was becoming the despair of his detective captain, who found him clumsy, naive, and too conspicuous for stake-outs; and he was simultaneously becoming the delight of his lieutenant, who enjoyed the young man's enthusiasm, basked in his open admiration, and was finding him very helpful indeed.

"What do you think?" Martinez asked him.

"I'm like this last one—I can't believe one of these little old people knocked her off. It just doesn't seem possible."

"I don't mean about the killing. We don't know enough about it yet to make a judgment. I mean about this Benbow woman. She's really something else, isn't she?"

Shorty shook his head. "If I'd made that comment about Mexicans, you'd probably have clobbered me. You know what she was trying to say about the beach people—"

"Sure I do," Martinez said, with obvious amusement. Of course, that little old lady was trying to be *nice* in her own way—She accepted me as an equal and she thought I'd understand and agree with her opinions." He paused and grinned. "I understood, all right."

"Who's next, sir?"

Martinez looked down at his list. "Hmm, let's see. Looks like Mrs. Herman Wingate . . . resident for more than twenty years . . . and if gossip is right, the queen bee around here. Well, let's see what kind of song a queen bee can sing."

A minute later, Martinez was thinking, "Some heavyweight queen bee," as the gigantic Caledonia Wingate settled in a chair that creaked dangerously under her weight. She was dressed as usual in a huge, flowing caftan, this one an awe-inspiring expanse of purple brocade shot through with copper metallic thread. Aloud he said, "Ma'am . . . I hope you can tell us something about what has happened around here . . ."

"Not a thing," Caledonia assured him. "I know what everyone else knows. That's all. But I hope you catch the son of a bitch."

Shorty blinked—not sure he'd heard correctly. Martinez bit his lip to keep from smiling. Caledonia sat, serene and unruffled, as though she were unaware of the effect she'd just created. "A defenseless little woman like that . . . it has to be somebody outside—one of the beach people, or . . . I hope you've interviewed residents up and down Beach Road, asking about strangers."

When Martinez gave no response except to listen politely, she barked, "Well?"

"We're trying, Ma'am, believe me. We're interviewing everyone about everything. Now, can you give us any personal information about the deceased?"

Caledonia looked at the ceiling, collecting memories. "She was always reading and passing on information. Some people thought she was a pest with her tidbits—but I thought she could be interesting. She was a gentle person, genuinely inoffensive, not the type someone would want to kill."

"What about friends, family, people especially close . . ."

Caledonia shook her head. "Nobody. And everybody. I mean, no relatives that I ever heard of. She seemed to be the last of her family. Friends? Well, we're all friends here, in a way—we have to be." She paused a moment then exploded with sound. "Hah!"

"Did you think of something important, Mrs. Wingate?"

"Oh, no. No . . . that was just—I was thinking how much more likely it would be if I was found murdered . . ."

"You?"

"Of course. Lieutenant, old ladies don't have much to keep them interested—not much within their own lives, anyhow. No matter how exciting or racey your life used to be, things quiet down when you get older." She saw one of his thin, black eyebrows arching skeptically.

"Oh yes," she went on, "though you wouldn't think so now, to look at us, several of us were real beauties. Several of us had adventure and excitement as our everyday fare . . . The dear old lady you saw with two canes to support her worn-out knees? She and her late husband were a fairly well-known team in mountain climbing circles. In fact, he died on the slopes of Nanda Devi— very sad. She came down alone, with just a team of Sherpas. . . . Nan was an actress in films . . . Paulette was a Miss America finalist in the 30s . . . I played tennis at Wimbledon one year when I was just nineteen . . . Angela did acrobatic dancing in her teens—I guess today they call it gymnastics. She was no Olga Korbut, but good enough, I'm told.

"But time takes it away from you. Especially activities that rely on a quick, agile body. So things can get pretty dull, if you're used to excitement and things happening . . . And one of the virtues of a place like this is that it gives us so many extra lives to get inter- ested in. Everybody knows something about everybody else . . . or they think they do. And they have their little jealousies . . . I'm very well off, as you may have noticed"—her diamonds flashed as she gestured to show them off—"but a lot of the people here aren't. So they envy . . . especially the girls do. For the most part, I think that's all right, even healthy. A little envy'll get the blood stirring—keep the interest keen and the mind sharp."

"But could anyone be so envious that they'd *murder* another resident?"

Caledonia gave him a bemused look. "Of course," she said. "I'm capable myself—not likely, but capable . . . You are—he is." She jerked her meaty thumb over toward Shorty, watching and listen- ing from his seat in the corner.

"But mostly old people are capable of murder because they resent change. They see change as a potential threat to what they are, to what they've achieved in their lives. Besides" she said, sigh- ing, "we're often ill and in discomfort, and because we feel lousy, we can be irritated easily—to the extreme—even by trifles . . ."

Martinez had a sense of *deja vu* that took him a moment to

recognize. He was being lectured, just as he had been in those college classes where you fought sleep to take intelligent notes. And here he was again, sitting without interrupting—half out of respect for the lecturer, half driven by his own pleasure in learning. "And I *am* learning," he thought.

"Oh, and another thing you might not think about," Caledonia was continuing, "we have much less to lose than a young person might, if everything were to go completely wrong and we got caught. I mean, a 'life sentence' would be a horrible prospect to a young man of twenty, facing maybe sixty years in prison. To us— what is a 'life sentence' but a matter of three or four years, maybe?

"No, Lieutenant, we may look sweet and harmless to you, but most of those sweet old things out there would crush you without any more thought than if you were a beetle on a rose petal, if they thought you were a threat to their last two, three, ten years on earth . . . Happiness—even just serenity, the ability to live out one's few remaining years in peace—is precious enough to preserve at any cost."

She thought about that a minute. "Contradiction, isn't it?" she said.

"What is, Ma'am?"

"Defend your life because there's not much left, and what little you have is precious—but take a chance, because there's not so much to lose if you don't make good . . ." She shook her head. "We're funny in the head when we get old, I guess. But believe me, that's all true—both sides of that argument." She swept herself upward and turned toward the door.

Martinez rose too, stretching out a restraining hand. "No, Mrs. Wingate . . . wait—I wanted to ask—"

"Young man"—she fixed him with a stern stare—"I have absolutely nothing of value to tell you. Believe me. It's been sweet of you to give me so much of your valuable time, especially when I have so little to contribute—and it's been nice to chat this way.

But I won't stay and impose on you any longer." Martinez shrugged and bowed slightly, stepping aside in surrender. She made her way past him and rolled majestically out into the hallway.

Next up were the Littlebrooks—"The Mud Fence" and her handsome husband. Len Littlebrook bent forward slightly, heels together, and lowered his eyes, rather than inclining his head— not a real bow, actually, but Martinez said afterward to Shorty, "I swear to God I thought he was going to salute. Or click his heels."

Len accepted a chair but Marian refused and stood just behind him to his right, her hand resting lightly on his shoulder.

"It's dreadful," Marian said with wonder in her soft voice, when Martinez asked if they could make any comment, offer any information. "It's simply beyond belief. Len and I have talked it over and we agree it must have been a hobo." She nodded emphatically.

Len nodded as well, "A hobo, surely."

Martinez cocked his ears—a touch of British accent in that careful voice, he wondered? Aloud he said, "We can't be sure yet. Are your rooms anywhere near the garden path? Could you see who came and went, to and from the beach?"

Len was shaking his head, and Marian explained, "Our suite is on the front of the building. It's terribly noisy, but we're both slightly hard of hearing, so it isn't too bad for us." As if to confirm what she'd said, she gestured at the flesh-colored plastic button lodged in her husband's ear.

"You didn't go out—down the garden path—yourself last evening?"

Len shook his head again and Marian said, "No. We walk in the mornings as a rule."

"Do you know anything about Miss Gilfillan's life that might make her a likely victim of murder?"

Len's head never stopped its gentle wagging, and Marian shook her head more vigorously. "No. No. Of course not . . . I mean, we never . . . We weren't even friends." She waved her hands in a gesture almost like the one Mrs. Wingate had used to show off her diamonds earlier. "We didn't know her. Not like you can know some here. No. We didn't. Len . . . come on, dear—time for medicine . . ."

Len flashed his white teeth at Martinez in a look that asked sympathy, understanding and forgiveness. "She's right, old man . . . sorry . . ." He stood up, and his wife fell in just behind him. Like his aide-de-camp, Martinez thought, instead of like a wife.

Stella Austin, their last interview before lunch, was (according to the notes they had cribbed from the residents' files in the main office) the widow of a banker, and the only child and heir of a wealthy Eastern family—so wealthy that even Caledonia's income faded by comparison. "Good thing I'm not jealous, eh, Beanie?" Caledonia often boomed. Stella would only smile. A member of the DAR, as she mentioned casually now and then, Stella boasted a family tree that went back to the *Mayflower*.

This terribly well-mannered lady, however, frustrated Martinez almost as much as the other witnesses put together. Smiling politely, never stopping her knitting, watching his face instead of her work, she listened to everything he said, answered every question in a modulated, well-controlled voice—and told him nothing. "Because I really have no information," she said, smiling. "But I'll answer whatever you ask, of course." And she fell silent again, waiting with bright, attentive eyes, her fingers moving constantly, playing out the yarn over the forefinger of her left hand, manipulating the needle with her right.

Martinez resisted with some difficulty the impulse to watch Stella's fingers—and to confide in her, rather than coaxing her to confide in him. "Funny what her not talking does to you," he told Swanson later. "You feel you *have* to talk when she doesn't. I bet people tell her all kinds of things."

Swanson nodded. "I know. I could feel myself starting to say something every time there was one of those long breaks between her answer and your next question. You were trying to wait her out, weren't you? And she just sat there, knitting like my mom used to, smiling and looking like she wanted to ask a question . . ."

". . . And pretty soon *I* was talking."

"Well, at least you asked the next question," Swanson said. "I'm not sure I could have stuck to business that way. All I knew was I wanted to say something, *anything*, every time."

"Thanks for holding on to your impulses," Martinez said. He fell silent for a few moments as they walked to Camden's main dining room for lunch. "The lady isn't really unfriendly, though," he said finally. "In fact, I suppose she's every man's dream of a wife—a woman who listens intelligently but doesn't say much."

Swanson grinned. "Just the opposite, I think. You'd find yourself confessing to all kinds of things—a beer on the way home, speeding on the freeway, smiling at another woman—it's hard *not* to talk to her."

"Yeah," Martinez said, "she makes you like her in spite of it all, doesn't she?"

Less than a minute later the two policemen arrived at the dining room and were shown to a table that had been set aside for them. Olaf Torgeson, Camden's ultra-efficient and universally disliked administrator, had decided it would save time—and it might make a good impression, soften up the police attitude toward the institution—if the two were invited to eat on the premises. Martinez had also decided they should dine with the residents in the main dining room—but for an entirely different reason.

Torgeson hoped the two detectives would realize how unlikely it was that one of his residents had turned to murder and that they would, in consequence, go away; Martinez hoped the residents, growing used to seeing them in innocent pursuits, would feel more comfortable sharing their confidences.

Except for the residents he had already met and identified as individuals, everyone in the dining room looked very much alike, even to his practiced policeman's eyes. You could tell the women from the men, of course—and he noticed that the women outnumbered the men about four or five to one. And of course a couple of them were bald, which made them distinguishable. But the women . . . If they weren't alike enough to be twins, they were certainly alike enough to be sisters! He noticed only two women in the room with hair any color but silver, white, gray, or salt-and-pepper—and one of those women wore an outrageous strawberry blonde wig tilted rakishly over one ear.

Martinez shook his head with a sudden sense of dizziness. It was as though a series of mirrors had been set up within the room, reflecting over and over different angles of the same person.

Then, even as he watched the other diners, he realized that he was beginning to distinguish individual faces, pick out different features: to his right, a hawk nose; to his left, a chart of country roads and streams, seams and lines from forehead to chin; by the door a pair of distorted eyes, viewed through their screen of thick, pebble glasses.

"I guess, after a while, they *don't* all look alike," he said to Shorty, "but I'm damned if I could tell 'em apart when I first looked at 'em. If one of them did it, he or she sure has the perfect protective coloration."

Shorty merely nodded, intent on savoring the last drop of a delicious cinnamon-flavored coffee.

The stream of useless noninformants passed in and out of the sewing room till late afternoon. And Martinez discovered for himself the major liabilities of old people as witnesses.

Mrs. Grant, for instance, nodded and agreed to anything he said, because she could hear few but the loudest, clearest sounds. Smiling and agreeing was her way of avoiding a problem.

Tootsie Armstrong, sitting down with her weak eyes facing the light, could not see his face at all and missed his casual question "Comfortable?" not only because she didn't hear it, but because she couldn't see his mouth moving to guess he'd said something. Mrs. Grant, at least, could see that something had been said.

"Reluctance I'm used to," Martinez said to Shorty. "But blind and deaf? We aren't going to have a witness that's worth a damn, are we?"

Mr. Grogan presented yet another kind of problem, one not really limited to the old. Grogan spent a large part of his waking hours drunk. On those occasions when he was sober, he suffered from perpetually bad temper, temper that interfered with his ability to see the same things others saw. One person might see a broken paving block in the sidewalk—Mr. Grogan saw evidence of civic neglect and incompetence. Another might grump about forgetting to reset his clock with the advent of Daylight Saving Time—Mr. Grogan saw it all as another wedge of creeping socialism: "Damn government interfering in what ought to be our own damn business . . . now they're trying to tell us it's already noon, when it's really only 11:00!" In short, Grogan sober was a fire-eater, while Grogan drunk was a bumbling, amiable incompetent.

When Grogan came to the sewing room for his interview, he was bleary with the last painful remnants of a hangover. Shorty could pick up the scent of stale booze clear across the room, and Martinez, standing beside Grogan's chair, winced as the old man spoke. Grogan was sober enough to be in a spectacularly vile mood. And as soon as Martinez got the drift of Grogan's splenetic perceptions, he was able to evaluate what was said—to filter it slightly, cutting down on the bias.

"That Gilfillan woman—I'd have killed her myself, if she kept bothering me with her infernal trivia . . . 'Did you know the earth is actually more pear-shaped than ball-shaped?' she'd say. Who the devil cares . . ."

Martinez dismissed Grogan with as few words as possible. He knew a dead end when he saw it.

The only fun the two policemen had all afternoon was when Nan Church rolled her pudgy self through the sewing room door. "Ex-movie actress, ex-beauty queen, ex-tap dancer, ex-short-order cook, and ex-anything else you can name," she announced, "that's me. I don't know anything about the murder, but I'll enjoy talking to two handsome young men. It makes a change from—" and she jerked her thumb over her shoulder toward the hall.

Martinez felt himself warming to her smile in spite of his determinedly professional manner.

"Actress?" he said. "I don't remember a Nancy Church . . ."

"Stage name," she said. "I mean I had one. Nancy Church is my real name. 'Nan' to you—and to everybody else in the world! I married Dr. Church in 1936 and a couple of years later I retired from the business . . . We didn't need the money and I didn't care for the work—not any more. I just wanted to please Doc . . . my husband. So I walked out one day and didn't come back. Well, all that is ancient history—you don't want to hear about me and my business . . . Let's get on about your business . . ."

But after a relatively pleasant ten minutes, Martinez was convinced she couldn't help them much more than any of the others.

And by the end of the day, Martinez and Shorty Swanson had exactly the same amount of knowledge about the murder as they had before—and knew not much more about Sweetie Gilfillan. Nobody had heard or seen anything unusual; nobody could imagine a resident of Camden-sur-Mer murdering Sweetie (though most agreed with Caledonia Wingate that there were people at the center who were quite capable of murder). Everybody—as though it had been agreed upon in advance—theorized that the murderer had been a beach bum down from Los Angeles for the surfing, the marijuana and the long weekend.

And the more they said it had to be an outsider, the more Martinez believed the opposite—but he could not have said why.

"This may be one that begins and ends with the murder, so far as we're concerned," he said to Swanson as they drove home that evening. "We may spend a lot of time on this, and get nothing in exchange . . . I'll bet you a cup of that cinnamon-flavored coffee we never get a break of any kind on this one."

But he was wrong.

CHAPTER 4

"I WONDER if Sweetie knew she was going to be killed," Mary Moffet said, her eyes looking past the gardens, over the land's edge, out at the noon-blue water where a tiny breeze chopped the waves into scalene triangles. "They say you have a premonition about death. Would murder be the same as dying naturally? Would you have a—a feeling?"

There was a pause, filled only with the complaining squeak of metal on metal as Nan Church slid her bulk back and forth in a wrought-iron glider, one of her still-tiny feet scuffling as she pushed against the red tiles of the patio floor. Caledonia Wingate, overflowing the redwood chaise with her jade green brocade, opened lazy eyes to half-mast, as though considering the matter. Stella Austin brought her eyes from half-mast to full-closed; it is possible she dozed off for a moment.

Several of the residents, waiting for the luncheon bell, were gathered just outside the lobby door that faced the garden, sitting in a miscellaneous collection of uncomfortable redwood slat chairs, drawn into a semicircle under the bougainvillea that formed a ceiling for the patio. It was one of the two or three favorite gossip-swapping times the residents shared, but on this occasion nobody seemed to have much to say.

Mary Moffet, eager for details and yet embarrassed to ask, tried again. "Dolly said—you know Dolly? The redheaded waitress with the two daughters in high school? Well, Dolly said at breakfast that Angela was given the third degree by the police. She fainted dead away, Dolly said. They had to carry her back to her room after she was questioned. Like a sack of potatoes, Dolly said." There was the smallest hint of pleasure in her tone, as she thought of the elegant Angela Benbow being cut down to size. "Could she have done it, do you suppose? Do you suppose they'd put handcuffs on her?" Mary was getting positively gleeful at the mental picture.

Caledonia opened her eyes fully. "Nonsense. She didn't get any more questions than the rest of us did. They questioned me too, you know . . . so I know there was no third degree about it."

The Littlebrooks, sitting off to one side of the patio, looked at each other and smiled. But Marian asked, "Are you so certain she didn't do it? How disappointing. We might have solved the whole thing and been done with all the questions—all this disruption. It's so . . . unsettling. To have the police here, I mean."

"Only if you have something to hide. They don't bother those of us with a clear conscience," Nan said cheerfully. "As for Angela, it wouldn't bother her if she *was* given the third degree. I'll say this for her. She's got guts. She—oh, hello, Angela. How're you today?"

Angela hesitated, posing in the lobby door, aware, with the sure instincts of a woman who has always been the center of attention, that she was being talked about. So she sighed deeply (and dramatically) before she answered. "Thank you, Nan, but I'm fine now. I was just tired after all those questions . . ."

"Everybody answered questions, Angela," Mary Moffet said, a bit sullenly. "There was nothing special about your questions—I guess."

There was another silence and then Nan Church laughed, "My God, Angela," she said, "you sound as though it was an honor or a severe trial being questioned. Mary's right: there's no honor.

And we all know it really wasn't bad, because we were all interviewed—you, me, Stella, Marian . . . I wasn't asking 'How are you' because I thought you'd been through any more than the rest of us. It was just—well, you know—a casual question. That's all."

Angela wasn't sure whether to pretend annoyance or to accept the remark at face value. She hated the feeling that anyone was laughing at her . . . but as she considered a response, the lobby loudspeaker sounded the first phrase of "The Westminster Chimes," and she didn't have to think about it any more. Dolores, the headwaitress, pushed open the doors to the dining room, and residents began to move in to find their places.

Angela and Nan edged along to their regular lunchtime table, settling themselves while the public address system crackled and whistled itself into life. Trinita Stainsbury, silver-haired, wearing silver-rimmed spectacles and attired in silver-gray crepe, held the chrome-plated mike in her hand to announce, between shrieks of electronic feedback, that tonight's entertainment would be a showing in the chapel of Robert Young and James Stewart as Annapolis plebes in *Navy Blue and Gold,* followed by a sing-along in the lobby before bed time. "Dear Mrs. Webster will play the old favorites let us pray," Mrs. Stainsbury said in a rush, catching Angela with her mouth full of iced tea.

"I think she does that on purpose," Angela complained in a strangled whisper, as Trinita began to intone a brief grace. But Angela bowed her head dutifully. When she looked up again, a fruit cup had magically appeared on her serving plate, and Caledonia and Stella had magically appeared in the third and fourth chairs at the table.

"I've been telling Beanie," Caledonia said, "that I've got an idea. Oh—no fruit cup, Dolly, thank you. I hate things chopped into little bits."

"It's all fresh, Miz Wingate," Dolly scolded, "an' you know it's good for what ails you."

Angela chafed at the cliche and at the implied vulgarity. Dolly hadn't actually mentioned the lower digestive tract, of course, but everybody knew "what ails you" was usually in that region, when you got over sixty. "Really, Dolly—" Angela started to protest.

But Dolly simply went about her business. She held a fruit cup up in front of Caledonia. "Melon and grape—a little kiwi berry— even some nectarine in it . . ."

"Oh, all right. Just don't fuss me about it, that's all. You sound just like my mother used to."

Dolly grinned good-naturedly and whisked the third fruit cup quickly onto the table, dexterously avoiding a spill as she wafted the little dish above the expanse of Caledonia's bustline. "How about you, ma'am?" she addressed Stella, in entirely more formal tones.

"I really don't think . . . Do you have a little of that delicious vegetable soup from last night?"

"Certainly. It won't take a minute," Dolly said, and headed for the kitchen.

Caledonia glared after her retreating back. "I don't know how you manage, Beanie. Everybody hops when you say to. You notice she didn't offer me any soup."

Stella allowed herself a soft laugh. "Oh, Caledonia, it's all in knowing how to treat servants."

"*Servants,*" Nan said. "The help here don't think of themselves as servants. Staff maybe, but—"

"You know what I meant," Stella said. "Besides, they wait on you exactly the way they do on me. Come on, now, Caledonia . . . I'm not going to let you tease me into an argument, much as you'd love it."

Caledonia, obviously pleased at getting any rise at all out of Stella, picked up her spoon cheerfully enough. "Okay, if I can't make you fight—you'll excuse me if I begin . . ."

Dolly was back in seconds with a small cup of brown soup, crammed with vegetables and redolent of beef—obviously one of

Mrs. Schmitt's own concoctions. Stella sipped, Angela picked daintily at her fruit, and Nan attacked her appetizer as though if she didn't move fast enough, it would rise from the cup and move to another table. "What were you saying, Cal?" she mumbled around a slice of honeydew. "An idea?"

"Oh, yes—my idea . . ." Caledonia made a pass at a wedge of plum near the top of her cup. "Well, what I think is, we'd all be happier if we got to the bottom of this mess. If we find out who killed poor little Sweetie."

"What exactly do you have in mind?" Angela asked. "Your ideas, Caledonia, usually mean as much trouble for us as they mean satisfaction for you."

Caledonia enveloped two strawberries whole. "The point is even *I* am getting a little nervous about this business. We don't know who killed Sweetie or why she was killed . . . so who knows who might be next? I think it's up to us to find out."

"It makes sense to be afraid, I suppose," Stella said. "But why is it up to us to investigate?"

"Who's better qualified?" Caledonia urged. "The police? They don't know us. Look at the silly questions they ask—like who went down the garden path and did we see anybody in the lobby. Even if you could find out the answers, I'm not sure they'd help a bit."

"I still think it has to be someone from outside Camden," Angela said. "These people here are all . . . they don't . . . I mean, we—we *know* them."

"Even Billy the Kid was somebody's baby, once upon a time. Everybody in town knew Lizzie Borden. They were still killers," Caledonia pointed out.

"I believe the latest thinking is that Lizzie Borden didn't actually kill her mother and father," Stella volunteered, and then looked sorry to have interrupted. She needn't have worried. Caledonia paid absolutely no attention.

"Knowing these people is exactly why we should look around. We can probably find out things outsiders couldn't."

"I think you're crazy," Nan said. "The four of us? Four widows in their eighties? . . . Still, it might be kind of fun . . ."

"I think we should try," Caledonia said. "We four have special knowledge, we're not physically infirm like some here, we still have all our wits about us—well, we may forget a name now and then, but that's nothing. And frankly, it's driving me wild not to know anything . . . not to be told. The police treat us like children—or as though we're so delicate, we have to be shielded from the real world."

"You have a point," Stella said. "We are being kept in the dark. I hate that!"

Caledonia grinned. "You must *really* hate it I haven't heard you express yourself with that much passion since the day Torgeson threatened to cut down the old eucalyptus tree in the garden!"

Nan controlled a smile, but Angela jumped to Stella's defense. "Well, Stella's right! That's a lovely old tree. You did blush, though, Stella."

Stella was blushing again and her eyes were downcast. "Mother trained me not to show my emotions," she said in an embarrassed whisper. "I usually manage to control myself. But it's just—I respect the old things, you know. Tradition. They're important."

Angela nodded. "I agree. Stella, once in a while you have to let fly at somebody, if you're right and they're wrong and they won't listen. But the problem is with all of this . . . Well, I'm not sure we're doing the right thing. Playing detective doesn't seem suitable, somehow . . ."

"I played a detective once," Nan put in. "I remember, there was a theft in a jewelry store, you see, and I—"

"That's completely immaterial," Caledonia said. "Stick to the point. We need to start investigating—finding things out . . ." She paused. "The problem is, how do we go about it?"

Angela suddenly pushed her chair back. "Excuse me," she said.

"You're not leaving, are you?" Caledonia asked. "We need your input."

"I forgot my calcium tablets," Angela replied. "That's all. I really should get them from my room. Calcium," she lectured primly, "does more good warding off osteoporosis if you take it all day long, than if you load up morning or night. And I should take it before the main course."

"Gee, thanks for the lecture," Nan said. Caledonia merely grunted and Stella smiled with amusement but said nothing.

Angela pattered off, out of the dining room and across the empty lobby toward her hallway. There was nobody at all to be seen—the residents, of course, were all at lunch; the staff appeared to be away from their posts and even the switchboard was unmanned. Crossing the lobby, Angela automatically felt in her pocket for her key clip. It was so embarrassing to forget your keys and have to ask at the desk to be let in.

She remembered the scorn with which she had greeted the little gift Caledonia had given several of them four Christmases ago—or no, it must be five or six years now. It was a little clip, like a metal clothespin, decorated with a gaudy stone, made to fit onto a belt or the edge of a pocket. From the clip dangled a short length of golden chain ending in a "split ring" to hold your door key.

"Lots of times I don't have pockets," Caledonia had explained, smoothing the liquid surface of an amethyst-satin evening caftan. "Like this—and what do I do with my key then? Try to carry it in my hand?—that's a nuisance. Knot it into the corner of a hanky? I always use Kleenex. Put it in my shoe? I don't want to limp around. No, this little gadget's been a life saver—I have mine clipped to my bra strap right now."

"I'm sure I'll find it very handy," Angela had said coolly, trying to look appreciative while privately convinced she'd never use the thing.

The next week, however, she barely caught the door as it started to slam shut, when she left the apartment to take the trash to the central bins down the hall. And she went straight back in, over to her little bureau; she unearthed the clip, fastened her key to it, and clipped it to her sweater pocket. It wasn't really growing forgetfulness that made her begin using the key holder; it was the thought of another accident that might actually lock her out, and would therefore make her *look* forgetful.

Besides, all "the girls" used their little clips, fastened to their belts or pockets . . . Tootsie, Nan, Marian, Stella and, she remembered with a feeling of discomfort, Sweetie . . . The little gold clothespin was becoming a fairly common sight. And if everyone else used one, Angela reasoned, it didn't look like you were the only forgetful one who needed it. So now she wore it—and always transferred it the moment she changed clothes. Well, at least she usually . . . She stopped and groped for the clip. Had she remembered? She had. She pattered forward again.

Her hall was elevated from the main lobby by four carpeted steps. As she swivelled around the wrought-iron rail to climb the short flight, she caught sight of a movement down the hall, and strained her eyes to make out a shape in the gloom, too far away to identify—someone moving slowly along, stopping, moving again, stopping . . . She thought, oh, it's one of *us,* someone who hasn't come to the dining room yet, and then thought again, nervously, that perhaps it was a stranger. The door at the far end of the hall, which led to the outside, was standing open now, a distant rectangle of golden light glowing against the hall's gloom. Wide open—why, anyone could come into the building. One of the gardeners, perhaps, or even a stranger . . .

The shape resolved itself into a friendly-looking redhead, a freckle-faced young man of not more than thirty-five or so, she judged, strolling down the length of the hall, glancing at the names on the doors as he passed.

"Can I help you?" Angela raised her voice a little above the level she would ordinarily call ladylike. "Are you looking for someone?"

"Yes, sure . . . Mrs. Nielsen. I'm her grandson. But she doesn't seem to be in her room," he said, waving vaguely back down the hall in the general direction of the Nielsen room he had just passed.

"Oh, she's in at lunch," Angela volunteered. "I'm sure if you went into the dining room . . ."

"Well, I don't want to be a nuisance. She isn't expecting me."

"You could wait in the lobby," Angela said, but at that very moment, Carla Nielsen turned the corner and started to climb the short steps into the hall, clinging to the railing to take the weight off her arthritic knees.

"Why there she is," Angela said, motioning with her head. "Carla, Carla"—she moved closer to bring her mouth directly next to the Nielsen ear—"here's a visitor for you, Carla. It's your grandson."

Mrs. Nielsen looked up from her painful climb, peering near-sightedly down the hall. "Don't have any grandson," she said grumpily. "Never had any children, let alone any grandchildren."

"But . . . he said . . ." Angela turned, frowning, and started an accusing "You told me you . . ." only to see the young man retreating hastily down the length of the hall . . .

"He wasn't exactly running," Angela told her friends, back in the dining room. "He was sort of walking very fast. I mean, why run? None of us could catch him, even at a walk. And there he went, down the hall, and outside and away."

"Didn't you do anything?" Nan asked.

"I yelled at him," Angela said sadly. "I told him to come back. Come back here this instant, I told him. Of course he didn't."

Stella smiled sympathetically.

"What would you have done," Caledonia asked, "if he'd turned around and come back?"

"Gone straight into my room and locked the door, of course."

"And left poor, lame Mrs. Nielsen out there all alone?"

"Better one helpless woman than two. I mean, we didn't know what he was up to, did we? And he could have taken our keys from us and gone into our rooms and stolen anything he wanted . . .

"Yes, maybe so," Caledonia conceded. "But the point is, would you really have run off and left Mrs. Nielsen?"

"Well, why shouldn't I protect myself?" Angela said indignantly, "I certainly couldn't protect both of us." The other three exchanged glances; none of them could think of a way to lecture her on her responsibility to a fellow resident without scolding. At last, Stella kindly broke the silence by changing the subject.

"What exactly was he doing in the hall? Who on earth was he?"

Caledonia took over with authority. "Sneak thief, that's who. Looking for an unlocked door. That's how he got Mrs. Nielsen's name. Off one of the doors he was trying. And he must have stopped trying to turn knobs when Angela came into the hallway."

Angela shook her head. "That was awfully quick thinking, to pretend to be someone's grandson . . . someone living here . . ."

"He's probably done it before," Nan said. "What really worries me, though, is that he seemed to know we'd all be at lunch, that he wouldn't be disturbed. It makes you stop and think, doesn't it? He wasn't picking places at random; he came here because he knew in advance we'd be easy to rob. He'd done a lot of homework on us."

Angela stiffened her back and raised her chin to a pugnacious angle, tightening down on her lips as she did so—what the late Admiral Benbow described as putting on her mule mouth. "The whole thing is frightening, all right. But it shows me that it's easy for a stranger to get in here—and so it was probably a stranger who killed Sweetie after all. And that means we can't do a thing about it. I mean, there's nothing we can find out. The police can find everything out better than we can, if it's an outsider. So why are we planning to—to—whatever it is we're planning to do?"

The others sat silent for a moment, then Nan finally spoke up. "You know, Angela may have a point. Detecting is fine and dandy as an adventure, but it's an adventure for the young. We're too old—and speaking for myself, of course, too fat—to go cavorting around hunting for clues."

"I agree," Stella put in, and then hesitated. "I mean, I agree we're too old, dear." She put a delicate hand on Nan's plump arm. "You're lovely the way you are . . . Not a bit too heavy. It's just—I feel every one of my years in my knees each morning now. It takes me longer and longer in a hot shower to be able even to walk without a limp. I can't imagine myself . . ."

It was by several words the longest speech Stella had made in days, and Caledonia should have been impressed. She was not. "Don't talk to me about 'old' and 'fat,'" she said, her voice rising. "I'm twice as fat as you, Nan, just for starters, and it never slows me down a second. And as for old . . . I am not *old*. I reject old and I reject anyone who's decided to *be* old."

She had said the magic word, of course, to push Angela into agreement. Angela's head was nodding emphatically as Caledonia said, "Now pull yourself together, girls. We are going to be detectives *because I say we are*. And that's the long and short of it."

Stella looked self-consciously around the dining room, but the other diners had finished and gone—and the waitresses, clashing china against silver, were far too busy clearing tables to pay the slightest bit of attention. Nan grinned and shrugged. Angela merely nodded.

"Then it's decided," Caledonia said. "We see this thing through to the end. No more excuses from here on out."

CHAPTER 5

IT HAD begun. The adventure of Angela's life was underway. She went into it with her feet dragging, her ears laid stubbornly back against her head, her jaw set. She would not, she *would not*, she *would not*—but she did.

The ladies met that afternoon in Caledonia's cottage for their first council of war. Incongruously, Caledonia served almond cookies and orange-spiced tea as they plotted against a murderer, identity unknown.

"It seems to me," Angela said, "we don't have the faintest idea what we're doing."

"Now don't start again," Nan said, shifting her bulk to a more comfortable angle on the little chintz love seat by the window. "We said we'd do this, so let's do it."

"But Angela's got a point," Stella said softly, breaking her almond cookie daintily into three small portions which she balanced on the edge of her cup. "We *don't* know what we're doing."

Nan took a big gulp of her tea. "Well, neither does anybody else, of course. The police certainly don't seem to be getting anywhere. I haven't seen them around at all today."

Stella sighed and bit a tiny corner from one cookie shard. "I suppose we need a plan. Some place to start." She sighed again. "Oh, dear, this is all so—"

"We need to do something—*any*thing. Doing nothing will be the death of all of us," Caledonia said, with an effort at firmness that was spoiled when she popped an almond cookie whole into her mouth, where it disappeared instantly, to be followed by another . . . and yet another.

"For pity sake, Caledonia," Nan said, "will you please stop eating? Take command."

"Well," Caledonia said, "the first thing is to find out everything we can, I should think."

"About what?"

"Well, about everything and anything . . . but mostly about the other residents."

Angela looked uncomfortable. "We know everything there is to know about each other. We know who has arthritis and who has a senile keratosis and who's constipated . . . Unfortunately, we hear it all in the dining room. We watch each other all the time, so we know whose children send presents and whose never even send a postcard . . . We see everyone who's going to play bridge or going shopping. We know who's still active because we see them on their way to swimming or take a walk . . . We know—"

"Yes-yes-yes . . . But do we know what they think? Who they hate? What frightens or threatens them?" Caledonia said. "Those are things that might tell us whether a certain person might be likely to murder or to fight back—"

Nan seemed confused. "Fight back. Against what? Why would anyone have fought back against Sweetie Gilfillan? She was such a—such a complete *nothing.*"

"The problem is that we just *thought* she was a nothing," Caledonia corrected. "Obviously she wasn't, to somebody. She must have made someone angry, or frightened or vengeful . . ."

"Well," Angela said, holding out her cup and nodding toward the teapot. Caledonia obliged with the rosy tea and a big slice of lemon. "Well, maybe that's what we do first then. Find out all we can about Sweetie."

Nan spoke reluctantly. "I don't know. I realize Sweetie's dead and all. But wouldn't that be invading her privacy?"

Stella moved uneasily in her chair and picked up her knitting from her ever-present tapestry bag. "It does seem like prying," she said.

Caledonia squinted at her. "This is no time to be squeamish. We can't ignore her or her background . . . not if we really want to know what's going on. That little woman had something about her that someone else couldn't put up with. None of us can guess what it might be. So we'll have to ask questions and find out."

Nan rolled herself forward in her chair. "All right, then, if we're going to do it, let's do it. We'll go ask everybody here at Camden what they knew about her." She jumped to her feet.

"I'll take the upstairs hall. Angela, you take the downstairs hall and the wheelchair wing. Stella, you talk to the staff. Caledonia, you can take the cottages. Well"—she clapped her plump little hands together in nervous excitement—"why are we standing here? Let's get moving." And as the others watched, open-mouthed, Nan propelled herself to the cottage door, apricot chiffon scarf and pumpkin georgette skirt flaring out behind in her self-created breeze . . .

"Come on, come on, come on," she called, bustling out, slamming the screen behind her and catching a corner of filmy skirt in the screen as it slammed. There was a pause, and then the triangle of georgette was yanked violently through as well, and the other three watched as Nan's fat little figure jiggled and swirled up the path.

"Wow," Caledonia said. "Who was that masked man!"

"I've never seen her sail into a project quite like that," Angela said.

"She burst out of here so fast, I didn't have time to tell her what I really want us to do this afternoon," Caledonia said.

"And what might that be?" Angela asked.

Caledonia smiled. "Break into Sweetie's room."

Stella's frown was tiny, but unmistakable. "Surely not . . ." Her knitting jerked in her hands as her fingers dragged the yarn tight.

Angela was startled. "Break in? You don't mean it."

"Ah, but I do."

"But how would we do it?"

"Something will occur to us," Caledonia said cheerfully. She heaved herself upright, and took another almond cookie in each hand as she passed the little tea table. "Let's at least see what would be involved."

Stella folded her knitting carefully over the pink plastic needles, and pushed the resulting bundle down into the tapestry bag. Then she rose and brushed invisible crumbs off her skirt, straightened nonexistent creases in the material, and pulled her jacket cuffs into place before she spoke. "Caledonia, I'm not going to come along with you. I'll talk to people—ask questions,—though I'd have preferred to be assigned to handle someone other than the staff, of course. But I'll do my part. All the same, I don't feel I can, in all conscience, break into another resident's apartment."

Caledonia was not impressed by the niceties of Stella's ethical code. "Beanie, come on. She's dead. She won't object. Besides, we're doing this partly for her sake."

Stella smiled. "Oh, Caledonia. I may agree to go along with at least part of your plan—after all, it's something to do, and we may actually end up being useful. But don't try to pretend it's for Sweetie's sake. If it's for anything, it's for us—for our amusement. It's because we're bored."

"Remember, it may even be for our safety, too. There's a murderer walking around out there," Caledonia insisted.

Stella smiled again. "All right, it's for our safety. All the same, I simply cannot break the law quite so casually. Commit burglary? My dear mother would turn in her grave."

"Stella, please . . ." Angela was a little surprised to find herself genuinely sorry to think of entering the adventure without her friends' company. "It's not the same if we go without you and Nan."

Stella touched Angela's arm gently in apology. "No, I'm sorry. I really couldn't. But I wouldn't try to stop you, and"—she smiled slightly in a kind of self-mockery—"you know I'll be eager to hear a complete report. Don't leave a thing out."

Angela nodded in grudging acknowledgment of defeat as Stella moved toward the door. "Good luck to both of you," Stella said, almost jauntily, as she went through the door and headed resolutely on up the garden walk.

"And then there were two," Caledonia said. "Unless—listen, you're not going to desert me, too, are you, Angela?"

"Well, no," Angela said reluctantly. Caledonia swung out of the apartment with Angela trailing behind her. "But surely the door will be locked, won't it?" Angela found herself a bit breathless as she pattered in Caledonia's wake.

"If it is locked, that just means we can't get in that way and we'll have to find another way, doesn't it? But we ought to look, at least."

The apartment Sweetie had occupied was in the second cottage on the right beyond the main building. Each of the structures lining the walk between the main building and Beach Lane was actually a series of small, one-story apartments joined under a single roof. Most of the cottage apartments had only two rooms and a kitchenette, though a few (like Caledonia's quarters) were especially large or intricately designed. Caledonia's apartment was actually two, joined together, making a king-sized apartment suitable to accommodate the Wingate proportions.

Sweetie's apartment, by contrast, was unusually small. It gave the impression of having been slid into the middle of its building, with two apartments on either side, almost an afterthought. While all the other apartments had big view windows through which the residents could watch their fellow residents coming and going through the garden—a lot more fun than most of the TV available at some hours (Saturday morning being TV's special "vast wasteland" for the elderly)—Sweetie's apartment had only a door, with two smallish windows placed one on either side of the door. Since they were obviously more for light than for the view, the windows were also placed high, to give the occupant some privacy. These cramped quarters had been Sweetie's since she arrived at Camden years before.

Now, as Angela and Caledonia sailed along the walk toward Sweetie's cottage, they saw Shorty Swanson coming away from it, whistling, a hammer and screwdriver in his hand.

"Oh damn," Caledonia muttered, "he's put some kind of lock onto her front door." All the same, Caledonia led the way to the door, since the iron bars that had been put across the cottage back windows years ago as a security measure would certainly be too much for them to move.

Caledonia reached the porch area first and began to laugh. "Look, Angela, look." Angela caught up and stood beside her, smiling as she realized what had happened. There was indeed a brand new shiny hasp and padlock affixed to a front door—but it was not on Sweetie's door. Shorty Swanson had firmly locked up Mr. Grogan's door, the second door along the breezeway, while Sweetie's—the third—stood unadorned.

"I'd love to be here when Grogan comes back and finds the mistake," Caledonia said with delight. "But there isn't time to wait around. Now, before that young policeman finds out what he's done and comes back, let's try the door. Angela, you stand here. Pretend to be talking to me. Smile, girl, smile. And move your mouth—pretend to talk . . ."

Angela's face took on the caricature of a smile, frozen and pained.

"Oh God, is that the best you can do? Well—move your mouth, anyhow. Make people think you're saying something.

Wave your hands around a little. And stand with your shoulders square to the wall . . . your body will hide the knob here."

Caledonia leaned casually against the door jamb and rested a large hand on the knob—which turned easily—and which, to her complete surprise, was followed by the door's swinging open. "Tch-tch-tch," Caledonia said softly. "Careless of them. The police must be as casual about locking things up as some of us are here at Camden—Omigawd!"

Both women stopped motionless. Inside the tiny living room, a whirlwind had been busy. Chairs were overturned, pictures hung crooked on the walls, the drawers to the tiny desk lay on the floor, contents dumped onto the rug. Magazines were scattered like autumn leaves after a storm. Books had been thrown helter-skelter onto the floor, and the small set of shelves that had been their home was empty, lying on its side.

"Angela," Caledonia said, gasping. "What could have . . . who would . . ." Suddenly she stiffened. "Inside. Hurry up." She grabbed Angela's elbow and pulled her over the threshold, closing the door so that it was only slightly ajar. She pressed her ear to the little crack and Angela—completely bewildered—leaned forward, listening as well.

Footsteps sounded, someone coming slowly up the walk toward the main building . . . then a tapping sound. "Someone with three legs?" Angela whispered.

"No, a cane with a metal tip," Caledonia said. "Quiet, it might be someone with good hearing. We don't want them to know we're here."

"Then stop whispering so loud," Angela said.

They waited until cane and owner had finally gone and then Caledonia straightened and turned to survey the wreckage of the room.

"This is really appalling. Poor Sweetie would die of a stroke, if she wasn't dead already. What could they have been looking for?"

"You don't think it was the police searching?" Angela said.

"Oh, I doubt it. They wouldn't leave this mess." Caledonia moved around the room, turning sofa cushions over with a foot, lifting a book, taking up a handful of papers . . . she held nothing for long, letting it fall or drift back down again. "I mean, the taxpayers would raise holy hell if their homes were turned upside down this way and not straightened up . . . Besides, it doesn't make for an efficient search. I mean, I'm not a neat housekeeper, but even I know that if you have things in this kind of order, you never know what you've already searched and what you haven't. You'd go back over some things a second time, and other things would get one short look and never be examined thoroughly. No, unless that Lieutenant Martinez is a lot dumber than he looks, which I doubt, this isn't the way the police do things."

"Should you handle things that way?" Angela asked.

"What way?"

"I mean, well, *any* way. Shouldn't you let them lay where they are?"

"What on earth for?"

"Well, if it really was someone else searching, the police will have to know about it. And there might be fingerprints . . . or a clue . . ."

"Don't be silly, Angela. Nobody leaves fingerprints these days—everybody watches television detective shows, and they give you perfect instructions about how to commit a crime and not get caught. Besides—fingerprints on sofa cushions? On paper? On rough cloth-and-board book covers?"

Angela was annoyed. "You're right of course, Caledonia, but I wish you wouldn't make such an issue of it. I mean, I do have *some* brains you know."

They stood facing each other across a mound of torn magazines, emptied wastebaskets and desk drawers. "For Pete's sake," Caledonia said. "You don't need to be told you're a valuable help in this expedition of ours—you should know it. You want me to compliment you and flatter you every minute? Is that what you want?"

"No, but I don't want you to treat me like a stupid child either."

Caledonia "humphed" loudly and sailed off down the oddly angled hallway to the bedroom, commanding, "Come along with me, girl. We haven't time for temperament . . ."

Hesitantly, Angela trailed along, trying to master her sense of injustice. At the threshold to the bedroom, she ran against Caledonia's broad back again, planted squarely in the midst of the opening. Caledonia was again staring into the room, holding the door jamb as if for support.

"What is it this time?" Angela whispered, raising herself up on tiptoe, trying to see over Caledonia's shoulder. "Have they been here, too?"

"Yes," Caledonia said, sighing. "But that's not it . . . Look, will you? I mean—just look."

"I'm trying. Can't you move? I can't see through you, you know."

"Oh, sorry, Angela." Caledonia's mass shifted sideways, so that Angela was looking into a scene of silken chaos. Dresser drawers were on the floor, closet doors stood open and clothing and contents had been dumped everywhere, intermixed with bedding pulled from the bed.

"I swear, it looks like someone went through this apartment with a giant Mix-Master," Angela said.

"Yes, but that's the least of it. Look at what's *in* that mess."

"What do you mean?"

Caledonia leaned forward and pulled a coral satin and lace negligee from a tangle of garments. "Look at this," she said.

Angela looked, and then looked again. "But that can't be Sweetie's."

"Ah, now you're seeing what I'm talking about. And look at

this . . ." Caledonia grabbed a cream crepe de chine slip with handmade lace on the bosom and along the skirt hem. "And this . . ." She dived into the pile again and came up with a wine-colored satin Chinese dressing gown, the brocade shot with gold thread. "And look at that jewelry . . ."

Angela moved forward and picked up a thin golden chain that lay in front of her feet. A large green stone hung from it, flanked by a pair of smaller stones of pale blue green . . . "This isn't bad," Angela said . . . "But is it Sweetie's? I don't believe I ever saw her wearing . . . it's . . . Caledonia! I think this is a real emerald!"

"And real aquamarines, then, I shouldn't wonder," Caledonia added. "And a real gold chain . . . And look at that pave-diamond bow . . ." She picked up a brooch that winked at her from under the bedside table. "Migawd," she said reverently. "This is set in platinum."

"Caledonia, what's going on? Sweetie had no money, or—I didn't think she did. Where did she get all these things? These beautiful, beautiful things."

Caledonia shook her head. "Obviously that little lady had more to her than books. She never earned the money to buy these things working in the library. Did she ever mention a rich relative?"

"Of course not. She had nobody—that's what she always said."

Caledonia grunted skeptically. "Sure, and she always said she couldn't afford to put up five nickles for the pot when we played bridge, too. But she was lying, wasn't she? Well . . . maybe she made some clever investments? But no, she would have had to have money to begin with—it takes money to make money, my husband always said."

Angela was still in shock. "Maybe salaries are higher in Duluth?"

Caledonia just glared at her. "Even if library salaries in Duluth were double what they are in the rest of the country, she wouldn't have earned money for real silk and platinum."

"And emeralds," Angela said.

"And emeralds," Caledonia agreed.

"What the bleeding hell . . ." An agonized roar from outside the apartment split the hush in which their whispers had, to that moment, sounded loud to them.

"What is it? Is someone in the living room?" Angela gasped.

"That's Grogan," Caledonia whispered. "He must have found the lock on his door. Hush and listen . . ."

Language that turned the air blue, punctuated by the blows of a cane against a door, a wall, a window frame, a porch railing, followed and continued until Caledonia wondered aloud if the old goat wasn't ever going to run out of breath.

If one could read between the bellows, one would gather that Mr. Grogan was both surprised and annoyed, and that—to put it in simple terms—he intended to do something violent about the situation. Grogan flogged his door twice more for good measure, and with a final, unprintable shout, flailed futilely again at the gleaming lock and charged off toward the main building and Camden's director Olaf Torgeson, whose daily afternoon headache was due to come a little earlier than usual today.

"We've got to get out of here," Caledonia said as Grogan's imprecations faded off up the path.

"Why?" Angela said. "He's gone now, and besides, he's not coming in here anyway."

"Because, simpleton—"

"There you go again . . ."

"All *right*. Listen. Because he's going to tell them they got the lock on the wrong door. And they're going to come running back—a bunch of them, if I'm any judge of Grogan—to take the lock off his door immediately, and put it on this one. And we won't be able to get out without everybody knowing we've been in here."

"Not to mention," Angela said, alarmed, "that if they put the lock on here, we couldn't get out secretly or otherwise. Those windows beside the front door are too high for me."

"And too small for me," Caledonia added. "Let's go."

"Wait," Angela said. "My purse . . ." She grabbed at the tiny sharkskin clutch that lay on the vanity bench, half-hidden under the foam of blue fox fur that Caledonia had been holding admiringly, but had dropped when the Grogan went off.

"Good God, Angela? You brought a purse along to go burgling?"

"Well, I didn't *know* we were going burgling when I started this afternoon, did I? And this shade of dark brown goes so nicely with this chocolate-and-blue linen, that I almost always—"

"Give me the fashion commentary later," Caledonia interrupted. "Come on." Caledonia pulled Angela to the front door, where she paused and, opening the door a slit, peered out. "Nobody coming . . . Quick . . ." She pulled Angela through and eased the door shut after them.

It had hardly settled shut when they heard distant thunder in the direction of the lobby . . . Grogan, baying like a hound on the scent, accompanied by the red-faced Torgeson, honking and gabbling like a gigantic and enraged gander protecting his nest against an attack by a fox. And behind them came Martinez, the sounds he made adding only a little to the general din. Caledonia was hard-pressed afterwards to describe the noise, when she related their adventures and narrow escape to Nan and Stella . . .

"I tell you, you had to hear it to believe it. Grogan swearing vengeance, Torgeson protesting innocence, both of them shouting for Martinez, and Martinez after them, yelling 'Swanson! Swanson!—except you could hardly hear him with the noise the two of them were making. Kirsten Flagstad and Lauritz Melchior accompanied by a police whistle obligato! . . ."

Nan was amused. "So what happened? They caught you coming out the door?"

"Not us," said Angela proudly.

Caledonia beamed at her. "Angela really used her head. Remember that freckle-faced, would-be sneak thief this noon?"

"The man Angela surprised in the hallway?" Stella said. "Of course I remember."

"Remember how he fooled her and made himself look legit by looking at the names on the doors—just like an ordinary visitor? Well, we did the same thing. Sort of. Angela said . . . You tell it, Angela."

Angela turned bright pink at the unaccustomed praise from Caledonia. "Well, I just suggested we pretend we were calling on the McCarthys in the first apartment. We just moved two doors over from Sweetie's door, and by the time they got where they could see us, we were knocking on the McCarthy door, all innocent."

"'Suggested' nothing," Caledonia beamed. "She grabbed me with one hand and pushed me with the other and said, 'Knock and look innocent'—and the best thing was, she had remembered the McCarthys were out for the day. Remembered they hadn't come to lunch because his sister's visiting and they'd driven down to San Diego. So we could say we'd been knocking a long time, and where were they . . ."

"And they believed it? That policeman, Martinez, too?" Nan asked.

"I think they were too busy with their own concerns to believe us or disbelieve us. They just sort of didn't see us at all. Of course they'd have noticed if we had been doing something suspicious, I suppose. Anyhow, that's what I think," Angela said.

"Quite right," Caledonia agreed. "I'm proud of you, girl. What quick thinking."

Angela shrugged and tried to look modest as she dug into her bag for lipstick, a gesture that always indicated that she was feeling smug and happy. As she rummaged, head down, Caledonia rubbed her hands and said, "I suggest we all deserve a little sherry to celebrate. Nan, we need to hear from you about your afternoon, and Stella, we'll have your report—and then we'll tell you what *we* found. I'll put that off till last because it . . ." Her voice trailed away as she looked at Angela.

Angela was very pale and she was holding the little sharkskin bag straight out in front of her. "This—this—" she was stammering, a look of distaste on her face that suggested strongly that something in the bag smelled very bad. "This isn't my bag."

"Don't be silly, of course it is," Caledonia said. "You told me how the color went with your dress . . ."

Angela was shaking her head. "I don't suppose I carried my bag today, after all. Well, how was I supposed to remember, what with Mr. Grogan, and burgling Sweetie's place, and . . . Anyhow, I think I picked up Sweetie's bag, when we were hurrying to get out."

"But it's just like yours?"

"I remember she admired mine and asked me where I got it and all. I told her, but I thought she was just making conversation, because she couldn't have afforded it. But I guess she must have gone and bought one just like mine. Because—well, now I know she could afford it . . ." She faltered, remembering the satin, the lace, the fur. "And all that jewelry . . ."

"What jewelry?" Nan demanded.

There was no point in waiting any longer; briefly Caledonia told the others about their find.

Stella shook her head in disbelief. Nan looked unhappy. "Why didn't she ever wear any of that stuff?" she said. "She always had that plain dark dress and an old sweater . . . She lived in that pokey apartment . . . Everyone assumed . . ."

Caledonia shook her head. "If she ever wore those clothes, she wore them when she was all alone and nobody could see."

"Maybe she never wore them at all," Angela suggested. "My great aunt, the old maid aunt, used to take the nice things we sent as presents and hide them in a drawer. 'Too good to wear,' was what she used to say about them. Then when a niece—or the daughter of a friend, or somebody—got married, Aunt Bess used to give the girl some of those gorgeous things for a trousseau . . . things she'd never had the heart to wear herself. When Bess died, there they all were—all the things we'd given her over the years. Anyway, what she hadn't given away to someone else—tons of lovely stuff that had never been used even one time . . ."

Caledonia disagreed. "Some of Sweetie's stuff had been laundered . . . and there was a makeup stain on that coral negligee . . . Sweetie wore it, all right. While she was at home alone, I'd say."

"But why . . ." Angela was puzzled.

"Oh, to make her feel good, I suppose . . . like, well, why do you lounge in a bath filled with blue oil, wearing a lacey net to tie your hair up? Nobody sees you—you aren't trying to impress anyone—you could wear a towel tied around your head—but you wear that lacey thing because it feels good." She held a tiny etched glass up, letting light glow through the amontillado it held. "Why do I drink from beautiful crystal, when I have a sherry before supper, even when there's nobody with me to be impressed? Because it feels good. I'll bet each of you has something you do that you do merely for your own pleasure."

Surprisingly, Stella spoke up, twisting her hands with embarrassment. "I—well, sometimes—I wear black underwear."

"Stella!" Nan was amused.

"Well, I only meant—I know what Caledonia means. Nobody sees it but it makes me feel—oh, I don't know—different. A little daring. You know—younger." She ducked her head and stared at her hands.

Caledonia's agreement was emphatic. "I understand. And I think Sweetie wore those clothes that way—for her own pleasure. We didn't know about them because she wasn't showing them off."

"But why not wear them around all the time?" Nan said. "We all thought she was poor. I heard Mary Moffet say over and over how sorry she was for 'poor Sweetie' . . . but there was Sweetie, obviously with money—at least with beautiful things—gloating to herself. You may think it's natural; I think it's unhealthy and mean-spirited. She could have let people know they didn't have to pity her. But no. She wallowed in that pity exactly the way she wallowed in the satins and lace in secret."

Caledonia shook her head. "You're being very hard on her, Nan."

"Not half hard enough," Nan said. "It's getting pretty obvious that we never even knew the *real* Sweetie Gilfillan. What we thought we saw wasn't really her—it was only a pose. I think she must have laughed at us behind our backs. At all of us."

"Girls—Girls—" That was Angela. She'd said not a word for a long time. Now she held out a creased square of aqua-colored paper with THINGS TO DO printed at the top. "Look at this. Look what I found in this purse."

Caledonia took the paper and read aloud. "1), call TV repair . . . 2), pick up wristwatch . . . 3), get cleaning . . . 4), talk to Sam, five percent—first; verify salary/office . . . 5), toothpaste, nail polish, bunion pads . . ." She looked up. "Well, so Sweetie took notes. So what? Most of us do. I can't remember a list of more than two things for five minutes without making notes. So what's the big deal?"

Angela was sober. "The 'Sam' she mentions on the list may be Sam our baker."

"So?"

"Well, lately he's been borrowing money from some of the wait-resses—Dolly said he told them he had a few gambling debts to pay."

"Okay . . . so?"

"Well, I'm not sure now it really is gambling debts. I mean, when I first got here, I heard there was something odd about Sam's wife's sudden death. I can't really remember—I think one of the waitresses said the wife fell out of a third-story window. For a while the police thought he might have had something to do with it, but the coroner's office finally said the death was accidental . . ."

Nan shifted uncomfortably. "Angela, I wish you wouldn't. I think I see where you're going with this, and—"

"I don't," Caledonia said impatiently. "Come on, what's the bottom line?"

Angela pursed her mouth. "I shouldn't speak ill of the dead, but suppose—suppose Sweetie was blackmailing Sam? Suppose she knew he actually *had* pushed his wife? Suppose she said she'd tell unless he paid her . . ." She took the note back from Caledonia and glanced at it ". . . five percent of his salary every pay day. And she would find out what he made because she'd check with the office, so he couldn't cheat her."

Nan groaned. "Honest to grandmother, Angela."

Stella shook her head. "Angela. Your imagination."

"Migawd, Angela, what a leap," Caledonia said. "From meaningless notes to blackmail—and from there, I suppose, to murder? You'd have bleary-eyed old Sam stabbing Sweetie with a meat skewer from the kitchen? Come off it. You're stretching. He's a gentle old thing, though he smells like a distillery. He wouldn't murder his wife—and he wouldn't murder Sweetie." She began to laugh. "You . . . you ought to write fiction, my girl. That's dumb . . . that's really dumb . . ."

Angela drew herself up angrily. "There you go again. Laughing at me. I asked you not to keep calling me stupid, but you insist you're the only one that knows anything . . . I have no brains at all, according to you. Very well, we'll see. I'm going to take this paper and find out what that note really does mean, and then I'll have the last laugh."

"How're you going to do that?" Caledonia asked, grinning.

"Well, I—I'm not sure. But I'll do it." Angela picked up the little bag and headed for the door.

"Wait," Nan called. "What else is in the bag? Did she have any other lists—things to do? Places to go?"

"Oh no, you don't," Angela said, clutching the bag close to her chest. "This is my clue and I'm going to follow it up. When I've looked everything over and figured everything out, I'll come and report to you. And not before. I'll see you at dinner." And she closed the door behind her firmly, with as much dignity as she could muster. She was really annoyed. She did not enjoy being laughed at, and as the late Admiral could have told the other ladies, when she got angry, she could walk straight through a stone wall.

Nan shook her head after the departing little figure. "That Angela!" she said. "Going to make something out of nothing if it kills her—just because you insulted her. You shouldn't do that, Cal . . . She's got more vanity than I've got pounds."

"Does her good to get riled—gets her circulation moving," Caledonia said, unremorseful. She drained her sherry. "Besides— the note's probably nothing. Would a blackmailer keep written notes? It seems risky to me."

"But as you said, Caledonia, all of us here have difficulty remembering things," Nan replied. "Maybe Sweetie thought it was a risk worth taking."

"Maybe . . . Well, what'd *you* find out on your travels today?"

"Absolutely nothing. I got a bunch of zeros. Almost everybody was out—and people I did talk to claimed they didn't know Sweetie well—had no close connections with her. I pulled a blank. So there's no report, and listen—" she heaved herself to her feet—"I think I'm going to be on my way. This georgette's pretty clingy for such a warm afternoon, and I'm going to lie back in some of that blue bath oil Angela loves so well, like you were talking about, and take a good soak before supper. See you then . . ." She started for the door.

Caledonia turned to Stella. "Well, did *you* find out anything? Did you talk to any of the staff?"

Stella bit her lip. "No. Not yet. I'm sorry, Caledonia . . . don't be cross. It's just—it's hard for me. I mean to do my part, but asking questions . . . Mother always said a lady shouldn't be curious about other people's business. And to ask questions of the help. . . ."

Nan grinned back as she swung the screen wide. "Stella, I shouldn't have assigned you to the lower claw-ses, should I? Tell you what . . . I'll do staff myself. You just nose around among the wealthier residents. Okay?" And she was gone, grinning widely.

Stella nodded gravely, the change of assignment obviously not as amusing to her as it was to Nan, and she too rose to her feet. "Caledonia, I think I'll leave myself—to change for supper."

Caledonia shook her head. "Why, Stella? Just tell me why? You always dress like you were going to the office—or to a cocktail party. Some day I want to see you throw on a pair of slacks—slap a pair of espadrilles on your feet—and we'll go to a bar and listen to the juke box till they close the place up. What do you say?"

Stella's smile was pained. "You're joking, of course. I see that, my dear. You know I couldn't do that."

Caledonia grinned. "Sure I know that. But it's kind of fun to think about. Well . . . maybe some day. . . ."

And the first day of the four great detectives ended with neither a bang nor a whimper . . . Just a sherry and fresh clothes for dinner.

CHAPTER 6

"**G**IRLS," ANGELA announced at breakfast, wide-eyed, "somebody tried to break into my room last night!"

It was "Waffle Day" at breakfast, and Caledonia, not ordinarily an early riser, was already at the table with the others, sponging up maple syrup with a block of buttered waffle. "Sure you're not exaggerating, Angela?"

"*Positive.*" Angela might have been the most reluctant of the four to get started with the investigation, but now that it was underway, she was clearly having the time of her life. "And it was Sweetie's purse they were after, you can bet on it. Pass the butter, Stella."

"Oh, Angela, come on," Nan protested. "You don't know it was Sweetie's . . ."

"Oh, don't I. Well, nobody ever tried to break in before. But now I have that purse—and twice during the night somebody was working at the lock on my door with something made of metal. I could hear it scrape and sort of jiggle around against the lock."

"Well, what did you do?" Caledonia asked as she poured cream into her coffee for the second time. "Don't keep us in suspense. Did you call the desk? Did you yell for the police?"

"Well, no," Angela said a bit sheepishly, "I was far too frightened. The first time I just lay there and held my breath."

77

"Whatever for?" Stella asked.

"Well, I thought if he didn't know I was there, maybe he'd go away. I know it doesn't make much sense, but at the time it seemed so sensible just to hold on and lie absolutely still . . ." Angela was a trifle meek about this part of the story. "But he did, you see. He did go away."

"And then what?"

"Well, I must have fallen asleep finally."

Nan snorted. "More likely you were asleep and dreaming the whole time and there was nobody at your door at all."

Angela was indignant. "You keep insisting I'm making this up. All you have to do is take a look at the plate on the outside of my door . . . It's a mass of scratches and gouges, and none of them were there before."

"All right now," Caledonia said soothingly, "then of course we believe you. Go on. What about the second time? Did you hold your breath again?"

"No. I decided to defend myself."

"Good lord," Nan said, "what with?"

"With a pair of scissors and my enameled metal footbath. I mean, I could stab him with the shears and hit him over the head with the footbath. Well," she went on defensively, aware of the broad grins of the others—even Stella, usually too kind to mock, was smiling, "it's all I had. I don't carry a knife or a gun—I don't even own a hatchet—or even a heavy frying pan . . ."

"And you chose to use the weapons at hand. Well done. Very brave."

Caledonia's praise went to Angela's head like wine on an empty stomach. Twice within twenty-four hours? She turned bright pink and went on, her voice husky with excitement, "It wouldn't have done him a bit of good, you know. There wasn't another thing in that purse . . . I mean, nothing strange or—you know—significant. There was a bottle of perfume. Giorgio—a full ounce. But we know now she could afford it if she wanted it."

Nan groaned enviously, "Oh gosh. And I love that stuff."

Angela continued, reading from a little list she brought from her sweater pocket. "I wrote each thing down. There was a pen, a lipstick, a little comb, a brooch with a broken clasp—she might have been taking it to be mended . . . There was a half roll of Tums . . . a snapshot of her with the Littlebrooks—it was funny because Len looked so grumpy and out of sorts—and of course that shopping list. Nothing odd about most of it, believe me . . ."

Caledonia was curious. "I'd like to see all that," she said. "Maybe the Tums were poisoned, or the lipstick was . . ."

Angela shook her head. "I gave it to Lieutenant Martinez already."

Caledonia started visibly. "You told him we were in Sweetie's apartment?"

"Of course not. I lied—I told him Sweetie'd left the purse in the sewing room, I'd picked it up and meant to return it, and now I thought he'd best have it." She waited a moment, then dropped her little bombshell. "I gave him the list with Sam's name."

"You didn't," Nan said. "Suppose you were right, Angela, and that was blackmail—not that I think it was, but just suppose— Sam might be in awful trouble because of that."

"Well, what else could we do?" Angela said. "I mean, suppose everything I said was true . . . You laughed at me yesterday, but suppose Sam *did* kill her. Would you want to protect him and keep quiet about it all then?"

"Of course not," Caledonia said. "You did absolutely the right thing, girl. Absolutely the right . . ." She was interrupted by Martinez, who was suddenly at her elbow.

"I'm glad you agree, Mrs. Wingate," he said, bowing slightly in her direction. "Ladies . . ." He nodded to each of them.

There was a moment's silence, and then Caledonia gathered her wits. "Won't you join us, Lieutenant Martinez?"

"Not today. Another time, perhaps," and he did the same little half-bow. "Actually, I couldn't help but hear you advocate cooperating—telling the police everything is always a good idea. We often are not efficient enough . . . for a variety of reasons, we fail to close a case. And as often as not, the cause of our failure is lack of information. We just can't find out enough to go on. I appreciate your turning the purse over to me. And now, if I might talk to you for a moment, Mrs. Benbow . . . In your room, perhaps?"

Angela felt absurdly pleased to be singled out that way by her Gilbert Roland, and she smiled her most coquettish smile—a little, triangular smile, bounded by tiny dimples. Martinez found himself, to his surprise, thinking of Vivien Leigh rattling on about Ashley Wilkes to the Tarleton twins at the barbecue. He half expected Angela to respond "Oh, fiddle-de-dee!" But she actually said, demurely, "Certainly, Lieutenant."

She pattered along ahead of him through the lobby, and at her door stopped so abruptly, he almost ran over her. The sight of her door made her think of her nighttime visitor. "Oh, Lieutenant, I wonder if you'd look at these marks. I think someone was trying to get into my room last night."

Martinez bent down and looked at them, bright streaks, obviously freshly incised across the corroded brass of the old lockplate. "Well, well . . . It would appear you are right. Why didn't you report this to me, Mrs. Benbow?"

"Well, I'm reporting it, aren't I?"

"I mean, immediately."

"Well, I declare," she said with her unconscious Scarlett imitation, "there's no rush about it. Surely to goodness the marks won't go away. I mean, I could have my breakfast first, couldn't I? And whoever made them is either still around or long gone . . . Either way, a few more minutes wouldn't help you catch him, Lieutenant."

He inclined his head in rueful defeat. "Any idea why someone would try to break into your place, Mrs. Benbow? I mean, did any of the others report a burglary or attempted burglary?"

"There was that young man yesterday noon," she said, suddenly aware that she had a few tracks that needed covering. A diversion, that's what was wanted. "Did they report at the desk . . ."

"Yes, they did. It sounded like Hotel Harry. A nice-looking, youngish-looking fellow, but nothing more than a sneak thief with the protective coloration of a gentleman. It wouldn't surprise me a bit, if he'd switched from hotels to retirement homes . . . You people don't exactly have security guards roaming the halls, you know. This place isn't what you'd call easy to defend. And on the whole, you're far less likely to be able to trip him up than a forty-ish business man from Toledo . . . that's the last hotel guest Harry walked in on. He thought the room was empty. He was wrong—and it cost him three years. I think he learned a valuable lesson. But maybe the lesson wasn't to lay off crime—only to lay off hotels. The description—clean-cut, sandy-haired, freckle-faced, well-spoken—it sounds like Harry, all right."

Angela responded eagerly. "Well, there you are. A professional thief. I dare say he came back last night . . ."

"Oh, I doubt it, Mrs. Benbow," Martinez said. "Harry may have thought better of doing his burgling in hotels, but his method of operating wouldn't change that greatly. He always entered empty rooms—or at least rooms he thought were empty . . . Once in a while he was mistaken."

"The gentleman from Toledo," Angela said.

"Right. The way Harry cut the odds against himself—he always did his burgling in the daytime, when the person renting the room would be at a meeting, or an office, out shopping . . . Never at night. You think of sneak thieves operating at night, of course. But that's when there'd be someone using the room.

"Anyway, our man Harry met the gentleman from Toledo in mid-afternoon. The problem was that Mr. Toledo was under a tangle of blankets sleeping off jet lag, he didn't wake when Harry first entered the room, and Harry didn't see him till he had both hands full of cuff links and credit cards. Then it was too late. I suppose Harry tried to run, but he got a slow start and the man from Toledo worked out regularly. He may have had jet lag, but he was perfectly capable of tackling Harry, who bumped his head and was knocked unconscious in the ensuing struggle. And that was the end of Harry's career. Until now, apparently."

Angela nodded sagely, hoping their discussion of Hotel Harry had diverted the lieutenant from the main question. But it hadn't.

"Well, Mrs. Benbow, if not Harry, then who?" Angela did not answer, but unlocked her door and entered the room, beckoning him to follow. Simply avoiding the issue—"Tacking to run before the wind," the admiral had called the maneuver—had often saved her trouble in the past. This time it didn't seem to work, though. "Maybe instead of asking *who* I should ask *what*. What do you think someone might have wanted from you?"

"Well," Angela said, deciding quickly that perhaps even a half-truth might be best. "I wonder if it was Sweetie's purse."

"How could anyone know you had it?"

"They could have seen hers—and seen me carrying mine. And assumed mine was . . . Here, let me show you." She darted to the antique chest beside the door where she kept her gloves and handbags. "Look," she said, pulling out the top drawer and fishing out the tiny sharkskin clutch. "It's exactly the same . . . same color . . . everything."

Martinez nodded. "Yes, probably that's it. Good thinking, Mrs. Benbow. You'd make a good detective."

She beamed at him. "I'm glad someone appreciates me. Caledonia often thinks I'm wilful and childish . . ." She stopped herself, realizing that was beside the point. "I looked into the bag, you know, before I gave it to you," she said.

Martinez smiled. "Of course. How else would you know it wasn't yours?"

"Oh." Angela was discomforted to realize he was one step ahead of her. "Well, perhaps you noticed a piece of paper there were notes on? About Sam? And his salary?"

Martinez did not answer, but he nodded, suddenly seeming

more guarded, a little wary. Angela did not notice, but plunged ahead. "I have a theory," she said. "I mean—I told Caledonia and Nan and they just laughed . . . But you take me more seriously. About the paper, I mean. I thought it was blackmail . . . About Sam's wife, I mean . . ."

Martinez' eyes opened a little wider but he kept an impassive face. "Why would you think that?" he asked.

"Well, we all thought Sweetie was poor, you know. I mean, I'm not sure we made that clear to you when you were talking to us the day before yesterday . . . was it Monday? No I think it was . . . Well, anyhow, I know I said she was only a librarian, and I'm sure that when you mentioned the diamond ring, I said she had no such thing. But I was wrong, you see. And so the question is, where did she get the money to go around buying diamonds. You see?"

"Yes, I think I do. Somehow or other you've got a look inside her apartment, haven't you?"

Angela froze, unable to think of anything—no lie, no evasion, no defense came to her. Finally she just said, "Yes. We—I—I did."

"Okay, Mrs. B. You'd better level with me. Who peeked in, what did you do and what did you see? Did you touch anything? And when was this?"

"Yesterday," she said. "Now Lieutenant, you're not going to be angry . . ."

"Just tell me about it. When yesterday?"

"Just before you put the lock on the right door. We were in there when Grogan found his door locked . . ."

Martinez closed his eyes quickly, and clamped tight on the corners of his mouth—at the mention of Grogan, he had started to smile in spite of himself. "Go on."

"We decided . . ."

"We who?"

"Oh," Angela said airily, "just a couple of the girls and I

decided . . . We wanted to try to find out about Sweetie, you know. I mean, we know each other here a lot better than you do—than you can in a short time. So maybe we could find out things you couldn't. We went down to see—well, we wouldn't have broken in or anything. But the door was unlocked and it just sort of came open . . ."

"Okay—go on. What did you think about what you saw?"

"I was frightened," Angela said. "It's so—so nasty, to think of someone pawing through your things and being so . . . so careless. She must have loved those soft furs and those silky things . . . but someone just dumped them out as though they were—garbage. It's—it's mean."

"Yes, it is," Martinez agreed. "It's an invasion of privacy. But then, in a way, so is what you did—prying like that."

"But we wanted to help," Angela protested. "It wasn't the same at all."

"Never mind. Just—did you touch anything?"

"Well, a few things, but we put them right back the way they were. Almost."

"You didn't mess the things up yourself, I take it?"

"Lieutenant. Please!"

"Okay—sorry—tell me about it . . . what you saw—what you noticed—"

"Well, we hadn't been in there much, before. Once or twice, some time ago, I seem to remember Sweetie having us in for tea and cake . . . but not for ages. And even if you looked in—provided you didn't open the drawers or the closets—you'd never have guessed about all those beautiful things. The furniture was ordinary . . . even shabby. Like her. Like the clothes she wore, with all the mended places in them . . ."

"She seems to have deliberately kept her beautiful things a secret."

"And the fact that she had money. I mean, she might at least have moved to a better apartment. But she didn't. So you see, hiding it was something she did on purpose."

Martinez nodded encouragingly. "The apartment wasn't very nice, was it? Not like this—" he looked appreciatively at a dainty antique secretary against one wall; a sofa bed so well disguised no one would ever have suspected its dual purpose; a handsome floor-to-ceiling wardrobe, deceptively roomy, fashioned of a magnificently rich fruitwood. And all of it tied together with the dove gray plush carpet and the soft bluish walls—the large windows catching morning sun and gently warming the room . . . a tiny breeze moving through, stirring expensive chiffon curtains . . . "You seem to have a choice spot, Mrs. Benbow. And your things are—so elegant."

She beamed again. "Thank you . . . just a few odds and ends—some I had before—" she waved in the direction of the secretary—"and some I picked up to help with the special problems of a small apartment."

Martinez was at his smoothest. "But such a lovely apartment . . . the location, with the good morning light . . . the size and proportion—it seems larger than most of the others. And," he herded her back on his chosen track, "certainly larger and more desirable than Miss Gilfillan's."

"Yes, that one is incredibly cramped. That's why I—we thought if she had money, she'd surely move. And her clothes—I mean, she wore that same old coat sweater, with the patched elbows, for years—really."

"Well, then, you and I saw the same things, I think, ma'am. That money was carefully hidden. She didn't have a single expensive thing you'd wear in public—except maybe the furs and the jewels—the fancy clothes were mostly night wear and underwear. Things she could wear and keep private—to herself."

"Just to feel good herself," Angela said, remembering Caledonia's description. "For her own benefit. But I thought . . . I felt— Well, never mind."

"No, go on, Mrs. Benbow. Impressions like yours—impressions from sensitive people—are extremely valuable. They can put us on exactly the right track. What was that feeling?"

"I—well, I felt it was somehow—gloating. Like she could laugh at us all. I mean—well, she could wear a platinum chain next to her skin, and a slip of *café au lait* satin, then put on that frowsy little rayon frock over it, and that old, mended sweater, and feel the touch of that luxury on her and know those things were there, but we'd all look at her and see the same old Sweetie. I thought— well, she was really having a kind of joke at our expense. Like she was—like she was wallowing in sensations she wouldn't share— two sensations really . . . one the touch of rich things . . . the other the . . . the gloating. Because she had them, and because we didn't know."

Martinez nodded. "Entirely plausible. It would give us a new look at her character, though. You all described her to me as sweet and quiet and studious—but now you're making her sound a lot less pleasant. It has an ominous feel to it, what you're saying."

Angela was eager in her agreement. "Yes . . . yes . . . that's what I feel. That sense of threat—I mean, I feel as though all the time I knew her, she had been—steering me, somehow. Manipulating me. Controlling what I thought and felt . . . Does that make sense?"

"Yes ma'am, it does. There are people, you know, whose chief pleasure is making puppets out of other human beings. The writers of anonymous letters, for instance—they get enormous joy out of being able to control others secretly, to make them suffer by remote control. And blackmailers, of course, who get more than money out of what they do. A number of them take genuine pleasure in their chosen profession. If your Miss Gilfillan was like that—maybe she pulled the strings on someone just once too often, or showed her pleasure just a little too broadly . . ."

Angela had sat down on the edge of the little Hitchcock chair and her bright eyes were half closed as she recited her responses . . . Suddenly she opened her eyes and looked up at Martinez. "Cocking her head like a little English sparrow," Martinez said to

Swanson later. "She looked right up at me and she said, 'Controlling people! Of course . . . It could be fun for her to control other people . . . just like you're doing to me, Lieutenant.' And she grinned like a little monkey."

Shorty smiled in appreciation. It wasn't often his boss could be found out, seen through, unmasked, when he was doing his "snake charming," which is what Shorty privately called Martinez's combination of flattery and gentle persuasion—especially effective with the ladies, as a rule. "I don't think they *want* to see through you, chief," Swanson had ventured to the lieutenant on one occasion, and Martinez had simply raised his eyebrows and smiled without comment.

Now Shorty looked straight ahead, concentrating on driving them back to the office through San Diego's evening traffic. "Getting as bad as Los Angeles," he said, swerving to avoid colliding with a car entering the freeway without yielding. A moment later, he said, "Well, was the information useful?"

"Yes and no," Martinez replied. "It gave me a better feel . . . Mrs. Benbow told me she'd suggested blackmail as a source of the Gilfillan fortune, because of the note about Sam, and she said everyone else—she didn't say who, but it had to be the silent one and those twin elephants she pals around with—everybody else laughed at her."

"Could be, I guess," Shorty said. "I don't know why they laughed. That old Sam actually was suspected of giving his wife the shove, one time. I checked the record. Would it have cost him his job here, if it got brought up again?"

"Probably, knowing Torgeson," Martinez said. "So blackmail is not such a joke, is it? Besides, I got a feeling, while Mrs. Benbow was talking about the Gilfillan woman's gloating. Benbow had nothing solid to go on but subtle things she can't put into words. She said it was—well, just a feeling, she said. I'd hate it if our Captain Smith asked me about it, but I tell you, I got a crawling sensation on the back of my neck. Somehow, what she was saying felt right. I mean, it makes sense when you think of the number of times the woman was stabbed, and the depth of the wounds. Somebody went at her wildly—and if she was blackmailing—and enjoying it—"

Shorty, eyes on the traffic, nodded. "If that Mrs. Benbow's right, the murdered lady wasn't a very nice person."

"To say the least," Martinez said. "But we still don't have any solid proof. The best thing to do now, I guess, is keep our eyes and ears open and—turn right at the next exit. You'll avoid a jam at the off ramp if you don't go all the way in . . ."

Shorty cut across two lanes of traffic that separated them from their exit by the simple expedient of flooring the accelerator and screaming ahead of the traffic flow. Over the sound of horns blaring behind them, Shorty asked, "Well, what's the next step?"

Martinez shrugged. "Look into this blackmail thing, I suppose. Start asking questions. If the lady was blackmailing the staff and the residents to get her little fortune and have a little fun doing it, she was playing a dangerous game. Blackmail victims get pretty desperate. I say we go back and look at that apartment again . . . and this time we really look at everything."

"I say we go back and look at that apartment again . . . and this time we really look at everything." Angela was emphatic.

"Well, aren't we the born leader," Caledonia said. Nan chuckled and even Stella smiled broadly. "Just a little while ago," Caledonia went on, "you were telling us you couldn't go breaking into Sweetie's place . . . and we were crazy to try . . . and now you want us to get back and do it all over again?"

"But that was before I knew we could. I mean, the Lieutenant didn't think my ideas were silly. In fact, he seemed very interested in what I was saying."

"Well, did he tell you there was anything pointing to blackmail as a possibility?"

"No."

"Did he tell you that her being a blackmailer sounded reasonable to him?"

"Well, not exactly, but—"

"Maybe," Caledonia said, "he acknowledged that you had brilliantly deduced what he'd been laboring to discover . . ."

"Caledonia, you're trying to put me down again. Now, you weren't there. I was. I tell you, he believed me. He *did* believe me. I bet he's looking into it right now. But I've been thinking—even if she was blackmailing Sam, she never got enough money from *him* for all those gorgeous things, did she?"

"Well, no. Of course not. And that's one of the reasons I thought it was such a silly idea. On his best day Sam couldn't have come up with enough to buy that brocade dressing gown, never mind the fox furs or the jewelry."

"So . . ." Angela was animated, positively glowing with excitement. "So that means she was blackmailing somebody else, as well. Maybe a lot of somebodies. Staff, residents, people in town . . . Anyhow, we have to start somewhere. So I say we go back to Sweetie's room. Nan—Stella—you haven't said one word this whole time. What do you think?"

Stella looked carefully at her knitting. Anyone who didn't know her would think she was checking on a missed stitch. "I don't believe you want to run that kind of risk again," she said. She bit her lip and looked earnestly down at her wool. "It's not just that it's illegal. It's . . . well, it's downright embarrassing."

Nan was not so reticent. She sighed and heaved herself forward on Angela's couch, till her stubby legs let her feet reach the ground. "Honestly, I hate the whole business. I hated it when you told me about it yesterday—and I still do. Breaking into Sweetie's place . . . it feels—bad."

"That's it," Stella said softly. "It's just not decent, somehow, poking around in a dead woman's things. In *anyone* else's things, alive or dead. I was brought up to respect privacy."

"Furthermore," Nan continued, "I don't like the idea that we might find out something we aren't supposed to know. Like about poor Sam. I mean, I didn't know he'd pushed his wife out a window . . ."

"Was only suspected of it, Nan," Angela corrected.

"Okay, okay . . . but the thing is, every time I eat a cinnamon bun or butter a slice of homemade sourdough bread, I'll think of that. It's ruined lunch for me, Angela, it truly has. And I don't know what else might be ruined by things we'd find out. Why, Nurse Washington might be an axe murderess . . . Our headwaitress might be an arsonist . . . Torgeson might be a transvestite . . ."

Caledonia snorted. "I'd love it! Don't tell me you'd mind anything Gilfillan might have had on The Warthog. Hah—I wonder what he would look like in a dress."

Angela held her hand up, like a child asking to recite. "We have to try, don't we? I mean, we've come this far . . . And you ate a cinnamon bun at breakfast, Nan, without choking, so I'm not sure I believe you about it spoiling your meals . . ."

"Of course I didn't mean it literally."

"You know," Stella interrupted in her diffident voice, 'if people want to share things about their life, they tell you. We might be looking into things people dont' want *any*body to know, let alone blackmailers."

Caledonia disagreed. "Anyway, I bet we can't find out a single thing we don't already know—or suspect. I don't believe there are any deep, dark secrets. Nobody here at Camden acts very secretive."

"Well, maybe not," Angela said. "But I say we should try."

"Even if you wanted to," Nan objected, "how are you going to get in? I mean, the bars are still on the back windows—and now they've locked the front door. There isn't any other way in, and that's all there is to it."

"Not true," Angela said, "there's always some other way." Her chin was thrust forward noticeably, at the angle the Admiral always called her fighting trim. "And if you don't want to do it, I'll do it myself. But you have to come along, at least . . . I may need help."

And thus it was that, late that night, when the last yard lights had gone off along the walk, and all the doors to the main building had been closed with a night latch except the garden door, Angela slipped quietly along her hall, tiptoeing along in her only pair of slacks and her one pair of sneakers, to meet her three friends by Sweetie's cottage.

CHAPTER 7

ANYONE ABROAD in the garden that night—not a thing common for the elderly, whose dimming eyesight made walking through the shadows treacherous at best—would have been fascinated to see a pair of legs, swathed in slacks and terminating in tennis shoes, sticking through the window six feet up and to the left of Sweetie Gilfillan's front door. The legs were thrashing, wriggling, kicking . . .

They belonged to the late Admiral Benbow's widow, whose upper body and head were invisible within the Gilfillan apartment. The visible portions of Angela's body included her hips, which seemed firmly wedged in the window, and her feet and legs, which protruded, moving in a kind of erratic butterfly kick, watched intently by Nan Church and Stella Austin, standing on the porch floor looking unhappy, and by Caledonia Wingate, looking equally unhappy and standing on a wooden garden bench that had been moved near to the Gilfillan door.

"Push harder," Angela hissed, frantically, wriggling and twisting against the window frame. "I seem to be stuck. Why I ever let you talk me into this . . ."

"What?" Caledonia said. "I can't hear you . . . Hey, you two, give us a hand. She seems to be stuck."

"Well, I can hear *you*," Angela said, grasping the edge of the door jamb inside the room with her one hand and using it like a lever to help turn herself, "and I wish you'd be quiet. All I said was, why did I ever let you talk me into this . . . "

It had seemed the only way to get in, finally, when they surveyed the possibilities. They had tiptoed through the darkened garden to the porch, only to find the door was indeed firmly locked, with Shorty Swanson's carpentry at last applied where it should have been. "Look here though," Caledonia had whispered, grinning, and directed her penlight at Grogan's door jamb, where pale tan plastic wood, not as yet painted to match the frame, filled up the offending screw holes Shorty had mistakenly created.

Nan had smiled in appreciation but Angela was impatient. "Shine that flash this way . . ." she said and grabbed Caledonia's hand, turning it so the light went back to the lock now on Sweetie's door. "Well, obviously, the door is out. What now?"

"If we had a screwdriver," Nan said, "maybe we could—"

"No we couldn't," Caledonia interrupted. "It's those funny ones they put in that you can't get out unless you drill, once they're in. They've thought of everything."

"Maybe not everything," Angela said, "let's at least look around out in back."

"You three go ahead if you want to," Stella said. "I'm staying right here." She seated herself firmly on one of the benches which had been placed every few yards down the garden path to help any of the residents who found walking hard and needed rest now and then, as they went to or from the main building.

"At least you didn't bring your knitting," Angela said, annoyed at Stella's defection.

Thus three cylindrical shadows of vastly different girth and height eased their way along the walkway between buildings A and B, and thence around to the rear of building B. There they came to a ragged halt as their owners faced a discouraging prospect: no doors—only a line of windows covered with wrought-iron security grillwork.

"All right—let me try the bars . . ." Caledonia whispered, grabbing the grill on the first window of the Gilfillan apartment. It shifted slightly in its concrete setting, but less than a quarter-inch—not enough to suggest they could ease even one bar free from the window ledge.

Angela tiptoed to the far end of the line and tested, while Nan worked away at the center windows . . . and in a moment their progress drew them together. "No luck," Caledonia said. "Well, what now? Do we give up and go home?"

"Not yet," Angela whispered. "Come on back to the front door again. There must be something . . ."

The cylindrical shadows moved off again, single file, around the end and again to the front of the building, where Stella rose silently to join them.

"No luck," Caledonia said to her, in explanation.

"How about those little windows?" Angela pointed out, once they had stationed themselves in front of the Gilfillan door again. "There—on either side of the door."

The others gazed upward skeptically. "Well, to begin with, they're too high. We might give someone a boost up from this side," Nan said, "but going through you'd fall. Be reasonable, Angela. We're too old for acrobatics."

Angela bristled. "*I* could do it . . . it wouldn't bother *me. I've* kept myself in good shape. Well, provided I went slow, of course." She glanced around—and spotted the bench Stella had just vacated. "Help me," she said, as she darted to it. "Come on, help me."

The three others, shaking their heads in unison, came off the porch together. Caledonia and Nan each took one end of the bench, Angela and Stella supported the middle, and taking tiny steps and puffing hard, they lugged their burden back to the porch and set it up against the wall. "This won't work," Nan was muttering, while Caledonia was saying, "The windows are locked anyhow," and Stella was murmuring tensely, "We must *not* do this. We simply must *not.*"

Bench in position, Caledonia, after one more *sotto voce* protest

("You couldn't even carry the bench over alone, Angela. How you think you're going to climb . . ."), gingerly hoisted her bulk up onto it, steadied herself with a hand against the wall, and pushed against the window, now straight in front of her face. It moved not an inch. "Locked!" she croaked, and carefully eased herself down again. "Well, that's it," she went on more cheerfully. "Let's move the bench back and go home. I was against this expedition from the beginning . . ."

"Now you just wait a second," Angela said. *"Wait."* And with agility born of anger, she took off one of her sneakers, clambered onto the bench, then eased herself upright. Stella and Nan both reached out, involuntarily, to steady her, both muttering, "Oh, dear" and "Be careful" as they grasped at Angela's tubby little form.

Once in position, one hand against the wall to steady herself, Angela swung the shoe like a hammer. It was soft, but she flailed with all her might and the glass gave way with a little pop, the pane flying inward and landing somewhere below within the darkened room, making only the smallest "chink" as it broke.

"Gosh," Angela said, as surprised as the others. *"Gosh."* But she strained to reach her arm around through the opening and fiddled with the catch till it fell open. Then she pushed at the window until, with infinite reluctance, the old paint around the frame let go, and the window swung inward with only a tiny creak.

"Okay. Okay, now—I'm going in," Angela said, her voice wobbling only the tiniest bit.

"I don't know about all this," Caledonia said. "I don't like to give in to anything—especially old age. But when it comes to clambering around where you could break something . . . Old arms and legs snap too easily."

"Angela, I wish you'd think again. I'm not sure—" That was Nan.

Stella merely moaned softly what might have been, "Oh dear, oh please no, oh dear . . ."

"You all can do what you like. I'm going in." Angela said in a muffled voice. She had bent over to retie her shoe. "Of course," she added, as she straightened up again and reached to grasp the window ledge, "I could really use a boost . . . I don't think I'm strong enough to lift myself up here . . ."

Stella recoiled, all the way to the outer edge of the porch, but with a resigned sigh, Nan and Caledonia each grabbed one of Angela's legs and lifted, and the blocky body rose silently and was inserted, head first, into the tiny opening. Head, shoulders (with difficulty), bustline—all scraped through, though barely. The waist was a very tight fit . . . and then came the hips, which jammed against the frame and held firmly.

"Push harder," Angela said. But it took a good deal more of her wriggling and their pushing—not to mention well-meaning instructions like "Tuck in, Angela—tuck in!"—for her to get her hips through the opening, at which point she fell with a sudden scraping noise through the window to the inside.

"Omigawd," Caledonia said. "Angela—Angela—answer me— are you all right? She's killed herself, Nan, I know she has. She fell through that window and down—" Standing tiptoe on the bench, Caledonia tried to peer into the shadowy room. "It's dark in there. I can't see her."

Nan was awed. "There's nothing under that window . . . nothing to break the fall. She'd go straight to the floor."

"Oh-oh-oh . . ." Not surprisingly, Stella was simply beyond words.

"Speak to me," Caledonia implored again, peering inside, straining to see through the gloom. "Oh, lord, we should never—"

Angela's stubborn little face appeared at the window, almost nose to nose with Caledonia. "Hush up, all of you. I'm perfectly all right. I was dazed because it happened so fast . . . but that's all.

I fell onto the love seat, Nan . . . the one I'm standing on now."

"There isn't any love seat there," Nan said.

"Well," Angela said, "the furniture's been moved around some probably the police did it when they were tidying up . . . Anyhow, I had a nice, soft cushion to catch me."

Privately, she felt shaken and frightened, and her stomach churned from the impact of the landing, which had knocked the wind out of her. She had bruised her leg—probably on the frame of the love seat—and she'd scraped a forearm. And she knew her back would be sore tomorrow—never mind that she landed on the couch. All she wanted was to go home and take a hot bath—and go to bed. But she would have preferred being flayed alive to admitting that she could be jolted so badly by a fall onto cushions—that she was, in fact, what they said she was—a little old lady.

"Give me that flashlight, Caledonia," she ordered, and Caledonia meekly passed it through to her, then watched as the light jiggled and jumped around the living room. Angela hardly knew where to start and what to look for, but she went to the first thing she made out in the light . . . the bookcase, now restored to its feet, with its books back in the shelves. She took the books out, one at a time, read the titles, and fanned the leaves to let any hidden papers fall out.

"That's a waste of time," came a whispered directive from above her head. "You know the books were dumped by whoever searched the room—he'd have found anything that was in 'em. And the police have handled them, too, to tidy up, if nothing else—surely they'd have found a paper . . ."

"You can't tell," Angela muttered, stubbornly, and kept looking.

Bunyan's *Pilgrim's Progress* in the fancy binding of the Franklin Library's one-classic-every-two-months, pay-only-for-those-you-keep offer. Nothing hidden between the pages.

Mutiny on the Bounty, and *Random Harvest,* and *Goodbye, Mr. Chips,* all in paperback. Nothing.

Burke's Peerage, and *Successful Investment for the Beginner,* and *The New Aztec Treasures,* and *The Nuremberg Trials,* and *Gettysburg Revisited*—no secrets here.

Last shelf—*The Arthur Legends,* and T. H. White's *The Book of Merlin,* and Leonard Maltin's *Guide to Movies on TV.* Ignoring several mail order catalogues, a fat phone book in a needlepointed cover and a stack of sheet music, Angela pulled herself to her feet. It was all very disappointing—Caledonia would appear to be right. Not even a Lifesavers' wrapper fell out of one of them. Angela went to the desk.

"Here's something," she said excitedly, holding up a small pack of letters, held together with a rubber band.

"Bring 'em over—bring 'em over." Caledonia waved her arm through the window, and Angela met her hand with the pack of letters. "Now go on searching, Angela—we'll read these later."

"Photographs?" Angela whispered, holding aloft a largish yellow envelope.

"I dunno—maybe—bring 'em here." And Angela ran those, too, across the room.

Back at the desk Angela found a bill for renewal of a *Smithsonian* subscription and a letter from the Publisher's Clearing House declaring solemnly that Sweetie could already be a winner . . . Angela gave a sudden, involuntary shiver. Sweetie would never win anything, now.

Angela shook off the moment and pulled out the top drawer. Disappointingly, it held playing cards, most still with cellophane wrappers around the boxes, a pack of tallies, several scoring pads and some pencil stubs, a dog-eared booklet outlining the Goren point count.

The middle drawer yielded a stack of warranty forms and owner's manuals for a hair dryer, an electric pencil sharpener, a Water Pik, a TV and for a heating pad with built-in vibrator. Angela tossed them back, unhappy to read the legend on the heating-pad manual—"Gives new life to tired muscles." But not for Sweetie, she was thinking. She shivered again as she knelt to reach the bottom of the little secretary.

The last drawer jammed, refusing to open past one-quarter of its length. She transferred the little flashlight to her neck, holding it by clamping between her chin and her chest, so she could pull at the drawer with both hands. Then, without warning, it yielded, coming completely out and thumping onto the floor. Loose snapshots flew everywhere. She turned the light down at them. What should I do with these? she asked herself, then, recognizing the subject, thought: Oh, gosh, these are mostly very old . . . and just of Sweetie . . . memories, that's all. She started gathering them and stuffing them back into the drawer, with only the quickest glance.

Sweetie at Yosemite wearing jodhpurs and a leather jacket. Sweetie wearing an incredibly slim, droopy-necked dress that boasted fur trim around the ankle-length, deliberately uneven skirt, and matching fur on each end of the wide, six-foot-long scarf she had tossed around her neck . . . One end of the scarf hung free near her knees, the other end lay across the edge of a roadster's door. (Maybe a Graham? Angela wondered. Surely, she thought, the Admiral had called for her once in one just like that.) Sweetie beside a pay telescope on top of the Empire State, her 1930s dress blown tight against a girlish figure, the New York air of a half-century ago looking clean, free of soot and murk.

Amazing, Angela thought, hesitating over that one, how much she looked then like she looks now . . . or rather, like she looked . . . Some people change so much you wouldn't know them. Angela was well aware that she was one who had changed—old acquaintances told her so, even though she couldn't see it. But she'd have known Sweetie anywhere.

Suddenly Angela was sick with sorrow for the girl that had been in those pictures. What a dull little old woman she had become. Or rather, how dull she had *seemed* to be. The thoughts made the hair on Angela's forearms prickle and stand upright with that sense of malaise she had felt before. She looked back at the picture of Sweetie, smiling into the wind. All the mischief in that grin had been channeled into . . . into what? Something ugly, Angela thought—something ugly and dangerous.

She pushed the pictures down into the drawer, closed it firmly, and stood up. One foot was asleep and her knees were stiff and aching. And after only just a few minutes, Angela thought ruefully. What could be wrong? She discounted the unaccustomed crouch to floor level that had folded her limbs into unusually tight and cramped positions.

"Should I look in the bedroom?" she whispered across to the big, dark silhouette in the window.

"Of course," the shadow hissed back in Caledonia's voice. "You're in there now—it can't hurt . . . Might as well be hanged for a sheep as a lamb, you know."

Angela trotted off down the hall, led by the bobbing circle of dim light from the pencil flash. She was vaguely disappointed to see the clothing folded neatly and stacked on the bed. It would be hard to look the things over, if one had to get those stacks back exactly without showing they'd been disturbed.

She went to the dresser. The fine jewelry had been taken away and all that remained were costume pieces. Still, some of that looked expensive and in excellent taste. She fingered a heavy black and silver Maltese cross on a silk cord that lay tangled with a set of red, white and blue bangle bracelets that she remembered seeing Sweetie wear this last summer on July Fourth . . . She grimaced, as she also remembered Sweetie saying, with what Angela now knew to be a fake sigh of regret, "Not like you girls with your lovely things—gems and gold and all, but nice enough for poor little me to dress up for the National birthday party. Right?" The self-pity had been distasteful at the time. Now that she knew it was mere hypocrisy, it seemed worse. What a liar Sweetie was, after all.

The drawers of Sweetie's vanity were empty . . . the cosmetics and prescription bottles swept away and probably now resting on some forensic technician's desk. She opened the closets . . . the hangers had been replaced but hung empty; no one would care now about keeping the clothes free from creases. She pulled open dresser drawers—all empty.

In the little bathroom the medicine chest stood empty save for a lonely tube of toothpaste and an over-used brush. The space under the sink yielded a roach motel (untenanted) and a box of Kleenex in one of those fancy wooden holders. Angela pulled out a tissue and touched her forehead . . . I really didn't realize it was so hot . . . she thought. I seem to be perspiring . . . Is this what they mean by "having nerves"? She pulled another tissue, and it seemed to jam in the holder, tearing raggedly. Angela worked a finger into the box to free the tissue—and her fingers touched something hard . . . not the side of the box, but—She pulled and twisted and with some difficulty, pulled out a small notebook that had been wedged between the tissues and the side of the ornamental box.

"A diary," she said aloud as she pried it out. "Sweetie must have hid it so nobody else could see her private thoughts."

But when she opened it, the book seemed instead to be a kind of miniature ledger. Indeed a label on the cover read "Charity Donations." Inside, each page of the tiny ring binder was headed with a name and divided into columns beneath the names. The columns seemed to be dates and amounts—very dull and ordinary, until you noticed the names heading each page. A bemused Angela read: "Dopey, Grumpy, Snow White, the Dungeon Master, the Red Queen, the Black Knight, the Arkansas Traveler . . ."

The book was certainly in Sweetie's handwriting. Angela had seen it often—on lists, on notes, on minutes of the Residents' Council the year Sweetie was secretary. Angela would know those tiny, pinched letters anywhere.

And suddenly she knew what this notebook was: a list of blackmail receipts. The revelation made her glance nervously around at drawers and shelves—no, nothing was out of place to let anyone see she'd been there . . .

Back down the hall she went, stubbing her toe as she raced around the corner into the living room, because the little penlight was growing dim. "Pssst—psst . . . I'm here . . . Caledonia, give me a hand . . ." She thrust the little notebook inside her blouse, wedging it firmly between her tightly brassiered breasts. Her loose shirt bulged only a slight bit more over the bosom. The penlight slid into her pocket.

Then, both hands freed, she clambered up on the love seat again, a bit more slowly than she had climbed on the bench to enter. To her disgust (though not completely to her surprise) her muscles were already stiffening from the unaccustomed use, as well as from the fall she had taken. She winced but grimly pulled herself up and thrust her face and arms through the opening. "Here I am. Take my hands somebody—" And she looked up to find herself eye to eye with Lieutenant Martinez!

The shock hit her like a glass of ice water. She couldn't think of a single thing to say.

"May I help you, Mrs. Benbow?" Martinez said politely, reaching his arms out to grasp and pull on her shoulders. "Easy, there, it's a tight fit . . ."

There was considerably less wriggling and twisting, with Martinez steadily pulling on her, and as she made it through, he picked her up in midair like a child and swung her to the ground to stand beside her three friends, silent and sheepish. "If you'll wait just a moment?" He turned back to the window and swung it shut, saw the broken pane, turned to Angela and shook his head sadly—"Mrs. Benbow! Tch-tch-tch . . ." Then he reached through and closed the latch. He jumped down and in one motion picked up the bench, which (to the ladies' dismay) he carried easily back to its place beside the walk.

"Whose place shall we go to, ladies?" he asked quietly, "Yours or mine?"

There was another silence. Then Caledonia spoke. "Mine, I guess. It's right there—across the garden in the first building on the other side, you know . . ."

Martinez bowed them ahead of him and the group moved off, considerably more briskly and openly than the four ladies had moved into the garden forty-five minutes earlier.

"Sit down, ladies," said Martinez, once inside. Assuming the role of host—or boss—seemed natural to him, and natural to all of them, for they meekly settled themselves in chairs circled around him. "Now I want an explanation," he went on, "and it better be a good one. What were you doing there? What did you hope to accomplish? And more importantly, what *did* you accomplish? Did you bring anything away . . . one at a time, one at a time," as they all began to explain at once. "Mrs. Wingate, you begin."

Caledonia had the good grace not to blame it all on Angela, though her self-protective instincts suggested that would be the most comfortable way. "Well, you see, we thought . . . that is, we were talking . . . and we thought . . ."

"You thought," Martinez helped her out, but his tone was sad, "that we were too dumb to know our business and you could do the detective work better. You thought we wouldn't scold you whatever happened because nobody scolds little old ladies. You thought—"

"No such thing," Angela interrupted. "It's just that we're all tired of being babied and kept in the dark. You act as though this is really none of our business."

"Well, it really isn't," Martinez said.

"Wrong!" Angela fired back. "It's our friend—well, anyway, one of our close acquaintances—who was killed. Well, you know what I mean—someone who lived right with us. We're all in shock over this . . . and scared to death—who knows what might happen next."

Martinez rolled his eyes to heaven. "Very good, Mrs. Benbow, very dramatic . . . I only wish it were true. I just wish you were a little frightened. Instead, you're running around in the garden in the moonlight playing detective—when there may be a killer loose. You ladies act like this was some sort of social event at the sorority house."

"And you act like you thought if you told us any details, we'd wilt like lilies in the sun," Angela said, defending herself with the tactic of attack—behavior that always won out, in the old days, against the Admiral. "But it's just the opposite . . . I mean if we knew for instance that Sweetie was killed because she made someone angry, we'd have no need to be afraid ourselves. If, on the other hand, it was a beach bum, looking for money—he might come back, you see. Some of this is bound to be 'our business'—and it's not just idle curiosity."

"Furthermore," Caledonia chimed in, "we decided we know more about each other and understand more about people in retirement than you'll ever be able to find out. We were the logical ones to find out what you couldn't."

Nan nodded her head vigorously. "We may have done it partly because we enjoy being active and in the center of things . . . not being left out and shoved aside . . . But mostly because we thought we could contribute something."

"We acknowledge it wasn't the right thing to do," Stella added, apologetically. "But if we found something you'd overlooked . . ." She stopped and looked embarrassed. "Well, you know what I mean."

Martinez looked from one to the other and shook his head. "I guess I don't have to tell you, do I, that I disagree? To put it mildly, a murder investigation is no place for an amateur. Besides, I'm not sure you would know a clue if it came up and bit you. Oh, you may be right about knowing other old people's minds—and specifically the others here at the center. But believe me, we'll solve this without you—and probably a whole lot faster than if you keep sneaking in and messing around with the evidence."

"We didn't 'mess around,'" Angela began.

But Martinez cut her short. "Sure. What's that in your hand, then, Mrs. Wingate? A peanut butter sandwich?"

Caledonia's jaw dropped slightly and she realized she had been holding the pack of letters in one hand, while the edges of the photographer's envelope protruded very obviously from the other. Even Caledonia's hands were not quite large enough to hide the evidence. "We—we were going to give these to you," she said and handed him the letters.

"Mrs. Wingate, I know you won't believe me, but we've read these all already. Since you're so curious—" He held up the envelopes one at a time. "The top one here is from a newspaper pattern service returning Miss Gilfillan's check for a Size 16 skirt and saying the pattern has been discontinued. The next is a bill for a Brazilian moss agate she had set in a cuff-bracelet. Under that is an ad for cut-rate panty hose . . ."

"*Enough.* We aren't stupid—we get the point," Nan said. "Do you mean to say there's nothing interesting there at all?"

"How about these pictures," Caledonia said, passing the yellow envelope along to him.

"Have you looked inside this envelope?" he asked.

"No."

"There are pictures of all of you—and a few other residents— taken at your costume party last month. Perhaps you remember Miss Gilfillan carrying a camera? You all posed in the 'cowboy and western' costumes you wore . . . and there's nothing there suspicious—except maybe," he said looking sideways at Caledonia, "where on earth you found those chaps you were wearing. You don't own them, do you?"

Caledonia grinned in spite of herself. "Weren't they somethin'? No, I got those from one of the handymen who does our repair work around the place. He rodeos, sometimes, and he's about my size."

Martinez would have preferred it if he could have stifled his grin—but alas, it got away from him. "Well, at any rate, take my word for it, you haven't got a thing here we haven't seen and examined and evaluated . . . and nothing's worth a hill of beans. But you risked getting yourself shot by the police guard . . ."

"What police guard!" Nan exclaimed.

"We didn't see anyone," Stella said. With no knitting to occupy her hands, her fingers worked together constantly, betraying inner agitation she could normally conceal.

"You weren't supposed to see him," Martinez nodded. "I'm glad to learn that he stayed out of the way. Incidentally, he is armed and a very good shot. Fortunately, though you may not have spotted him, he recognized you. Instead of taking precipitate action, he phoned me . . . which is how I happened on the scene."

"You frightened us," Angela complained, squinting up at him.

"Good," Martinez said. "I'm *glad* I frightened you, Mrs. Benbow. You went in where you knew we didn't want you to go—not once, but twice. You handled things—moved things—changed lord knows what hint or clue. If we never find who killed your Miss Gilfillan, it might well be because *you* obscured some pointer. . . ." He turned to face the others. "Chipmunks in a vegetable garden couldn't wreak more mischief than you four."

. Angela's mental picture of Caledonia and Nan, dressed in sweatshirts and caps as Alvin and Theodore, made her choke back an audible laugh. (Stella she could not visualize in chipmunk disguise at all.)

Martinez turned at the sound she made. "Did you have something to add to the discussion?"

"Well, actually, I do," Angela defended herself. She had just remembered the hidden notebook again, because its corners had begun to dig into her tender skin. To Martinez' obvious amusement and Stella's obvious disapproval, Angela wriggled a little, unbuttoned the top of her shirt, and reached down inside.

"I've got something here I bet you didn't know Sweetie owned . . ." she said as she did so, and glared as Nan muffled a laugh. Caledonia grinned as well, but Martinez managed to keep a smile from his lips as Angela pulled out the little book with a flourish and handed it across, without apparently realizing what her words and gestures had implied.

"Hey . . ." Nan forgot her little laugh at Angela's expense. "What's that?" Stella and Caledonia craned their necks to see as well. But the writing was so small and cramped they could scarcely make out, at that distance, that there was anything written on the pages at all. They could not even read the label. Martinez read it aloud.

"Mmmm . . . 'Charity Donations.'" He flipped it open and looked at the notations penned into the pages. "Well, well—this seems to be a sort of record of accounts. Mrs. Benbow, your wild guess about blackmail may be worth some investigation after all. Perhaps it's not so wild as it seemed. Where did you find this?"

"Hidden inside her Kleenex box," Angela said. "Pushed up from the bottom and wedged beside the stack of tissues. She has one of those fancy carved wood holders that take the boutique size tissues. After you've taken their outer box off, you slide the tissues up into the ornamental holder."

"I can understand her concern that nobody see the book, if it really is a record of blackmail victims' payments. But why hide it inside her own apartment?" Martinez seemed to be thinking aloud as he spoke.

"Well, if you and Angela are right," Caledonia said, "she may have been hiding it from the maids. They come once a week to clean inside our apartments, Lieutenant, and they do a thorough job. They'd see anything we left out—and a book might fall and come open . . . See what I mean?"

Martinez nodded. "If they read it, they might ask awkward questions, even if they didn't understand what it meant."

"I guess it all makes sense," Nan said slowly. "She wouldn't bother to hide something that wasn't pretty sensitive. But what a hiding place! Who'd ever think of a Kleenex box?"

"I still don't understand," Stella said. "What is that book? What's in it?"

Angela was eager to share her guesses—especially with the lieutenant an attentive listener. "I don't *know*, mind you, but I think it's her ledger recording blackmail payments. I think the charity she mentions on the label is *her*. That was a joke she made all the time, remember? When some group came through asking for funds—the Girl Scouts with cookies or the Salvation Army at Christmas. She always said—we thought she was poor, you see, so it made sense—she always said, 'No, I save my money for my favorite charity: *me.*' And we always smiled, even though we'd heard it a million times."

"We laugh at all the old jokes, here, for each other's sake," Caledonia confirmed to Martinez.

"What does it say? Are there names?" Nan asked, standing up and actually walking toward Martinez.

Martinez pushed the little notebook smoothly into his pocket. "Mrs. Church, unless names from fairy tales mean anything to you, you couldn't tell a thing from this. There isn't a real name here, and I suppose we'll never find out who some of these stand for. Oh, we'll find out a few, if she really was blackmailing any-body, as Mrs. Benbow thinks she was—but never all of them. Now, if you'll excuse me . . ." He straightened and moved to the door.

"Ladies, promise me one thing. You WON'T DO IT AGAIN. Now, I mean it. I'll do more than scold, next time. It's hard and cruel to take a lady to jail—any lady—and especially a genteel lady of advanced years. But all of you will go to jail—and not just as a one-day object lesson—if there is any more breaking and entering. Or tampering with evidence. Is that clear?"

Eight solemn eyes stared at him unwinking. Four grayed heads nodded in unison.

"Ladies," he said, bowing slightly, "I wish you a pleasant good evening," and he whirled out, closing the door behind him. Again in unison, all four ladies fell backwards into their sofa cushions, feeling intense relief that they were not to be punished . . . not this time.

CHAPTER 8

I T WAS the next morning that Mr. Grogan fell down the back stairs on his way to breakfast.

Angela had joined Nan and Stella over a slice of sugar-sweet cantaloupe, French toast with boysenberry syrup and a cup of excellent coffee. Caledonia, who ordinarily treated sleeping late as a sacred duty, had managed—in honor of their exciting evening adventure—to rouse herself this morning, though she entered the dining room after her friends were well into their meal. Caledonia poured herself a water tumbler full of cranberry juice from a carafe at the breakfast bar—where one could also serve oneself from a steaming pot of (she shuddered and looked hastily away) hot oatmeal—and walked over to settle herself at the table.

"Not much today, Dolly," she boomed as the waitress came up to take her order. "Two eggs over medium, bacon and sausage, four slices of whole wheat toast with unsalted butter—Gawd, I hate that stuff, but the doctor says the salted kind is bad for me— oh, and bring me some of those tiny pancakes . . . but no syrup. I'll use the marmalade today—I use too much when I pour the syrup on . . . You ought to watch sweets and salt, too, Nan, with your bad heart." As Dolly left, Caledonia drank deep of the cranberry juice. "Good potassium in that stuff," she said, smacking her lips.

"Besides, now that I've got used to the flavor, I actually like it."

Nan nodded and went on pouring boysenberry syrup.

"What's on the schedule today, Caledonia?" Angela asked eagerly.

"I'm not sure. You know, I wish there was a way to find out who those people were in that book you gave Lieutenant Martinez, Angela. Then we'd be getting somewhere. Those people might tell us things about Sweetie . . ."

"Wait a minute—wait a minute . . ." Nan banged the little syrup pitcher down on the table so hard, the others jumped, and Stella gingerly picked the little pot up to see if it had cracked and would leak. It hadn't, and therefore wouldn't.

"Problems?" Caledonia asked.

"I'll say." Nan sounded angry. "I was right in the room with the rest of you last night when the Lieutenant told us, 'No more playing detective!'—and he said it in no uncertain terms. If you didn't hear him, I did. And if you heard him and didn't understand him, ask me what he meant."

"I agree with Nan," Stella said primly. "We ought to forget about this now—pay attention to the Lieutenant."

"Oh, come on, girls," Angela coaxed. "You aren't going to let that man scare you out of this project, are you?"

"Martinez said he'd throw us in jail," Nan went on stubbornly. "And he meant it. You can't possibly intend to go on snooping around."

"Oh, nonsense, Nan—thank you, Dolly," Caledonia moved off and took the fresh coffee from their waitress, then waited till Dolly moved off out of earshot. "You surprise me. I expect timidity from Beanie"—she smiled fondly at Stella—"but you? Well, I for one haven't had so much fun in years."

Angela's little face was pink and her eyes were bright with excitement. "It *has* been thrilling . . . I mean, it was really scary to be alone in that apartment. With shadows everywhere and the silence . . ."

"Loved it, didn't you?" Caledonia said. "See what I mean, girls?"

Nan held her ground. "He said that guard might have shot us."

"Well, then we just have to avoid the garden at night, that's all," Angela urged. "There are plenty of other things we can do."

"Like what?" Stella was skeptical.

Angela leaned forward. "Like do what Caledonia said—find out who those names in the book belonged to. I was thinking—Sweetie must have written the accounts down because they were too complicated to keep in her head. But she was afraid that even if she hid the book, someone *might* see it some time—so she wrote those names in a kind of secret code."

"Well, if it's a code," Nan said stubbornly, "then she didn't mean for anyone to be able to figure it out. You can't expect to decipher—"

"But we *can*. At least, I think so . . . I believe she must have chosen those names because something about the person reminded her of the character . . . or the other way around. So it should be possible for us to figure it out. It had to be something fairly obvious. I mean, what's the use of choosing a secret code name for somebody if it's easily forgotten?"

Caledonia smiled. "And that's one thing we surely would all do, if the connection wasn't perfectly apparent. I mean, you know what they say around here: 'First it's your hearing, then it's your eyesight, and then it's your memory for names.'"

"But Martinez has the book," Nan said. "You didn't make a list or anything . . ."

"Well, I think I can remember a few of the names," Angela said.

Stella was still playing the role of Doubting Thomas. "We-e-ll, then," she said, "what were some of them?"

Angela screwed up her eyes and furrowed her brow with what the Admiral had always called her "Plotting the Course" expression. "Let me see . . . Well, there was 'The Black Knight' and there was 'The Dungeon Master' and then something-or-other from *Alice in Wonderland*. Oh, and 'Snow White'—so of course there was 'Doc' and 'Sleepy'—the seven dwarfs, you know. And there was . . . well, there was 'Grumpy' . . ."

Nan shook her head. "Impossible. You'll never get anywhere. I mean, how would you ever guess which one of us was 'Grumpy'? It could always refer to someone who doesn't even live here. And even if it does refer to us—well, we're *all* grumpy, day in and day out. The worse the arthritis hurts, the grumpier I get . . . the later the mail comes, the grumpier Emma Grant gets . . . the hotter the weather, the grumpier Mary Moffet gets . . . the smaller the portions of food, the grumpier Caledonia—"

"No, no, no: It would have to be somebody who was monumentally grumpy—whose chief characteristic was being grumpy. A code name wouldn't be any good unless it could only refer to one person. So it can't be someone like us—not plain, everyday grumpy," Angela said. *"Think.* If you had to choose just one person in this whole place and call him or her 'Grumpy,' wouldn't that be—"

The air was split with a wild yell that seemed to come from the other side of the wall that formed the back of the dining room . . . a series of terrible thumps that started near the ceiling and moved erratically down toward the floor . . . the crash of broken glass . . . and at last a stream of incredibly inventive curses in the loud and unmistakable voice of Grogan.

"Lord help us," Caledonia said. "The man seems to have fallen down the back stairs."

The stairs at either end of the lobby were broad and carpeted, well lit and bounded by sturdy railings. Residents were warned by signs to "Watch Your Step," and to "Grasp the Railings Firmly." Even so, from time to time someone fell, and the thickness of carpeting had been doubled in an effort to cushion bodies against the inevitable bruises—and worse. In fact, residents were encouraged to use the rickety old elevator, and to avoid the stairs altogether.

But in four places besides these two main stairways, there were steep, narrow, utility stairs, which could be used to short cut through the building. The maids used those stairs. Medical staff and occasionally an ambulance crew or rescue squad, and once in a while the police and firemen, also came and went rapidly and privately by these steps. One such set of stairs ran between the second floor and the kitchen, and was especially useful when nurses took a food tray from the kitchen to a sick resident on the upper level.

If residents found the broad, well-lighted front stairs treacherous, these back stairs were nothing short of lethal. After any number of people stumbled and fell while trying to short-cut to the back door of the dining room, big signs were posted saying RESIDENTS FORBIDDEN TO USE THESE STAIRS, and a metal, accordianfold gate was put across the upper access. But the gate was only closed, never locked, and older folks get into the habit of believing that they know best, and that regulations laid forth for the general populace really don't apply to them. So from time to time a resident appeared in the dining room through the back door, and the diners already seated pretended they didn't notice that someone had once more defied the order and used the back stairs.

On this morning it was Grogan, wandering through the upper hall on some errand or other, who slid back the metal gate and stepped off into space . . . and pitched head first down the stairs, ricocheting off the walls and shouting imprecations against various vindictive gods as he went. He came to rest athwart the bottom step, accompanied by the sound of breaking glass, his spectacles crooked on his nose, which was bleeding copiously, and one arm doubled back at an odd angle.

"Don't move, Mr. Grogan," the cook was shouting.

"I bloody well *can't* move," Grogan said. "I'm half-killed, I am."

"Get a doctor—get a doctor—someone get a doctor," Dolly was shouting, dancing around the fallen Grogan. "Oh, Mr. Grogan—oh, Mr. Grogan . . ."

"Oh yourself!" Grogan shouted back. "I'm bleedin'—I've broken every bone in my body—I'm dying . . . Now *SHUT UP.*"

The shouts died out as Dolores, the headwaitress, glided to the connecting door and closed it firmly, shutting off sight and sound from the fascinated diners. "We're taking care of everything," she announced smoothly, "now, just go on with your meals."

"Is he hurt badly?" Angela called hastily, as Dolores sailed past their table.

"There'll be an announcement posted on the residents' bulletin board by the desk," Dolores said easily. "We'll let you know later. Please continue eating, ladies." And she whisked out toward the office, no doubt to report to Torgeson.

For a moment there was a hush in the dining room, and then gradually the sounds of silver on china, cups in saucers, and humming conversations began to resume normal patterns.

Nan said, "God must have been listening to your question, Angela. That was a direct answer for certain."

"Question?" It had been driven straight out of Angela's head.

"About who we'd call 'Grumpy' if we had to choose."

Angela nodded and Caledonia sighed. "No doubt about it," she said, "if that's a blackmail list, then Grogan was being blackmailed, because he's 'Grumpy' if there ever was one."

"I wonder, though," Stella murmured, "how we'd find out for sure."

Angela had the answer. "I'll ask him," she said pertly. "If he lives, of course."

But Angela was underestimating both the hardness of the Grogan head, and the floppy resilience of drunken arm and legs. Grogan's skinny body was purple with bruises, and he had acquired two giant black eyes that made him look like a white-haired raccoon. He was also aching from top to bottom. But later, after he had undergone a full battery of X-rays and tests in the small health care facility across the street, it was determined that all he needed was bed rest. He was very far from dead.

"The way the nurses watch him," Angela reported, "I suspect they're also keeping him there to dry him out—to keep him from taking a drink. The other two nodded assent.

Angela had walked across the street to see Grogan as soon as the notice went up that he was mending satisfactorily, all things considered, and that (Torgeson was using this opportunity to give them all a reminder) residents *must not* use the emergency stairs.

"No reason you can't see him," Aretha Thomas, the head nurse at the nursing facility, said. "If you want to. I mean, why anybody would want to visit that old curmudgeon beats me. Still," she went on, when Angela neither backed down nor commented, "everybody to their own poison." She beckoned Angela behind her, and led her down the hall. "I wonder, was he always this nasty?" the nurse said. "Or did he grow that way over the years? I mean, it takes time to make someone that rotten . . . Here we are. First door on the right. Knock before you go in, Miz Benbow . . . no telling what the old goat is up to." She went off cheerfully, whistling "When Irish Eyes Are Smiling" as she went.

"Are you in, Mr. Grogan?" Angela ventured at the door, peering carefully around it.

"Where the bleeding hell else would I be?" Grogan said. "Don't hide behind the door . . . come in where I can see you . . . Oh, it's you, is it? Well, come in, come in . . . Came to see if the old drunk survived the fall?"

"Oh, uh . . . w-well, hardly th-that," Angela stammered, taken aback. "I mean, I did come to see how you are . . ." She looked at the figure in the bed and winced. Grogan lay on his stomach, wearing a turban of bandages, as though to keep his brains from leaking out of his skull. His wrist was taped up and his face was discolored and swollen—but other than that, he seemed in fairly good condition. She took a deep breath and went on, "That was such a dreadful fall . . ."

"Damn right," Grogan said, his voice filled with pride. "Would've killed anybody else in the place."

"How did you fall to begin with?"

"Oh," Grogan said nonchalantly, "I was drunk as usual . . . put my foot out and there was nothing there . . . I mean, I missed the step, somehow . . . I knew I was going—I could feel myself fall—and there wasn't a damn thing I could do about it. At the time it seemed as if that fall took forever."

"It certainly seemed so to us, Mr. Grogan. You didn't miss a single step on the way down—we heard you hit every one. Is—is your wrist sprained?"

"Yup," Grogan said. "Sure is. Hurts like hell, too, I'll have you know."

"Do you—do you have a skull fracture?"

"Not as far as they can tell. Bandages can't hurt, they said. Nose might be broken, too, and I've got some bad cuts in my southern end where I sat down hard on my pint bottle of bourbon. I crushed it . . . and I've got the lacerations to prove it. Oh, and they tell me I hit my face bad, and that I have a pair of shiners. I haven't been able to check in the mirror yet. How do I look?"

"Mr. Grogan, I have never seen anyone look more like a giant panda and less like a human being."

Grogan cracked a painful smile. "Oooh, that hurts. I think I'll keep a straight face, Mrs. B. I can't bear to grin at you. Besides, it's out of character, anyhow. You'll have to take my word, I'm smiling inside . . . It was nice of you to come calling. What brought you?" he added, returning to his customary paranoia. "Did somebody I owe money to ask you to see if I've been turned into a bad debt?"

There seemed no tactful way to bring the matter up, so Angela plunged straight ahead—one of the few directions she ever seemed to use. "Well, in a manner of speaking, that's exactly it. Mr. Grogan, were you being blackmailed?"

"Wh-wha-wh-" Grogan began to splutter and though the bruises made any red in his face invisible, Angela could see the color sweep up his neck.

"You see," Angela pressed on, "we found a book Sweetie Gilfillan had—an account book with several names with money amounts. Like a record of payments. We thought—I thought," she amended, "it was a blackmail list. And I want to confirm my suspicion."

"Damn," Grogan said. "Damn-damn-double-damn. . . . Well, if my name's on that list, I suppose you really know already, and there's no use denying it. But Mrs. B.—for God's sake" —Grogan's voice was lowered—"how may others know about this?"

Angela was surprised at the strangely altered tone of his voice. In response to his husky half-whisper, she dropped her briskness and spoke softly as well. "The police have the list, Mr. Grogan. I—well, I just happened to see it by accident. It doesn't matter how."

"Anyone else see it? Please, Mrs. Benbow . . ."

"Well, the four of us—Nan Church and Stella Austin and Caledonia Wingate."

"I see. Well, they're good women—I know they won't tell anyone if you ask them not to. Promise me . . . please . . ."

Angela nodded, a little humbled by the results of her quest. "I don't see any reason the girls and I can't keep it a secret. But what—I mean—why did you . . ."

Grogan sighed. "I had a wife and daughter, Mrs. Benbow. Separated from them, of course, because of the drinking. After I left them, I was involved in a hit and run . . . not nice. Not nice. I left a young fellow dead in the road. Of course they caught me. I did time for manslaughter. I was lucky and got out while I still had a couple of years left to live outside that prison . . . But of course I wouldn't want my wife and daughter to know. I've done enough to them, believe me . . . They don't need to know what became of me. Grogan's not my real name, you see."

"But how did Sweetie find out, then?"

"That harpy . . . that damned blood-sucking woman . . . I spent a lot of time in the library, Mrs. Benbow—our own library, in the main building, I mean. I read the newspapers, I read Westerns— we really have a lot of pretty good stuff—"

Angela nodded. Like the other Camden residents, she had— shortly after moving in—donated most of her own books to the library they maintained in common, when she discovered how little room there really was in those apartments. All the residents had free access to the library, and Sweetie had acted unofficially as curator of the collection—dusting the books and sorting them, scolding the careless readers who returned a mystery to the shelf that held romances, bullying donations from the residents for new bindings on some of the well-worn favorites and for magazine subscriptions. Olaf Torgeson was a world-class tightwad, but he did subscribe to several newspapers every day for use in the library—it saved having the paper boys traipse through the halls disturbing the late sleepers.

"I've seen you there, Mr. Grogan. But I always thought you were . . ." She hesitated.

"Asleep? Dead drunk and passed out? Well, sometimes I am . . . and that's how she caught me. I don't remember talking to her about my past—but obviously I did. It had to be one of those days—and there are more and more all the time—when the Irish mist is on me . . . I don't remember doing it, but I told her my hometown and my real name, may the Lord forgive this sinner. I've been a damn fool many times in my life—but seldom that bad.

"Well, she came sidling up to me one afternoon when nobody

else was in the library." He closed his eyes. "I can see her standing there with that cheesecloth pad she used to dust the books, and that phony, sick-sweet smile she used to hang on her face . . . And she said how would I like everyone back in Spokane to know I was a miserable drunk?

"Well, I just laughed at her. I told her they all knew it already—and that was why I'd left. She couldn't do a thing to me with that information, I said. And that was my mistake. I never did know when to let well enough alone and keep my sloppy mouth shut. I said she'd have to do better than that if she wanted to see me upset—and she got mad as hell. She glared at me and she said she'd see about that and she slammed out of there. I figure she really liked to see people get upset and grovel and ask her to lay off—and I hadn't played the game the way she wanted it played. Because she went to a lot of trouble, then.

"She must have spent hours in the San Diego library—and out at the University using their microfilms of back issues of newspapers from Washington State. . . . It was weeks and I'd forgotten all about it. Then one day I was in the library reading Zane Grey—I don't think I'll ever read *Riders of the Purple Sage* again without remembering how she came walking over and pulled my book down and laid a picture in it, on top of the pages, so I could see. It wasn't very good—just a Xerox of a newspaper shot—but you could tell it was me . . . coming out of court after the trial. And there was an article about my arrest and conviction that went with it.

"So then she smiled again and said, 'No, Mr. Grogan, who's laughing now?' And she showed me a letter addressed to my daughter. 'Your father is not just a drunk, but a murderer and a jailbird as well. He killed a man by hitting him with his car and then he drove off and left the man to die in the road. He was sentenced to twenty years.'" He fell silent. Then he turned partly over so he could look at Angela's face.

because I spend my life ashamed. It's to keep people from knowing what I'm really like inside. And I drink a lot—it kind of dulls my memory. And I guess I'm a coward as well, because I did what she wanted—I begged her. I broke down and cried. I swore I'd do whatever she asked . . . and finally, I paid blackmail because I'd rather starve in the street than have my daughter know what her father is. And Mrs. Benbow, I really think that woman enjoyed my tears more than the money she got from me every month."

Angela had started the day excited and eager and with a sense of fun. As she walked down to Caledonia's cottage, she moved slowly, in time to some unheard, distant funeral march. Nan and Caledonia were as silent as Stella while Angela recounted her interview with Grogan.

"It was terrible," she told them. "I felt—guilty. I felt—ashamed of myself. As though—as though *I* had done something wrong. He stopped blustering, you see. And he was so defenseless. It was like—like when you were little and you caught a turtle and turned it over. He was pitiful."

"But you were right, Angela," Caledonia said. "Sweetie was blackmailing him."

"I can't believe you," Nan said. "You have the devil's own luck, and that's the truth. We could have gone on forever and not found that out. But you get a flash of intuition . . . and it's all there, laid out like a story in a novel. You see that shopping list and your little mind jumps all the logical steps. You think 'blackmail.' And against all reason, it turns out to be true. And what did you have as evidence to go on? A hunch, that's all it was . . . a lousy hunch."

"Finding the book to confirm it was just luck, too," Stella put in. She and Nan shook their heads almost in unison.

"Martinez will be fascinated," Caledonia added.

"Listen," Angela said urgently. "We aren't going to tell any of

"Mrs. Benbow, I'm noisy and I'm a bully, I know. But it's partly

this, are we? Please . . . I mean, you know I don't care for Grogan. He's such a—well, ordinarily he's such a dreadful man. And he reeks of whiskey . . . and he doesn't shave close enough . . . and his nails are dirty . . . But when he was telling me about this, he was so—so sad."

"Of course we're not going to tell," Nan agreed. "Let Martinez find this out for himself if he has to. Why should we rat on that poor man? I mean . . . well, that is unless he's the one who killed Sweetie, of course."

"Well," Angela told them, "I asked him if he did it, and he swore to me he didn't. In fact, he'd just paid her for this month."

"Just curiosity," Caledonia said, "but how much did he pay?"

"Well, he gets a little pension of some kind—he doesn't get Social Security. Is that because he was in prison or something?"

"I don't know," Caledonia said. "Go on"

"Well, he paid her fifty dollars a month out of his pension, and that just left enough for him to pay his rent here . . ."

". . . And to buy some whiskey, obviously," Caledonia snorted. "He wasn't as hard up as he made you believe. He could afford booze, all right."

Angela nodded. "But you know, fifty dollars isn't really very much, and I was thinking . . . If I was a blackmailer, I'd be reasonable like that, too."

"Reasonable," Caledonia said. *"Reasonable?"*

"Reasonable?" Stella echoed faintly.

"I mean reasonable in the amounts I'd ask for. I mean, what's the use of killing the goose that lays the golden egg? Why make it impossible for people to pay? The trick would be to get yourself a lot of 'clients,' but make each one pay just a small amount. That way, you see, I'd make a lot of money—at least, a really good, steady income—and they—the people who paid me—wouldn't start to feel frantic, and run away, or go broke or anything . . . And most important, they'd keep paying . . ."

Stella had the same expression of distaste on her face that she would have assumed if she'd found a cockroach in her salad. Nan shook her head. "You've got the mind-set for a good blackmailer, all right. Getting a good income without breaking the bank. That shows a cool head, I'd say."

Caledonia shivered. "A cold one, I'd say. My God what a way to get spending money—by making other people suffer. That woman must have been a Gorgon inside. I didn't know they grew 'em that tough in Duluth."

"You're right," Nan agreed. "It takes a special sort of nastiness to enjoy watching somebody in pain. She certainly seems to have had that, all right."

"It's amazing to me that I never realized any of this was in her," Angela marvelled. "You'd think it would have showed on the outside, somehow."

"Well," Caledonia suggested, "maybe you'd have seen it, if she tried blackmailing you the way she did Grogan."

"That's another thing," Angela said. "About the payments, I mean. If she just asked for those small amounts, it kind of shows she got something more than money out of it, don't you think?" She looked at the others solemnly. "She went to a lot of trouble to find out about Grogan, and it would have been natural to want a big pay-off for her efforts. But she was willing to take smaller amounts to keep him paying . . . I think because she enjoyed it so much."

"Camden's answer to Lady Macbeth," Caledonia said with distaste.

"What were the amounts entered for the other names on that list?" Stella asked.

Angela screwed up her face again, thinking hard. "I don't remember anything with three numbers . . . they were all below one hundred. But I don't . . . oh, like $25 and $30 and $75 . . . I don't really remember exactly. I'm sorry."

They sat still and silent for a long while. Finally, Caledonia stirred herself. "Well. So much for Grogan. It sounds to me as though that Sweetie Gilfillan was a woman looking for trouble. I would think blackmail would be terribly dangerous. At the very least you're liable to get yourself beaten up."

Nan shook her head. "Nobody would do that. Because then Sweetie would have gone ahead and told everybody everything. I mean, she'd have told whoever it was you didn't want to know, whatever it was you didn't want them to know."

"Say that again?" Stella said, slightly confused.

Nan ignored her. "The way I see it, Sweetie's victims had only two choices: to pay or to get rid of her."

To everyone's surprise, Stella joined the discussion.

"Nan does have a point. There is such a thing as self-defense, you know, and you'd be defending your life, in a way."

Caledonia sighed. "Okay, okay. I really don't know . . . and I'm glad I don't. All I think is, we ought to sit down and figure out some of the other names from that list."

Nan threw up her hands. "You're balmy, Cal. You saw how bad Grogan made Angela feel. She felt horribly guilty for making him tell his secrets. She was making him tell her about the one thing in the world he didn't want to tell anybody. And he suffered, too, just going over the story for her benefit. It seems to me that if we keep on nosing around, maybe a lot of people could get hurt."

"I see things exactly the way Nan does," Stella said. "We're prying where we have no right to pry."

"You're wrong," Caledonia said. "I mean, we might as well find out. It's all going to come out eventually anyway."

"Who says," Nan put in.

"I say! The police will find out. They would have found out about Grogan, for instance."

"How? How would they?" Nan stood up, the better to challenge

Caledonia—not nose to nose, however, because Nan was so much shorter. More nose to bosom, perhaps.

"Well, fingerprints, for one thing. Police have records on who goes to jail, you know."

"But would they think to match his fingerprints up with their records?"

"Maybe—and maybe not. But if not that, then something else . . . Believe me, all we did was make the truth come out sooner."

"And," Angela said with a note of satisfaction, "we made sure we'd know the story. I mean, if the police found out about it for themselves, they wouldn't tell us a thing. This way, we found out about Grogan . . . and we know a lot more about Sweetie . . . and we know that Grogan didn't kill her."

"Wait a minute." Nan turned around indignantly to face Angela. "On what grounds did you decide *that?* Just because the man *told* you he didn't?"

"Well, you didn't talk to him. I did. He's—I don't know— different somehow, when he's sober . . . Though of course," Angela conceded, "he's a perfectly dreadful man when he's drunk."

"He's awful even when he's not drunk," Stella said with distaste. "Those displays of violent emotion . . . You know, I was taught as a girl not to show what I felt. Mother always said . . ."

"Not healthy to bottle things up," Caledonia said, as she almost always did when Stella got on that subject. "I always say . . . Let *go!* Fly off the handle once in a while. It clears the sinuses, if nothing else."

Stella made a tiny face, acknowledging the old argument between them, but Angela ignored their byplay completely. "Maybe he is a bad-tempered, selfish old man. But I still wouldn't like for him to be the one, somehow. I just *know* he's innocent."

"Great." Nan flung herself back in the arm chair. "Just great. Why are we doing detective work at all, if all we have to do is ask Angela how she *feels* about someone."

"Come on. No squabbling." Caledonia came back to the main discussion. "Look, we know the police would turn up their noses at intuition, but that's part of what we're counting on to help us learn things. Of course, Nan has a point, Angela. We can't absolutely eliminate Grogan, you know, just because you don't want him to be a murderer."

Angela wriggled as though literally to settle her ruffled feathers, and whispered sulkily, "I know what I feel, though."

"Enough. Next subject," Caledonia commanded. "Move ahead."

"To what?" Nan asked. "Ahead to what?"

"Nan, I told you. We want to think about that list. Go on, Angela . . . the names you remembered?"

"The Black Knight."

"Hmmm. We have one black resident, but she's a she, not a knight. I don't think that refers to Mrs. Goodbody, do you?" Caledonia asked.

All the other three shook their heads emphatically. Mrs. Goodbody was their only black resident, a sweet little birdlike woman of ninety, confined to a wheelchair in the special wing . . . The thought of her stabbing Sweetie was ludicrous to begin with. The idea that she might have rolled her chair to the top of the bank, met Sweetie there, stabbed her, and then pushed the body down the beach steps seemed about as likely as the possibility of a Martian invasion.

"How about our black staff members?" Stella said.

"Well, there are two black nurses," Nan said tentatively. "But Sweetie wouldn't call them 'knights,' I don't suppose."

"There's Charles, the volunteer who drives the van for us on Wednesdays," Angela reminded them. "He's black."

They turned inward eyes on their memories of Charles Tidwell. "But he's a minister from San Diego," Stella said. "Would a minister . . ."

Caledonia said, "Well, a minister might not murder someone, but he could be blackmailed, I guess, even if he's not a murderer. Ministers must do some things they wouldn't want their congregatons to know about. Remember Jim and Tammi Bakker? Wasn't there some threat of blackmail or something, somewhere in all that mess?"

Angela nodded. "I guess we put him down as a 'possible' on 'The Black Knight.'"

"I'd have nicknamed him 'Easy Rider,'" Caledonia said, grinning. "I mean he is the best—the smoothest driver we have. When Torgeson drives, it's like he's in some kind of race."

"How about Torgeson? He's got black hair . . . maybe 'The Black Knight' means black-haired, not black-skinned," Angela suggested.

"Oh dear! I didn't think of that. But no," Caledonia reminded them. "We decided it had to be an obvious nickname . . . so you'd remember what the nickname was and who it applied to. We have so many staff members who have black hair you'd never get it straight."

"Listen, how about Torgeson?" Nan said, suddenly. "Now, there's a man who ought to have a shady past. I mean, the way he acts . . ."

Caledonia agreed, "And we'd all feel no regrets if we discovered some terrible secret about him. But who on that list would he be?"

"Wait! He's 'The Dungeon Master,'" Angela said, her voice ringing with conviction. "Naturally. He is in charge of this place."

"And Sweetie used to call her apartment a prison," Stella said. "Prison—dungeon. Remember how she used to complain about those bars on her back windows . . ." She lapsed into embarrassed silence again.

Nan chimed in. "You're right! You're right. I know it. I feel it. That Torgeson has some secret . . ."

Angela couldn't help but gloat. "You're all on my side now, aren't you? I knew you'd see it my way."

Caledonia put a big, traffic cop's hand up, palm out, between them. "Cut it out. No crowing. What we have to do now is find out something about Torgeson. But the question is—how?"

"Well," Angela said doubtfully, "I suppose we ought to look around in his office . . ."

"Sounds about right," Caledonia conceded. "Well, then, girls— let's make ourselves a plan."

CHAPTER 9

ANGELA WAS to ask for an appointment to see the administrator in his private office, ". . . To case the joint," as Caledonia told her. "Find out where the files are, if he has a safe . . ."

"But what'll I ask to see him about?" Angela asked.

"Oh, that'll come to you," Caledonia said. "Make something up as you go along."

"I don't like this," Stella muttered, as she had several times.

"Why not?" Nan said. "Torgeson deserves it. He's a complete toad."

"A foul lump. An excrescence," agreed Caledonia. "And that's what makes it so nice, Stella. We'll be fooling him, you see, while we get information. He really deserves to be bamboozled."

None of the ladies had ever forgiven Torgeson for replacing the previous manager, a mild-mannered courtly little man of middle age and of exquisite manners but poor money sense. Their delightful Mr. MacLeod had left after overspending his budget three months running, and Torgeson had marched in, taken firm command, and immediately antagonized all the residents by issuing an order to use less toilet paper.

Expenses have risen alarmingly, Torgeson's notice began. *There are very few corners that can be cut in food and services, for we have been careful stewards. But in one unusual area, this retirement center has a noticeably large expenditure that it could pay us all to examine carefully—our use of bathroom tissue. So the message for the week is "Think! Will two sheets do instead of three?" Stop and contemplate, before you tear.*

"I don't believe this. Who does he think he is," Caledonia had complained. "Is nothing sacred?"

"Well," Mary Moffet had said, giggling and blushing, "I understand Mrs. Winkler used up two whole rolls polishing her car. And Tootsie Armstrong was using it to stuff pillows for the craft sale . . . I'm sure that's what he was talking about. I mean, they do furnish it for us and I suppose it's getting expensive . . ."

"I wouldn't know about that," Caledonia said, "because I haven't bought any since I moved here years ago. I mean, when I was buying it, good toilet paper was only ten cents a roll. But be that as it may—there are some things in life that ought to be beyond the reach of even the most officious manager—and toilet paper's one of 'em."

The next indignity was Torgeson's trying to economize by firing the old man who was their full-time van driver and having the van driven by a rotation of other staff members, on their regular duty hours, and by a few volunteers. He tried to make it look more acceptable by putting his own name on the driving roster, but that didn't help. The residents missed their old driver, and worried about the part-time substitutes.

Some of the drivers—like Mr. Tidwell, the Presbyterian minister who was one of the volunteers—were fine drivers, and wheeled smoothly to the front door of the bank or doctors' offices to let their passengers out easily. But some were less than fine. It wasn't that they were fender benders; it was that residents were let off at distant corners to limp to their bank—vans appeared late or had to be cancelled and doctors' appointments were missed—and a pile of speeding tickets accumulated in the office. Torgeson raged, but stuck to his "economy measures," and the residents grumbled and smoldered and blamed Torgeson each time a van stopped too far from the curb.

The last straw, from the residents' point of view, came the day Torgeson gave Dolores, the headwaitress, a frightful bawling out for opening the dining room eight minutes early. Residents usually waited on the patio or in the lobby for the bell that announced their lunches and dinners. They would be assembled and impatient long before the Westminster chimes told them they could enter the dining room. On the day in question, everything being ready inside the dining room, Dolores simply thought that if she let them in, the diners would finish early, and the dining room staff could clean up and set for supper all the sooner. Besides, she was a friendly, caring sort of woman—and pleasing the residents by opening early seemed to her to be a small kindness.

Unfortunately, Torgeson had a guest. Torgeson and his visitor had been sharing a little glass of sherry in the back office—and when they wandered out at what would have been a fashionably late arrival for the meal, they met residents already finished and leaving the dining room. Torgeson somehow felt it made him look bad. Nobody made Torgeson look bad with impunity—so he hunted down the culprit and to her embarrassment, and to the fury of the residents with whom she was popular, Dolores got told off in public.

Since that time, Torgeson could do very little right in the eyes of his residents. If there was too much salt in the stew, someone would insist it was at Torgeson's orders—that he was trying to kill them all with hardening of the arteries so he could replace them with richer clients.

If the hose was forgotten, carelessly stretched out across the garden walk, and someone tripped, the victim blamed Torgeson's new work schedules, which gave the gardeners less time to tidy up.

If it rained on their birthdays, the residents declared it was somehow Torgeson's fault!

And this was the man Angela intended to meet face-to-face, to try to incriminate as a blackmail victim and a potential murderer. She wasn't afraid, of course—she assured the others she didn't mind facing him down. "The only thing I regret," she told her co-conspirators, "is that he's so nasty it *can't* be him. I mean, it's always someone you don't suspect, right? And I'd suspect him of anything. But . . . but . . ."

"But what?" Caledonia asked, urging her toward the door.

"But I still don't know what I'm going to say."

"I tell you, you'll think of something . . . you're good at inventions. Go, girl, and keep your eyes open. Tell us everything you see and hear." And Caledonia pushed her out the door in the direction of the main building.

So it was that about midway through the same afternoon, having asked for and received an appointment to see "Olaf The Terrible" in person, Angela marched into the inner area behind the front desk, an area usually avoided by the residents if possible.

Seated at desks that faced each other from opposite ends of the outer office were Torgeson's perpetually harried secretary, Tish, and a calm, aging bookkeeper named Patty, both of whom Angela knew slightly. The room was lined on three sides with filing cabinets, leaving barely enough space for the doors to operate. Angela's heart sank—would they have to look into every file?

Like most of the others at Camden, she seldom came into the office; most of her business would be handled in writing, or by the secretary's or the bookkeeper's coming to her room. She glanced around; there was an open arch in the center of one wall, and she could see through to the area the residents knew best, the front desk where the mail slots and the switchboard lay. As she announced herself to Tish, Angela could hear Clara on the phone outside: "Camden-sur-Mer, may I help you?"

"T-Ti-Tish." Angela stumbled with distaste over the name. "I'm to see Mr. Torgeson at 2:15." It wasn't the woman she minded so much as the necessity of seeming familiar with the staff. Unless one wanted to say "Mrs. Martin" to the secretary and "Miss Vogel" to the bookkeeper, one had to use first names—and that presented a difficulty, since both women were named "Patricia." Angela loathed using nicknames for subordinates, but refused the formality that seemed, to her, to denote too much respect. She waited stiffly to be recognized.

"You'll have to wait a minute or two, Mrs. Benbow, I'm afraid," Tish said, tucking her blouse back into her skirt-top, where it had worked free. Her other hand worked away at the wispy hair straggling outward from between her ear and the bow of her glasses. "He's on the phone . . . to the carpet people about that new rug in the lower hall. It wasn't tacked down right."

"No problem," Angela said airily and sat herself down in a shiny maroon office chair near the door to the innermost office where Torgeson lurked. She immediately regretted it, for the chair was stiff and unyielding, and the imitation leather slippery. She was perched on a little vinyl mountain in the center of the seat, and her stubby little legs did not reach far enough for her to touch the floor. Slowly she slid forward on the steep mound, until her feet touched carpet and she was barely on the seat at all. She grasped the chair arms and wriggled herself backward to the center of the chair, feet sticking forward like a child's—and the slide began all over again. There seemed no way—short of winding her arms through the chair's arms and gripping hard—to stop herself. With all the dignity she could muster, she stood up and moved across the room to gaze at a pair of imitation-Godey prints on the wall. "I've been sitting watching television practically all day," she lied. "It would feel better to get up and move around."

"Suit yourself." Tish redid the middle button on her blouse, which had come undone, and worked at her wispy hair a little more, all the while she tried to keep typing, first with one hand, then with the other. Angela tried to look the other way; she was beginning to find the perpetual fidgeting unbearable.

At last the buzzer sounded on the intercom. Tish tugged at a slip strap to correct the flash of white nylon that hung below her dress hem . . . smoothed a cowlick with the other hand and said "You can go in now, Mrs. Benbow," and immediately reached behind to yank at the seat of her panty hose, which seemed to have twisted. Angela looked straight ahead to the inner office, and almost ran toward it—escaping into the presence of The Terrible Torgeson with something approaching gratitude.

"You wanted to see me?" Torgeson said briskly, gesturing a hand to an empty chair. "Let's see now, you're—uh—you're—uh—"

"Angela Benbow. Mrs. Douglas Benbow. First room in the south corridor, ground floor . . ."

"Oh, to be sure." Torgeson's smile flashed on and off, like the beam from a lighthouse—brilliant for an instant, then disappearing without a trace. "Now . . . I'm certain you want to get right to the point . . ."

Angela wanted no such thing. She had hoped for a little casual, introductory chitchat that would allow her time to look around— and time to think. She still hadn't decided what to say. "Well," she began uncertainly, "it's—it's—it's—uh—about—" mercifully a tiny inspiration came, at last. "It's our sale of handicrafts."

"Oh, of course. Very worthy projects." Torgeson beamed again, and this time the smile stayed on. Perhaps this little woman was not going to complain about something. That would be a welcome change. "We have enjoyed your finished products—real works of art. But even more, we've enjoyed the things you ladies have done with your earnings . . . The new coffee machine in the dining room, the big-screen color television in the lobby, the silver tea service for our little monthly receptions, the prize for the 'Custodian of the Month'—all very welcome help to us, I assure you. Now, what about the handwork sale? Is there some problem?"

Angela felt herself entering on somewhat dangerous ground, for she had invented only the general subject for a conversation, so far. But she tried to assume a nonchalance she certainly didn't feel. "Well, not really a problem, Mr. Torgeson. More a request. The ladies feel—well, several of them do, though not all—I speak, however, for a majority, you understand . . ." Her eyes darted wildly about as she tried to absorb details of the office, searching at one and the same time for inspiration and for a safe— concealed behind a picture, perhaps, as in all the Charlie Chan movies on Saturday afternoon TV.

Torgeson was getting impatient, but he fought it back. "Yes, yes, Mrs. Benbow. I'll take it that you speak with the voice of several. But what exactly do you—do *they* want?"

"Yes, exactly," Angela said, inspiration not forthcoming. "What, exactly."

"Yes, what?"

"That's what I said," Angela said.

"No, that's what *I* said," Torgeson corrected.

"Well of course, you said it first, but after that I merely repeated, as a preamble, you see . . . I mean, *I* wasn't asking 'what,' though you were." Angela was getting quite pink in the face with desperation, and Torgeson was growing purple with repressed impatience.

"Mrs. Benbow! Please! I don't like to rush you, but as you see, I have work. I am at your service, of course, but if you could just tell me what it is you want from me?"

"Yes. Yes. Well—"

"About the sale of your handicrafts?" Torgeson prompted hopefully.

"Yes. Ah—we were wondering if this year . . ." She jumped to her feet and walked across the room to the window. Nothing outside gave her an idea, and she turned back, her eyes rolling frantically around the room.

"Yes? You said 'this year,' Mrs. Benbow?"

"Yes. This year. We were wondering . . ." suddenly she found herself staring at the carved wooden Mexican masks Torgeson had hung on his wall. "Yes . . . If this year we couldn't have a special theme. Perhaps a Mexican theme. I mean, decorate the main lobby—maybe sell food at a booth—have entertainment—call it 'The Camden Fiesta,' and make a big party out of it. Combine an open house, a party, and the sale. You see what I mean?"

"We-e-e-ell." Torgeson thought a moment. "It sounds splendid, but wouldn't it be a lot of work?"

"Oh, the residents would do the planning and the publicity. We couldn't lift things, of course, and we'd need you to ask the staff to help out, you see. That's why I'm asking you." It was all so simple, once an idea had struck. She sailed ahead, beginning to be quite enthusiastic about her own invention. This was all going rather well. "I mean, we could help in the kitchen, I suppose . . . but I thought of us, the residents, as being the salesmen. Manning the booths, you see. The staff would have to help putting up the decorations, but we could make them. Of course we couldn't hang garlands and things, for instance . . ."

Torgeson's eyes were gleaming. "Yes, I can see it now. We could sell tickets at the door—not much, but a little—to cover overtime wages for the staff who were helping . . . and to pay for wear and tear on the carpets."

"Of course," Angela said smoothly.

"The proceeds from the ticket sales would have to go to the company—to pay for the cost of the food, the cooks' time, and so on . . ."

"Yes, naturally."

"But you'd make the profits from your craft sales—and that would go into some project for all of us."

"How about entertainment?" Angela was entering into the spirit of the thing. "Couldn't we have music? A mariachi band? Somebody to sing?"

"We'll have to see," said Torgeson, suddenly cautious, thinking of talent fees. "Perhaps some of the staff . . ."

"Well," Angela said, "you can count on me, of course. And the other ladies. I think they'll be so enthusiastic!" And she moved toward the door.

Torgeson jumped to his feet. A heavy man, his leap into good manners was accompanied by a thudding sound. "Let me see you out. It's so seldom we get anyone to volunteer to head a project . . ."

"Head?" Angela was suddenly dismayed. "Oh, but—no—you see, I didn't—that is, I was only suggesting. I thought you—someone—"

Torgeson hurried on. "Let me see, the term 'chairman' is considered sexist these days, isn't it? So we can't call you the 'chairwoman' either, can we?" He laughed immoderately.

"Well, actually," Angela said faintly, "I hoped that you wouldn't call me either one. You see—"

"How about if we call you 'The Chair'? Yes, that's it. The Chair. Ah, Mrs. Benbow, thank you for coming in today. This is such a sad, confusing time for us all. It's really cheered me up a great deal to have you volunteer to lead this project. And I wish you good day."

Angela was led firmly out through the exterior office and found herself deposited in the lobby. A little dazed, she made her way back to her friends, waiting at Caledonia's.

"The *Chair*," Caledonia said with amusement, interrupting Angela's report. "He makes you sound like a maple rocker." Stella raised slim fingers to her mouth, hiding a smile.

"Or a Lazy Boy recliner," Nan said kiddingly. "Oh Angela, you've been taken advantage of. I mean, you went up there to snoop on him, and you ended up heading a fiesta. Who else is on the committee, Chair?"

"I don't know," Angela said mournfully. "I only know I had to make up something—and I did, just like you said—and all of a sudden I'm putting on some party for the general public."

"Don't worry, Angela," Stella said. "We'll all help you, if it ever comes about. I had a lot of experience back home with charity bazaars and things like that. My family used to sponsor a tea dance every year in support of the local children's hospital. It was the social event of the season . . . My mother's family started it more than a hundred years ago. Before the Civil War! The Shalford Ball, it was called, and we used to . . ."

"Stella!" When Caledonia used Stella's real name, instead of calling her by her nickname, "Beanie," everyone knew Caledonia meant business. But Caledonia's rebuke was mild. "You're rambling a bit, dear . . ."

"Oh. Oh, dear . . . I'm so sorry . . ." Stella's dreamy expression changed to a more alert look as she came back to the present. "Of course. We—we were talking about . . . What were we talking about?"

"Angela's being put in charge of a party here . . . at Camden," Caledonia said gently. "I was just telling her not to worry about it. By the time the party is supposed to come off, Torgeson may be in jail for murder. I mean, we still have to look into him and his background and whether or not he's being blackmailed . . . What did you find out, Angela?"

"Find out? Oh, nothing really."

"Oh, come on Angela, surely something struck you. Describe the room."

"Well," Angela said, closing her eyes to make the picture in her memory clearer, "his desk is a mess—piles of paper everywhere. We can look through that without his ever knowing we've done it. The drawers are all ajar, because he's got so much stuff stuck into them, they won't close properly. I don't think we really have to worry. If we can get in, we can search."

"No safe?" Nan asked, sounding disappointed.

"Well, maybe, but I didn't see one."

"There aren't going to be any secrets, then," Caledonia predicted. "But we still ought to look, you know. The question is how to get inside the office."

"Oh, that's easy," Nan said. "My front door key opens the office door."

"What? How could that be?"

"Well," Nan said, shrugging, "One day I wanted stamps. It was a Sunday, so the office was closed. That red-haired clerk, Clara, was on the switchboard. She was talking to a friend—personal gossip—and she didn't even look up when I went around and tried the office door. It was locked, all right . . . nobody answered my knock either . . . and I don't know why—just a hunch, I guess, that just about any key could turn an old lock like that—but I tried my key, and it worked! Maybe everybody else's key would work as well. How do I know? Anyway, I went to Tish's desk, left my money, took a stamp, and walked out."

"Did they ever find out?" Angela asked.

"How would they find out? I locked the door after me. Nobody ever knew I'd done it."

"Well, that settles it," Caledonia said. "We'll look through that office tonight. Agreed?"

"Agreed," they said together, and this time, even Stella, who disliked Torgeson every bit as much as the others did, didn't say no.

So that night they set out together. There was a night clerk on duty at the desk, of course, every night. But it was old Sarge Nelson's turn—Sarge was fat, diabetic and slightly deaf. He was a retired Camden policeman, which made people feel safe, even though everyone knew he mostly slept as he sat at his post. He badly needed the job to add to his tiny pension, and he jollied the ladies along and smiled a lot, which made everyone feel happy when they talked to him. So he was a more or less permanent fixture behind Camden's desk three nights a week. Sarge wasn't likely to be any problem to them.

They met again at Caledonia's place and moved silently up the garden and through the sliding glass door, which stood open as always—as though there had been no trouble of any kind, let alone a murder. Nan's key easily opened the outer office door, which was around the corner from the desk area, so that Sarge never saw them enter. Once they were safely inside, there was just enough light coming into the room from the desk area to keep them from falling into wastepaper baskets or kicking chairs, so they moved through silently. Sarge snored blissfully on.

The inner door to Torgeson's office was tightly closed. Nan put her key into the lock, it turned partway, they heard a tiny click— and nothing happened. She jiggled the key around and turned it again, putting pressure on it. Nothing. "Okay," she whispered, "that's it. Let's go home."

"Wait a minute. Let me . . ." Caledonia elbowed her aside and turned the knob, lifting as she did so . . . and the door opened. "You have to know how," she breathed, pushing the others ahead of her and easing the door shut behind them.

Their eyes were already adjusting to the gloom, and Angela remembered seeing a desk lamp. She got it switched on—Stella hastily drew the drapes shut—and they looked around.

"Wow, were you right about the mess on that desk," Nan whispered. The erratic piles of paper mounded left and right had slid and slithered in random order, completely obscuring the work space. Under one mountain on a forward edge of the desk protruded the corner of an "IN" box. From another the telephone cord ran to the wall.

"How can he find anything?" Angela said.

"Who cares? The question is, how can *we* find anything," Caledonia replied. "This is the most perfect burglar-proofing in the world. He could have a stack of atomic secrets in there, and the cleverest spies in the business wouldn't know it and couldn't locate 'em if you told 'em." She sighed. "Nothing for it but to try, I guess . . ." And she plunged one huge arm into a nearby pile of papers, pulling up a tangled handful and starting through them, one at a time, but rapidly.

Nan sighed too, but started working on the desk at the opposite end. Without a word, Stella went to work on a small side table, where more papers had been stacked—or perhaps dumped would be more accurate. And Angela, after a moment of hesitation, went to the bookshelves and started through the books . . . pulling one, reading the title, fanning the pages and shaking, replacing, taking the next . . . Caledonia watched her and shook her head, but said nothing and kept working.

It was perhaps five minutes later that Stella said suddenly, "Here's something."

The others stopped work. "Well, read it aloud," Nan said.

Dear Sir, the letter ran. *This is the third notice about your delinquency. If you do not make payment on your account within seven days after receipt of this registered letter, we will be forced to turn the matter over to a professional collection agency.*

"He couldn't pay his bills?" Angela said. "But he makes a big salary here, I thought."

Caledonia nodded. "Maybe his bill for blackmail was higher. Okay, he had a bad credit rating. But that's not something to have to keep secret, is it? I mean, it wasn't enough to pay blackmail over. At least, I didn't think it was. A lot of people owe money, what with credit cards and things, these days—and it's no big secret."

Stella shrugged, put the letter down on the pile, and went on sorting. Another minute passed in silence. Then Angela called them, "See this, girls." And she came over to the light carrying a newspaper photograph. There was Torgeson with an arm around a lovely blonde in an evening gown, and they appeared to be hurrying into a taxi. They both looked straight at the camera; the young lady looked dismayed, Torgeson looked angry. And the caption said, *Beauty queen in divorce case forgets her troubles with a night on the town. Of the business man who was her escort, Beebee Morgan, "Miss Idaho Potato" for 1949, said "We're just good friends."*

"Oh brother! Just good friends? That line went out with celluloid collars, didn't it?" Caledonia said.

Nan said, "But is this blackmail material?"

"For her, maybe," Caledonia said. "According to this, she was in the midst of a hot divorce case. But there's nothing here to say Torgeson was ever really involved."

Angela sighed and carried her find back, replacing the clipping in the book and the book onto the shelf.

They worked on in silence for a while, and finally Nan said in disgust, "I give up. He wouldn't keep private papers on top of his desk or dumped onto a table, would he? You can joke all you like about nobody being able to find anything here, but it's no place for real secrets. I'll try the drawers." She eased herself, panting a little and groaning softly, onto the floor behind the desk and started opening and pawing through drawers that were every bit as disorganized as the desk top.

"He dropped his membership in his lodge," Caledonia whispered, waving an envelope with a big logo in place of a return address.

"Did you know he had been married?" Angela whispered, holding aloft a picture of a slim young Torgeson in uniform posed beside a bride in white, her hair in an unmistakable 1950s beehive.

Caledonia grunted softly. "I didn't think he'd ever been young, let alone know that he was married."

They worked along another five minutes, and Caledonia began to tire of standing and sorting. Her sense of time was also giving her warning signals—they'd been there entirely too long. The longer they were in that office, the more uneasy she felt—and the more certain she felt that they should move along. She had just put down a handful of paper and started to say, "Come on, let's go," or something like that, when she was aware that Nan was sitting rigid, a letter held out in front of her.

"I think this is it," Nan was saying. She looked unhappy. "Oh girls . . . oh girls . . ."

All three moved to her and together, peering over her shoulder, they took in Sweetie's tight little signature at the bottom—"Sara Jane Gilfillan"—and Nan read aloud:

Dear Mr. Torgeson:

I shall be pleased to accept your offer of a free room here at Camden including free meals and medical services. I consider that most generous. Believe me, I do not require a large cottage. I am quite content with my little rooms.

Of course, if you could install a new refrigerator in the kitchenette and a microwave oven as well, I would be most grateful.

I hope your daughter is doing well in the drug rehabilitation program. Naturally I understand why you wish to avoid publicity. And I shall honor my promise not to tell. I certainly wouldn't want your wife to be pained by your daughter's recent setback. Sick as she is, bad news might be too much for her. I agree with your judgment that this should be kept from her at all costs. . . .

Nan stopped reading. "That *witch*," she said. "That-that-that—"

"She *was* awful," Stella agreed, pink with indignation. "She really was."

"I feel awful myself," Caledonia said. "Poor Torgeson . . . the terrible things I've said about him. And all the time she was . . ." She rose to her full height, her eyes blazing and pronounced sentence: "That woman was a dreadful creature."

"Put it back, Nan," Angela whispered. "He should never guess anybody else found out."

"That's so rotten," Nan said between clenched teeth. "How the *hell* do you suppose she found things like that out, anyway?" She buried the letter halfway down in the right-hand bottom drawer, at least approximately where it had been, and eased the drawer shut.

"Remember all those hours she spent in the library researching Grogan? Odds are she did the same for Torgeson," Caledonia said.

"I suppose," Angela added, "that he made her mad over something. He made *everybody* mad over something."

"And then she went after him. With a vengeance."

"More like *for* vengeance," Angela corrected.

Caledonia ignored her. "Drug arrests are sometimes news. The business about his daughter might have been in the papers."

"But how would Sweetie know about his wife's illness?" Nan asked. "None of us know about it."

"Well, of course she might have heard the staff gossiping about that—some of them would be bound to know." Caledonia had seated herself in Torgeson's chair behind the desk. Now she heaved herself up with difficulty. "Time to go home, girls. I really don't feel well enough to poke around here any more. The whole thing sort of turns my stomach."

Angela nodded. "The picture of Sweetie collecting gossip and filing it away to use to get at people—it kind of spoils the fun of gossip, doesn't it? I'm not going to be able to enjoy the next tidbit I hear. All I'll be able to think about is what *she'd* have done with it."

"She'd have gone to the library and worked till she got the

documents to back it up, that's what she'd have done," Nan agreed, and led the procession to the door. It slid open silently, and they tiptoed out. Sarge was still snoring behing the desk, and they made it to the garden door, where they parted—Nan and Caledonia to the cottages, Stella to her two-room suite on the second floor.

"Goodnight," they whispered to each other and Angela moved silently away, across the shadowed marble floor toward her quarters. It *had* been a good night, she told herself—it was important, finding out about Torgeson, although thinking about the blackmail again made her shiver slightly as she let herself into her apartment.

"We accomplished *so* much! It's really quite satisfying to be doing something about all this, instead of just waiting for something to happen. It certainly makes a change. But . . . I suppose I should be sorry to be so impatient . . . I should be ashamed of all the snooping and prying. This is a sad, dreadful business. Yes, that's it, sad and dreadful!" But underneath that prim thought, she had enough honest self-evaluation to sense the presence of another feeling. She was enjoying herself.

Enjoying herself? Surely not. Enjoying the loss of her peace and quiet? Enjoying peering through the private business of other people? Enjoying a sense of urgency? A sense of danger? Surely not.

It had taken her only a moment to get ready for bed. As she pulled the light sheet and cotton blanket toward her chin, she was amazed to find herself smiling. It didn't take her three full minutes to fall into a deep, contented sleep.

CHAPTER 10

TO ANGELA'S surprise, when she woke the next morning, the sky was gray. It was too late in the year for what Southern California fondly calls its "rainy season" (two days in January), but during the night, a gently drizzling rain, already slackened off, had stained the sidewalk and turned the dust-grayed palm fronds green again. In the old days, she'd have said this was a good morning to sleep in. She might have shut off the alarm, turned over and skipped breakfast in favor of two more hours of napping lightly, sliding in and out of sleep, with the luxury of knowing she did not have to rise if she didn't want to.

This morning was different. She almost hopped up out of bed, feeling a sense of purpose, and her fingers were clumsy with haste as she slipped into a "working uniform" (low-heeled, rubber-soled shoes and a dark blue, cotton blend shirtwaist dress, suitable for a morning walk—or for burgling).

Before she left the room she phoned Nan . . . no answer . . . Probably already at breakfast, Angela thought. She dialed Stella's number—then hung up before it rang. I'll just get her out of the shower if I ring through now, Angela thought. She really doesn't need me to call anyhow, I guess. She's never been late to anything in her life. But Angela wanted to be certain her fellow conspirators joined her for the morning's plot-making, so she risked dialing Caledonia.

"Hmph?" Caledonia answered the phone.

"It's me. Are you going to breakfast?"

"Who's me?" the lazy voice growled.

"Angela. Caledonia, surely you're not going to sleep late today, are you? Are you going to breakfast?"

"Eventually. Is there any rush?"

"Yes. Of course. We need to make today's plans. Figure out what to do next."

"Oh." There was a long pause. Finally Caledonia said, a gigantic yawn audible in her voice, "Oh, all right. See you there. They don't usually set me a place—because I don't usually come to breakfast. But have them lay out the utensils and we can talk while we eat. But *after* I've had coffee, Angela. Please don't talk to me before coffee. Not this morning. I didn't sleep at all well last night."

"That's too bad. I did. Slept like a baby. See you there." Angela was out the door almost before she hung the phone up.

The Camden dining room didn't open for breakfast till 7:00, and this was inconvenient for many of the residents. The old may nap, off and on, through afternoons and evenings, but by and large, they tend to be early risers. There is a feeling that, if they stay in bed, they are wasting precious time, when time is probably the one commodity they have far too little of. So at least half the residents were up, walking around the block or watching the morning news on TV or working the crossword puzzle in the morning paper, for as much as forty-five minutes to an hour before they could enter the dining room.

All the same, breakfast was the one meal where one was allowed to arrive late. Breakfast was a "free" meal; that is, one could order anything, within reason—unlike lunch and dinner, when one simply received at one's place whatever was that day's fare. In addition, there was "open seating," so residents could occupy whichever table they liked, unlike the assigned seating at the other meals. The theory had been, as explained to a skeptical Residents' Council by an eager young activities director, that the residents would enlarge their circle of friends by sitting with new people during at least one meal a day. But she was very young and did not understand; habits succeed in taking hold of us because they are comfortable—and comfort is high on the list of priorities among the elderly. Almost all the residents took the same places they used at lunch and supper.

Since residents could start breakfast when they pleased, so long as they did so between 7:00 and 9:00—and since they had their seating pre-arranged (despite the earnest hope of the activities director)—they did not crowd the lobby waiting for the dining room doors to open in the mornings. They stayed in their rooms instead, or took what passed for their morning exercise, until they felt like going to breakfast—then strolled straight in without waiting.

Angela found the lobby empty, as usual, with the exception of Mr. Brighton, shuffling painfully along with his cane, making slow but steady progress toward his breakfast.

"Good morning," Angela sang out as she sailed past him.

His "good morning" was not as sunny as his usual greeting. In fact, he croaked it out.

"Arthritis bad today?" Angela asked.

"Mmmm . . . When I was a young man"—Angela slowed to listen to his strained and husky voice—"we'd have called this 'the rheumatiz.' We believed rain made it worse. Well, the rain—or something—surely got me a good lick today."

"Do you need any help?"

"Ah, no . . . there's not much you can do short of throwing me across your shoulder and carrying me to the dining room . . ."

"A wheelchair—"

"*No thank you.* When I take to a chair, it's probably going to be to stay. And they'll make me leave my nice room back there . . ." He waved his hand toward the back wall of the lobby, indicating the general location of his airy little corner room on the south wing. "I don't want to be in with the crew in the wheelchair wing yet. Go on ahead—go on ahead—I'm not going to be able to keep up, and I'd rather you didn't hear me puffing along."

Mrs. Benbow nodded with understanding and picked up her pace, pulling ahead of him and entering the dining room, while he kept struggling along behind her.

She went to the service bar, set up across from the main entry, poured herself some cranberry juice and carried it to her table. A thermos pot of coffee already sat there, and she poured some out, adding sugar and cream. Then she sat back and looked around . . . Neither Stella nor Nan had appeared yet and . . .

"That's odd," she thought. "Not a single waitress. I wonder where they all are? Is this Sunday?" On weekends they operated shorthanded in the dining room, and it wasn't unusual for one girl to handle the entire room—slowly, of course. But Angela recalled that it was in fact Friday. All right then—maybe a holiday? On holidays, staff duties were carried out with only a skeleton crew. I may be a wee bit forgetful now and then, she conceded to herself, but I'd remember if it was Thanksgiving or something. It's only October . . . there's no holiday in October, surely. "Oh, good morning, Stella."

Stella slipped diffidently into her customary chair. "I thought I was going to be late, but nobody else is here yet, either. I mean— well, you're here, my dear, but we seem to be about the only . . ."

Just then Nan puffed in from the garden entrance closest to her cottage. She was not too winded to pour herself some juice before she came to the table, but she panted, settling down, and her voice wheezed slightly. "Sorry I'm late," she gasped. "Rain stopped, so I thought I'd join the walkers out around the block today . . . Damn near killed myself, I tell you. I won't do that again. Have you ordered?"

"No," Angela said. "I haven't seen a waitress yet. I was wondering if the staff has gone on strike, like they did four years ago."

Nan was surprised. "Oh, I don't think so. I mean, they warned us of that for weeks in advance, trying to get the company to improve their wage package. They talked about nothing else. We've been keeping ourselves pretty busy, this week, but we'd have heard about a strike, all the same. Pass the coffee, anyhow."

Stella passed the thermos, Nan poured, and Angela craned her neck, looking for the waitress. And while they waited, Caledonia marched glumly in, stopped to get herself a water tumbler full of apricot nectar, and made her way to their table. "I thought," she grumbled, grabbing silverware and some china from a nearby table, "you girls were going to have them set my place."

"We would have," Angela said in an injured tone, "but we have yet to see a waitress. I think they're on strike. Nan says not, but where could they be?"

Just at that moment, the door from the kitchen swung wide, and three waitresses burst out at once, each heading for a table, pad and pencil at the ready, to take orders. "Hmph," Caledonia said. "Torgeson's been laying down the law in the kitchen again. Remember that time he called them all together before lunch to tell them to quit giving seconds on desserts to save money? Lunch was twenty minutes late that day."

"I thought we were going to lay off Torgeson now," Nan protested.

Caledonia grinned in spite of herself. "Well, you know, I got to thinking about that last night. And I decided, once a toad, always a toad. I mean, I may feel sorry for a fly if someone pulls its wings off to torture it—but I'm still going to swat it dead, if it gets into my house. Sweetie was giving Torgeson a hard time, no doubt about it—but when I got to thinking it over . . . well, I feel sorry for him about that—but he's still an absolute warthog."

Dolores, the headwaitress, appeared at their table with a pad and pencil. "Morning, ladies," she said. "What are we having for breakfast?"

Nan ordered hotcakes, Caledonia asked for her usual bacon and eggs and waffles and syrup and toast, and Stella and Angela both ordered a poached egg on an English muffin. "But wait!" Angela stopped Dolores, who was just moving away. "Where were you all, when we first came in?"

"Oh, just out in back. You know." Dolores waved generally at the kitchen.

"Torgeson again?" Caledonia asked.

"No," Dolores said. "There's been . . . a little accident. We waited till—someone came to take care of it."

"Accident?" Stella asked.

"Not those stairs again," Angela said.

"Well, yes," Dolores said. "Look, they asked us not to talk about it, you know?"

"Who was it? Surely you can tell us that much . . ."

Dolores grinned ruefully. "They didn't tell us not to do that, I guess . . . It was Mrs. Piper. You know—"

"Paulette?" Angela was shocked.

"I guess that's her first name. She has the center front apartment on the second floor . . . you know. That lady."

Caledonia nodded confirmation. "That's Paulette Piper, all right. On the stairs you say?"

Dolores nodded.

"Was she—is she badly hurt?" Nan asked.

Dolores looked around at the kitchen door, but nobody appeared to be watching her. She leaned down over the table, so she could talk very softly. "You act surprised when they tell you now, officially like . . . But she's dead. Stone dead. Broke her neck falling down those stairs, just like Mr. Grogan the day before. Except he didn't. Break his neck, I mean. Maybe he *should* of, but she *did.*" And she hurried out to place her orders with Mrs. Schmitt.

If they hadn't known from Dolores that something drastic had happened, the three ladies, craning their necks toward the swinging door that led to the kitchen, would have guessed it within a short time, because only a couple of minutes later, Martinez and Swanson walked in from that swinging door, deep in serious conversation. Swanson managed to nod and smile as he passed each table; but then, he was mainly listening and occasionally scribbling in his ever-present notebook. Martinez, doing most of the talking, only lifted one hand in half-greeting to those diners he recognized and moved steadily ahead, weaving a crooked path through the crowded tables, which had gradually filled with diners, each one every bit as aware as were Angela and her group that "Something is up!"

The men put themselves down at the guest table that had become, by common consent, their preserve at meals, and kept talking, too low to be overheard. All the while they sipped their coffee and ate their meal.

Angela watched them quite openly. Everyone in the dining room did. Curiosity was something even the politest resident did little to conceal. Curiosity was taken for granted at Camden. Perhaps the two policemen were not used to being watched so closely, but by the time he was halfway through his bacon and eggs, Swanson was shifting uncomfortably in his seat and Martinez had stopped looking around the room. Every place he turned he had met inquisitive eyes, until at last, he protected himself by glancing only at his plate and his coffee cup, and—once in a while—at Swanson.

"I tell you what,' Angela said finally. "I'm going over and ask them about it. That's what I'm going to do." And she stood up abruptly, tossed her napkin onto her plate, and marched across to the guest table.

Both the men lurched upward to a half-standing position, bumping the table almost simultaneously from two sides. "Sit down. Please sit down, gentlemen," Angela said, waving graciously at them.

"Do you have something to tell us today, Mrs. Benbow?" Martinez asked as he sat back down.

"No, I don't," Angela said, taking a seat beside him. "But you two seem to be trying to keep secrets from the rest of us. I told you before we don't like 'the kid glove' treatment—partly because we're scared half out of our wits, with a murderer running around loose—partly because secrecy itself makes us fearful, I think."

"Oh, come now, Mrs. Benbow. What makes you think that any secrets—"

"Don't do that," Angela interrupted. "You're babying me again, treating me like I haven't got all my brains in working order. We all know something's going on, when we come to the dining room at 7:15 and there isn't a waitress around. Then they all come in at the same time, all flustered and out of breath. And we'd have to be pretty dumb not to know there's some kind of problem. All you're doing is delaying our finding out . . . and making us more nervous than we have to be."

Martinez nodded. "I suppose you're right, Mrs. Benbow."

"Of course I am," she said. There was a pause. "Well?"

'Well—all right." Swanson's eyebrows raised slightly, though he said nothing; he wasn't used to seeing the boss cave in before anybody, let alone before little old ladies, no matter how formidable. "We told everybody not to talk about it till we'd made some determination of cause. But I really don't suppose—Another resident is dead by violence, Ma'am. Mrs. Piper."

He looked a question at Swanson, who affirmed, "Paulette Piper—second-floor front."

Martinez said, "She fell down the back stairs . . ."

Angela shrugged and spread her hands. "Well, there's your causation. Death by falling down stairs. It's a wonder Grogan didn't break his neck yesterday, and it's no wonder at all that Paulette broke hers. Whatever is in doubt about the cause of death?"

"Oh, there's no doubt she died of a broken neck. And there's no doubt she fell downstairs. The only question is, what made her fall?"

"Oh. I see. But then, what made Grogan fall? There's nothing really wrong with the stairs, Lieutenant, except that they're dark and narrow and steep. We residents—well, some of us don't see very well, and several of us are tottery and uncertain on our feet. Someone's always falling. Which is why they told us not to go near those stairs."

"But Grogan and Mrs. Piper did."

"Well, yes," Angela said. "But Grogan was hurrying down to lunch, you see, from visiting somebody upstairs, and the back stairs are a shortcut."

"Well, then Mrs. Piper was trying to take a shortcut, I suppose?"

"Certainly not," Angela protested. "Her front door is almost opposite the head of the main front staircase. She'd be going out of her way, to nip around to the back stairs."

"She had probably been to visit somebody," Martinez said. "Didn't you say Grogan had? After all, he lives in the cottages, as Swanson here has reason to remember." He nodded toward his assistant, who gave a sheepish look.

"The question is," Martinez went on, *"why* did she fall? Grogan fell because he was blind drunk. And probably that's also what saved his life. Mrs. Piper was grasping at things as she fell. She tore her nails and there are bruises on her arms . . . and fresh scratches and scuffed places on the railings. So she was holding herself rigid, fighting the fall. That usually doesn't save you—and it can kill you. But what we need to know is what made her fall in the first place. Was she unsteady on her feet?"

"N-n-no," Angela said. "I don't remember her ever having a dizzy spell, though some of us here do once in a while . . . not me, of course. And she doesn't—she didn't drink at all, that I know of. Did she have on high heels, did you notice?"

"I thought of that. Flat heels. There's a small tear in the carpet," he went on, "just up there on the second step from the top, and it's bad enough to catch a heel in—but not the heel of a moccasin-type shoe."

Angela shook her head. "Unless of course she had a stroke. Mrs. James in the third cottage keeled over on the walk and banged her head, two weeks ago. When they got her up, her side was numb and all—stroke on one side. These things can happen pretty fast."

"We'll keep that in mind," Martinez said.

Angela squinted wisely at him. "You mean your autopsy will look for it, I suppose," she said. "You needn't hide that kind of thing from us, either, you know. We understand about autopsies and things like that."

For the first time that morning, Martinez smiled. "In other words, share everything we know with all of you, is that what you want?"

Angela nodded. "Well, certainly I realize you have to have *some* secrets. But within reason . . . I mean, you did ask for our help and cooperation, you know, and if we're to operate as part of your team, you should treat us like part of the team. You'll get more out of us."

Swanson opened his mouth and started to say something—but Martinez held up his hand and glared a quick warning, as he said, "Well, thank you for the advice and the information, Mrs. Benbow. We'll be talking with everyone, of course, trying to find out what Mrs. Piper was doing down that hall—and who can help us with why she fell. But in the meantime, you've given us a great deal to think about." He rose, obviously dismissing her, and Swanson struggled up in imitation.

"Oh, and don't hesitate to tell your friends about this conversation. I think you're right that we shouldn't hold back," Martinez added as she turned away.

When she was well out of earshot, parked at her own table, her hands moving in animated discourse as she (undoubtedly) filled in her three friends on the details, Swanson turned to his boss. "Sir, do you mind my asking why you let her think she's . . . what she said—part of the team?"

"Why contradict her? Did you see how she spoke right up this time? When we asked her questions the first time, she didn't know anything, she couldn't think of anything and she didn't want to talk to such as us. Now that she's declared herself in on the action, so to speak—now that she's decided she's really interested and it's not 'beneath her' somehow—she's told us a lot we needed to know. She actually volunteered information. Now that's what I need—a lot of people simply aching to tell us things. Let's get started up in that second-floor meeting room again . . . go arrange it with Torgeson, will you? I'll just finish my coffee here . . ."

Swanson left to do his job, with only one regretful glance backward at the half a cinnamon roll still on his plate.

When Martinez followed him fifteen minutes later, not another diner had left the room. Heads bent forward, meeting over tables; conversation buzzed; eyes rolled, watching Martinez for any sign of what he was thinking. He rose and strolled toward the exit, feigning a casual air he could not feel because of all the staring eyes. On his way out, he detoured by the table where Angela and her co-conspirators were still talking and eating and talking.

"I wonder," he said gently, "if you ladies would mind 'breaking the ice,' as it were, for the other residents? That is, if you'd come up to the room we're using for interviews, and give me—oh, say ten minutes apiece—first—then perhaps the other residents would understand this is really only a rather casual inquiry. After all, we don't have any reason to think today's death is other than a sad accident. But, whatever our reasons for being here, we seem to alarm a lot of these people. Questions bother them, and yet we need their complete cooperation. So will you be my bellwethers?"

"Judas goats, you mean," Nan said.

Caledonia glared at her quickly, then turned a wide smile on Martinez. "Certainly, Lieutenant. Glad to. Angela's told us how generous you were with information to her, and we're delighted to share whatever we know. It's being kept in the dark we don't like."

"About fifteen minutes then, ladies?" And Martinez bowed gracefully out.

"What's the matter with you, Nan?" Caledonia asked. "If we're going to find out what they know, we have to let 'em think we're cooperating, even if we don't tell 'em everything."

"Like about our trip to the office last night," Angela agreed.

Nan was sulky again. "I don't like talking to them at all," she said. "I don't know if this man is any good at his job, do I? I don't know how he's going to take whatever I tell him. Maybe he'll end up arresting someone here . . . and maybe it'll be because of some fool thing I said that I didn't mean to say . . . I don't like it."

Caledonia soothed her. "I don't like it much, either; I'm as worried as you are about what he'll think and do. But you have to trust somebody, after all . . . The police are as good to trust as anybody, I guess."

"Oh, I know," Nan said. "I just feel so—uncomfortable."

"I agree with Nan," Stella said, buttering a tiny wedge of dry toast. "Talking to the police. Involved in a murder investigation . . . Nothing like this ever happened in my family. Why, if my dear mother knew I was talking to police about a murder. . . ." She shuddered.

"Well, my family was never involved in a murder investigation either," Angela declared. "But it doesn't bother me. It fascinates me."

"We've noticed," Caledonia said through a mouthful of bacon, egg and toast.

"I'll go first, okay?" Angela tried not to sound over-eager. "And then maybe you won't feel so bad about it, Stella. Caledonia, you come next . . . I'll call you in your room when I'm done, shall I?"

And they went their separate ways . . . Angela across the length of the lobby to the elevator. Much as she hated the creaky old thing (she had to her fury been trapped there one afternoon for nearly an hour—and with Tootsie Armstrong, of all people), it was still preferable, considering all that had happened, to taking the stairs—in either direction.

Angela's conversation with Martinez was polite, and they simply repeated much of what they'd already said. It was only when Torgeson's name came up that Angela inadvertently added to Martinez' mental file on the red-faced administrator. Martinez was asking about repairs . . . like to the torn carpet on the step . . . Surely, he implied, that was Torgeson's responsibility? and Angela sighed, "Well, the poor man has had other things on his mind, I'd imagine." She did not elaborate, and he did not follow it up . . . but the words stayed with him.

When Caledonia rolled into the room and was safely seated in the largest chair available, Martinez began with the same questions he'd asked Angela. Did Mrs. Piper use the back stairs regularly? No. Why would she be using them now? Caledonia didn't know. Was Mrs. Piper given to fainting spell or was she weak of leg or dim of vision? No, probably not enough to cause a fall.

Caledonia said, "But there is one thing. She turned her ankle rather badly last year when she was wearing a new pair of very high heels. If she had on those stilts . . ."

"No, they were flats. Moccasins. You know—walking shoes."

"Oh, of course. I remember—last night before supper someone was talking about the jogging craze. Somebody else said walking was plenty for them . . . said something like how they walked twice around the building every day before breakfast. Paulette spoke up and said she was going to start exercising, too. She planned to go walking regularly—starting tomorrow—that would be today— very early. She asked if somebody would join her."

"And did anybody say they would?"

"Well, not then, anyhow. But you see, some of them start out together from the west end of the building—just nip down that back stairs through the kitchen to the loading doors—and that's where they start the circle around the block. The virtue of starting by the kitchen is that when they're completely 'whoofed'—which usually happens about three fourths of the way around the building—they can peel off and come straight through into the dining room, sit down, catch their breath, and start breakfast feeling virtuous. If they started at the garden door, for instance—well, that's right in the center of the U—you see, they'd have the length of the walk to go before they could start the outside circuit. If they started at the main front door, they'd have to go all the way around to get back to the dining room."

Swanson was shaking his head trying to follow the geographical description of the walking routes, but Martinez seemed to understand. "So they use that dangerous back stairway in spite of the signs . . ."

"If they live on the second floor and they're among the morning walkers. Certainly."

"What time do these walks begin?" he asked.

"Oh, around 6:45, give or take five minutes or so. It's very informal. If two people show up at the same time, they start off. The next one finds himself alone and waits for a companion . . . anybody . . . to arrive."

"I see. Was Mrs. Piper an early riser?"

Caledonia shook her head. "Now that I don't know. I didn't live close to her, so I never saw her in the garden or the hallways before breakfast. But I kind of think not, since she made such an issue out of getting up to go walking today. You know—when she was telling us about it, I mean."

"Well, one of the walking crowd found her. The kitchen crew arrived for work at the usual time—around 6:30—and they didn't hear anything. So, she must already have fallen. None of the kitchen help went into the little closet where the stairs end, so the next resident to come down for the morning walk—Mr. Littlebrook—he found her. And she was dead then and had been for some little time, I'd guess. We'll know later, when the doctor reports, of course. But the signs . . ." Caledonia shivered hugely. Martinez jumped ahead to his conclusion, "I'd say not an hour, but more than a couple of minutes. So she was going walking very early—perhaps between 5:45 and 6:15."

Caledonia just shook her head, marveling. She herself knew only one 5:30—and that was in the evening. "My sherry time," she called it fondly. She had never understood people who enjoyed watching the dawn—and she said so before she left.

Nan seemed less cheerful about what Angela called "their new status as partners," than the other two had, but was no less polite and apparently no less forthcoming. Yes, Paulette lived at some distance from the back stairs. No, Paulette had no illness that would cause dizziness.

"I hear she'd decided to be an early morning walker," Martinez suggested, trying to get something more than a minimal response.

"Really?" Nan was still not 'giving out' with any enthusiasm.

"Tell me something about her," Martinez suggested.

"Like what?"

"Well, some way in which she was different from the other residents."

Nan gave a sour laugh. "Well, she was kind of stuck-up. She thought she was younger and better preserved than we were. Of course, she did have her hearing still, which is better than most of us can boast. So in that way, she was better preserved. But we didn't like to have our noses rubbed in it. And she was on the prowl for every single man around here. I figured she was trying to get rid of the 'widow' label and be someone's wife again."

"At her age?" Swanson blurted out, in spite of himself, and then ducked in embarrassment.

Nan did smile, then. "You sound like Hamlet, Officer Swanson."

"Hamlet?"

"He told his mother to try to refrain from 'the marriage bed' of her new husband, who was also his uncle—her former brother-in-law, you understand? Hamlet thought his uncle Claudius had murdered his father, you see, and that made it twice as bad to Hamlet that Mother and Uncle Claudius hurried up and got married right after Daddy died.

"So Hamlet tells her to keep clear of her new husband, the suspected murderer. And Hamlet tells his mother it won't be so tough to do, because 'At your age, the heydey in the blood is tame.' Now, I always thought his Mom should have taken a hairbrush to him. She should have said, 'Oh, is that so. Well, wait till you're my age, Sonny, and then tell me that again.'

"So you—you're like Hamlet, because you think everybody over forty loses interest in the opposite sex. And some day, you're going to find out for yourself how wrong you are. Old people like me still have romances—we get stirred up and feel sexy once in a while—and old people get married every day. Some of them for the first time, and some for the second or third or . . .

"So, that's why it's perfectly possible. I mean, I really thought Paulette was husband-hunting. It would have been her fourth."

"Really," Swanson said, obviously impressed. Martinez just glared at him and nodded a "Go ahead" sign to Nan.

She took a deep breath. "Listen, I know you think we're all sweet little old grannies and grampas, and we ought to be tied to one mate for life—and then call it quits. That's what everybody thinks about senior citizens—like we were all lavender and lace. And of course it's perfectly true of some of us. Some women are like me—we are one-man women. That's kind of old-fashioned now, isn't it? But it's not just the generation we were born into and the training we got as kids. It's that—you see, we are the lucky ones. We get the right man, the perfect man, for us—by blind chance—and we'll do anything we have to, to hang onto him."

She waved a hand in generous concession. "Of course some

women found the right man, but they were unlucky—they lost him, somehow. To death—or to another woman. Then there are some who never found the right one, and gave up after a few tries—married or otherwise.

"And then there are the Paulettes . . . Those are the women who try one man, they don't like him, they throw him out and try another . . . And they simply never stop trying. Vain hope, maybe, but even when they're her age—and mine—they don't give up. I think she had her eye on Brighton. You know—cheerful old goat with a lovely smile and a bad limp . . . severe arthritis. You know which one I mean?"

Martinez was torn between a smile of amusement and a frown of intense interest. "Yes, ma'am, I remember Brighton."

"I don't suppose any of this matters. But you did say you wanted to know what she was like."

"You didn't care for the lady, I gather."

"Not much. She was pretty vain, for one thing. Of course, maybe she just wanted all that new makeup because it'd help her in her hunt . . ."

"New makeup?"

"I guess you'll find it when you search her rooms. You do search rooms, don't you? Well, I think she came through the lobby here every day this week with a box or a bag under her arm, boasting about some new lipstick she'd bought that was guaranteed to make her lips look moist and inviting like sweet sixteen. Or the next day it would be the perfect eyeshadow she'd found to disguise crinkled lids. Or a new wrinkle cream made with bee droppings or unborn-calves-foot jelly. Or a marvelous new French perfume that would turn men into satyrs . . . She never did get around to hair dye or false fingernails—but they would probably have been next. Well, anyhow, I thought she was really trying to bait the trap."

"We'll make a note of it, Mrs. Church," Martinez said, keeping a straight face. "Do you have anything else you can think of we should know?"

Nan laughed sourly. "I don't think you should even know *this* much. It can't really have anything to do with her accident. But you asked what I thought . . ."

As Nan waddled toward the door, Martinez, standing politely, said, "Oh, Mrs. Church—one more thing. Didn't I hear that your husband, Dr. Church, is still living? I haven't seen him with you at meals, or . . ."

Nan turned slowly back. "And you won't," she said, in a softer voice. "He's across the street in our little hospital-nursing home. It's Alzheimer's, they say. There's nothing much there, now, but his body—and even that is fading away, a little at a time."

"Oh. I'm sorry. Really sorry."

"Yes. Well. There's nothing anybody can do for the poor souls who get it, you know. Just—let 'em go, with as much dignity as they can retain for as long as they can keep any. And as much comfort as you can give them." She bit her lip and struggled with tears. After a moment, she won. And she turned back to them. "I wish you could have seen Doc Church in the old days. God, he was handsome. A dentist—maybe you've heard—And he was tall and tanned and in that white coat he wore, you know . . .

"I was an actress. I think I told you. I wanted caps on my teeth—thought it might get me better parts in films. Nowadays, of course, they all have capped teeth. There isn't a twisted eyetooth or a gap between the front incisors in all of Hollywood, these days. Of course with all the flouride and stuff, the whole country will have perfect teeth. I think the next generation won't need atomic weapons to win World War III. They'll be able to just go on out and win by biting through the enemy tanks. Or by blinding 'em with their dazzling white smiles.

"Anyhow, I heard Doc Church was the fellow to do the caps—all my girlfriends said so. And the first time I saw him, I knew why the girls had recommended him. He was a—he was so—" She gave up the attempt to find the perfect word and just sighed deeply.

"And you know something? I know you wouldn't believe it to look at me now"—she spread her arms, making her ample form look even wider—"but I used to be pretty good-looking myself, in a kind of sweet and innocent way. A sort of Mary Pickford type, you know . . . Golden curls, Cupid's-bow mouth, big round innocent eyes. I looked ten years younger than I was. And it was literally love at first sight for both of us. And we each let the other know it, too—No coy lead-in for us.

"We went straight from his office out to dinner . . . I don't remember where. Then we went from dinner to the old Coconut Grove, dancing." Her eyes were dreamy. "You had to dress to get in, back then, you know? But that was okay—we used to dress up fancier in the daytime than the kids do now. So we looked okay, I guess. We danced till the place closed. Then he drove me to Malibu . . . He had a Packard convertible . . . There weren't so many houses along the beach then. We took off our shoes and walked along the edge of the water holding hands and making plans . . . We were married three weeks later."

She was looking over Martinez's shoulder at the wall behind him, but he knew her eyes were focused on moonlit Pacific water, a tall young man, a tree bending gracefully, its leaves stirring in the sea breezes of a night fifty years gone. . . .

Martinez smiled gently. "That was moving pretty fast, wasn't it? You didn't know too much about each other."

"Enough. We knew enough to know there'd never be anybody else, not for either of us. And there hasn't been. And it's been wonderful . . . all of it. Well, until now, of course. It's kind of hard to go over there and sit with him and not be sure he even knows who I am. He used to be cheerful and he talked to everybody. He didn't really know where he was, but he seemed to know me. At least, he always seemed glad to see me." She sighed. "But maybe he was just glad for someone to pay him attention and hold his hand and rub his back. Like—anybody would have been welcome.

"Then, even that slipped away. He got a bit cranky and it seemed like he was frightened. He couldn't figure out where he was and why he couldn't go home. Funny—Doc didn't even know where 'home' was, by that time . . . but he kept crying and fussing and asking to go home. And he didn't really know who I was. He'd cling to my hand—so tight. And he'd just say 'Take me home. Please let me go home' over and over . . .

"And then, within these last couple of months, you could see even that slip away. He's starting to have a hard time eating— even with someone feeding him. He has to wear diapers. And he's . . . He's so small. He sits in that wheelchair—he has to be held in with a strap, because he doesn't know enough to sit up and hang on, you see. He slumps there, strapped in, looking like a little old wrinkled doll someone threw away. He doesn't look at anything in particular. He can't talk and nobody's sure how much he can understand of what we say to him . . . I wish I did know that. God, I wish I knew how much he knows—how much he understands. I hope—I even hope he's what he seems to be—completely out of it. But you know, there still are days I'm sure—I'm certain he knows what is going on, what I'm saying to him."

"It would be a comfort," Martinez said nodding, "to know that he *didn't* understand . . ."

"What?" Nan looked at him directly then. "Oh, yes. Of course. Like hoping someone just dies without knowing it's coming, so they're not afraid. But of course he did know, for a while. At first. They told him it was Alzheimer's. At least, they told me, but they said it out loud so he could hear it. They didn't bother to whisper. They acted like he was deaf, too. Doctors can really be cruel, you know? Prime bastards . . .

"He was still himself back then—at least, most of the time. It was just that he got confused and he forgot things. Well, after he knew what it was he had, he'd cry at night about what was happening to him. He didn't cry so much for himself, you know. He was sorry for *me*—worrying about what it would do to me. Just like him, you know. He was always so generous. He took such good care of me. I always wanted a way to pay him back for how good he was to me . . . Well, now I've found one way . . .

"See, I've told them 'No heroic measures.' If his heart stops, it stops. They're not to start it up. If he has a stroke, if he gets pneumonia, they're to make him comfortable, but not to give him a respirator."

She fell silent, and Martinez seemed at a loss for something to say. "I'm—I'm really sorry," he muttered.

Nan drew a deep, deep breath that expanded her shoulders and pulled her head back so that she was looking up and straight at Martinez again. "Don't be," she said. "I love him very much still—but you see, he's not there in that awful, flabby body—in that withered brain. What he needs is to be rid of them, so he can be truly free. The day he dies, I'll drink a toast to freedom . . . his freedom." She turned and walked out the door, pausing as she reached it to turn and say softly over her shoulder. "Good day, Lieutenant."

"Damn," Swanson said. "That's . . ."

"A great exit," Martinez said, shaking his head. "She must have been some actress."

Swanson looked unhappy. "Lieutenant, she wasn't faking that."

"No. Of course not. It was all real and all true. I checked up a little on Doc Church. Read up on Alzheimer's, too, a while back. And I believe every word she said. But she couldn't help but make an exit, could she, for all the genuine emotion? She paused in that doorway at exactly the right second to break that exit and give us one more look at her face . . . She knew exactly how to time it."

"You really don't sound like you feel sorry for her."

"On the contrary. I feel very sorry for her . . . and for Dr. Church, though he's past caring one way or the other, I imagine. I think she's stretching it when she thinks maybe he picks up on anything she says to him. He's like—like a six-month-old baby, and getting 'younger' in his actions and abilities by the minute. Going backwards in time. He probably doesn't understand the words she says—just the tone of voice. Even a newborn can recognize a friendly presence, though he has no concept of 'mother.'"

"Or 'wife,'" Swanson said.

"Or 'wife,'" Martinez agreed. Both men shook their heads and by common consent observed their own few seconds of mourning silence.

"Okay," Martinez sighed at last. "Let's talk to the next one."

Stella had changed the informal brunch coat she wore to breakfast and had on her usual Sunday-go-to-meeting wear by the time she arrived at the interview. She seated herself in the straight chair Martinez indicated, crossed her ankles and tucked her little feet under her ("I bet she was brought up to think no real lady ever crossed her legs at the knee," Martinez told Swanson later), carefully took out her knitting, counted the stitches on the right-hand needle, and then began to add to them. "Now," she said brightly, "you wanted to ask some questions?"

Despite her expressed willingness to cooperate ("I'll really tell you anything, Lieutenant. You have only to ask!"), the interview was as sterile as their earlier encounters. Martinez labored at being charming—a task he usually accomplished with no effort at all. But somehow, in Stella's presence, he felt his armpits getting slick with perspiration and his brow beading with moisture.

If Stella really looked down on a plebeian like a member of the police force, she was too polite to let it show. She kept her little smile firmly in place, her fingers moving steadily along her work. But the only time she yielded information or a reaction worth noting in Shorty's little book was when Martinez asked about Paulette's flirting. "Mrs. Church seems to think Mrs. Palmer was in the market for another husband," he began.

Surprisingly, Stella spoke right up, laying her knitting down and looking him full in the face. "She was a wicked, silly woman, Lieutenant. Imagine—at her age."

"You don't approve, Mrs. Austin?"

"It's hardly up to me to approve or disapprove the behavior of my fellow residents, Lieutenant. Nevertheless, one had to notice. All that makeup . . . Those dreadful stilt heels . . . The shameless flirting . . . No *lady* would ever behave so blatantly." She pressed her lips together. "Forgive me. I shouldn't pass judgment . . ."

"On the contrary. Honest reactions are what we want here. Every scrap of information—every impression . . ." But Stella had said what she had to say. She was not going to volunteer any more.

Martinez asked her the questions about Paulette's health and balance that he had asked the others and received monosyllabic responses. "I take it from Mrs. Wingate that Mrs. Piper's announcement that she was going for a morning walk came as something of a surprise to all of you."

"I am never surprised by anything that woman does. Did!" Stella said. "But as for her saying she was going for a walk—I really don't recall hearing that. Did she tell people that?"

"Apparently so. That explains why she took the back stairs, you see."

"Oh." Stella counted the stitches on her needle and resumed her work. "Of course. That would make sense." And that approving remark was the end of her contribution to the interview.

The remaining interviews were about equally unproductive. "Well, it looks like we've got our work cut out for us with this one, too," Martinez said, sighing.

CHAPTER 11

THAT NIGHT when the pre-dinner crowd gathered in the lobby, there was a division among the members of one "conversation group." One segment—led by an argumentative Angela and an almost surly Nan—maintained that Paulette Piper had died an accidental death. The other identifiable faction—captained by a nervous Tootsie Armstrong, supported by a grim-faced Marian Littlebrook—argued that Paulette was the second murder victim. Hovering around the edges of the two groups, uncommitted and unable to make up her mind, was a twittery Mary Moffet.

Len Littlebrook and Mr. Brighton, his arthritis eased with a day's medication, sat silently near the back of the patio, just listening for the most part, and not apparently taking sides. In a shaft of light from the lobby door sat Stella Austin, using the glow from the lobby to check her knitting, and as usual, merely listening. And seated almost midway between the factions, which had drifted into physical as well as argumentative alignments, was Caledonia—a magnificent referee in a silver lamé caftan, toying casually with the extra-long, extra-heavy string of fine pearls she inevitably wore, swinging them like a pendulum to make a point or punctuate an argument.

"We know of absolutely nothing to connect the deaths," Angela said.

"But two, so close together?" Tootsie put in.

"That doesn't make a scrap of difference," Nan said. "In a place like this people are always sick or having accidents—and they're always dying. I mean, it's a rare month when someone doesn't die of a heart attack or a tumor or complications from phlebitis or emphysema. Things are busy killing one or the other of us all the time. And the management even counts on it. How would they stay solvent, if it weren't for the big entrance fees the new people pay, taking over those vacancies? We have to die off and let new residents buy in, or the management'd go broke. And we oblige. Constantly. Of perfectly natural causes."

"That's enough of that kind of talk," Caledonia snapped, jerking her pearls in an impatient twirl. "Let's get back on track here. What about our current problems?"

"Well, it just isn't logical there'd be two women dead in one week in such unusual ways . . . one stabbed, one falling down those awful stairs. It doesn't make sense," Tootsie insisted, her frizzy hair seeming to rise in spirals of protest.

"It makes sense if they had something in common. Something like . . . Oh, a treasure map that someone would kill to get hold of. I saw the same thing on the late movie last week. But Sweetie and Paulette didn't have one single thing in common, and you know they didn't," Angela argued.

"What map? What treasure? What are you talking about?" Tootsie asked.

"There *isn't* any map, Tootsie. I was just trying to think of a hypothetical example," Angela said, looking for support to Caledonia. She realized her illustration had made little sense, but she had wanted to explain her point with something as far removed from blackmail as possible. That was still their secret—theirs and the police's of course.

Caledonia came to her rescue. "Oh, I know what Angela is try-ing to say," she said. "She means, what could there be about both women that was bad enough to make someone murder both of them because of it?"

"Right," Angela said, nodding gratefully. "And we can't imagine any way at all they were alike, those two. Sweetie was from Duluth and Paulette was from . . . Where was she from?"

"Roseburg, Oregon," Marian Littlebrook said. "At least, that's what she said, one time."

"Well," Nan said, "that doesn't sound like a connection."

"Sweetie was a librarian—" Angela began.

"Well, at least, till she got fired," Mary Moffet interrupted.

"Fired? Who says so?" Angela asked.

"She said so," Mary said. "I complimented her on the way she kept our library here, and she said it was a pleasure to be working with books again. She'd missed it when she'd had to leave the county library in Duluth because of the trouble."

"What trouble?" Caledonia's eyes showed sudden interest. "What happened?"

Mary sighed. "I didn't really understand. She didn't tell me a lot. She just said that she'd been . . . Well, she said 'forced to retire.' She said it was some kind of what she called 'unpleasant-ness.' Something to do with her finding out the county council's books weren't quite right. I didn't know a local government had library books, did you?"

"She probably meant account books, Mary," Nan said kindly. "That she'd discovered some discrepancy in money coming in and money going out."

"Oh. Oh, I see," Mary said. She paused. "Well, no, maybe I don't see. Why would they want to fire her for that? They should be grateful."

Tootsie Armstrong seemed even more bewildered. "Wait," she said, her frizzy hair bristling out as though to register her puzzlement in question marks. "Mary, you're saying Sweetie had lost her job back in Duluth because she found out something damaging about her boss and his accounts . . . Is that right?"

Mary nodded. "I guess so. If the county librarian works for the county council. Well, of course, all this probably doesn't have any importance. I probably shouldn't even have brought it up. I'm sorry."

Angela shot a glance at Caledonia—a glance that was what is known in Victorian romances as "fraught with meaning." She intended to convey that she'd talk to Caledonia later about all this . . . And she was annoyed to see Caledonia grin in amusement. Angela returned to the debate.

"That's interesting, but I don't see any connection there with Paulette Piper, do you? Unless maybe Paulette was a librarian? Or fired from her job, too? What did Paulette do before she came here to live?" she asked.

"Nothing," Nan said, registering disapproval. "Nothing but get married. I mean, she wasn't even qualified for the title of 'House-wife,' because she probably had maids to do all her work; they must have had a little money, all those husbands of hers."

"Oh, I don't think so," Tootsie said. "It seems to me she said once that the first one was a gambler and lost his money, the second failed in business, and the third left her only their house and just enough insurance to buy in here. I think she said Social Security and the money she'd earned from the sale of her house were all she had each month to pay her rent. She never had a cent left over."

There was a slight pause. "But . . ." Marian protested . . . and then stopped.

"I know what you're going to say," Angela said, jumping in. "She had enough money lately to indulge herself. She bought a lot of things . . . junk jewelry . . ."

"Cosmetics," Nan added. "Tons of warpaint."

"That's right," Mr. Brighton chimed in. "And she had just got herself a small electric organ for her apartment, too. She invited me in to see it."

"Sistnered wreck! Ceased . . . ceased . . . auk-shy-sick—ick—" Len Littlebrook bellowed suddenly, entering the conversation for the first time with an explosion of confused sounds. His usually handsome face was flushed and contorted. "Abba—abba noon see toe test!" he shouted. "Noon is ceased toe it!" His voice caught in a strangled gasp and he began to laugh harshly, "Cease, tote! Cease, tote!"

"Len," Marian commended, her voice nearly a shout. "Len! Stop this instant. Think. Think where you are."

"What did you say, Littlebrook?" Mr. Brighton asked. "What was that?"

The dark red slowly receded from Len's nearly unlined face, and the clenched jaw muscles slowly eased. "I—I—oh, I say. I— did I say anything to upset . . . Oh, I do beg your pardon. I had no wish to offend . . ." Marian touched his arm and he rose from his chair. Caledonia could not tell whether Marian was guiding him or pushing him as they edged away from the group together. "I— I'm so frightfully sorry . . ." Len was muttering as they moved off. And as they mounted the stairs, moving steadily away from the lobby, Marian began to whisper to him, inaudible even to those with the best hearing.

"What on earth was that all about?" Angela asked.

Mary Moffet edged forward. "I've never seen Mr. Littlebrook so angry. Never. And he wasn't making any sense at all."

"Well, I understood him," Tootsie said. "I could hear every word. He said someone's sister'd had a wreck. I didn't quite get it all. You know, I thought maybe he meant that Paulette had a sister."

"No," Nan said. "He was talking about testing her toe. I think he was trying to say Marian was wrong and we were right, that we'd find Paulette's shoe was scuffed, if we ran a test. Maybe her toe did catch in that carpet . . ."

"That isn't what it sounded like to me," Angela put in. "I thought it was something about her being shy and sick. Maybe he meant she got woozy and dizzy and fell down the stairs."

"What are you talking about?" Mary Moffet said. "None of it made sense at all. We were talking about music and suddenly he started yelling about testing toes, and stopping toting something, and wrecks and . . . You want to know what I think? I think Mr. Littlebrook's had a nervous breakdown, that's what I think."

"Doesn't any of you here speak German?" Caledonia asked.

"I do," Mr. Brighton said. "Ah . . . I think that perhaps you heard what I heard . . ."

The Westminster chimes signalled that the dining room doors had opened, and the group moved off to join the other residents streaming in to find their places for dinner.

Caledonia lingered a moment beside Mr. Brighton. "I have no idea what he *really* said, but I know what I *think* he said . . . When he wasn't just bubbling and fizzing and spluttering. I did study German for four years in high school and later we were stationed for a while in Germany—at the embassy—between the wars, of course." When Caledonia referred to "the wars," she, like everyone else at Camden, meant "World War I" and "World War II"; nothing since had made much sense to them. And it was getting hard to differentiate between Korea and Viet Nam . . . between Nicaragua and Lebanon . . . only the big ones really mattered.

"I thought," Caledonia went on, "that he was talking in German and cussing, and he said something about death."

Brighton nodded. "That's what I thought myself. He said . . . 'She is just garbage'—you know, like trash. Then he definitely said, 'But now she is dead.' Of course he was all worked up—he was stuttering and laughing when his wife interrupted him."

"Exactly," Caledonia agreed. "He said . . . 'only garbage' and then—of course I've forgotten most of the German I know—but then, didn't he say something a little worse . . ."

The courtly Mr. Brighton turned pink. "Well, I thought he used . . . an unfortunate word. Better not translated, I think. He was so overwrought . . ."

The surge of hungry humanity caught them up and swept them along. Mr. Brighton and Caledonia had been moving rather slowly toward the dining room, talking while they went. As they neared the door, they were parted as it were, by the tide. Caledonia grinned at Brighton and shrugged her inability to carry on their discussion, then eased her way across to where Nan and Stella and Angela had already seated themselves and gingerly lowered her tonnage onto the remaining chair. ("Not nearly sturdy enough," she had pronounced ten years ago, the day the new chairs first appeared in the dining room. She was still waiting for them to break apart under her weight.)

"Okay, what was all that about Len talking German?" Nan asked.

"It *wasn't* German," Angela maintained. "I heard English words. I certainly don't speak any German, so I wouldn't have been able to understand even a couple of words, if what he said had been in a foreign language."

"Listen to me carefully," Caledonia said. *"Aber, nun sie ist tot.* Now, what did you hear me say?"

"Sounds like what Len said," Angela replied. "You said 'abba noon cease tote'—which makes no sense at all."

"I was speaking German," Caledonia said. *"Nun sie ist tot,"* she repeated. "Or, in plain English, 'Now she is dead.' That's all Len was saying. Or, well, not exactly all. He threw in a couple of swear words to describe her. He said she was—well—dirt. *Nur Dreck.* Only garbage. Refuse. That's near enough. You just assumed he was speaking English."

"I think I see," Stella said.

"Well, I suppose it could have been in German," Angela said, reconsidering. "Oh, thank you, Dolores." The waitress put down their plates—a savory pork chop, dill carrot strips, tiny new potatoes—and moved away. "I just don't understand," Angela went on, unfolding her napkin daintily and putting her fork firmly into the mound of carrot strips, "why Len would speak in a foreign language. He never has before."

"It obviously upset Marian," Caledonia said. "Look—she and Len haven't come to the dining room yet." She gestured across the room at the Littlebrooks' table, standing empty.

"There's something fishy about this, girls," Angela declared. "I've never seen Len Littlebrook act in the least disconcerted, let alone lose control like he did a few minutes ago. You know what I'm thinking?"

Caledonia nodded. "That we should pay a call on the Mud Fence and her husband tonight."

"Exactly," Angela said, and as she sat back in her chair the corners of her lips turned up in the same smile the Admiral had always labeled her "going into battle" smile. She had no doubt about this one.

CHAPTER 12

TO ANGELA'S and Caledonia's dismay, Stella and Nan both flatly refused to accompany them on their visit to the Littlebrooks. After dinner, the four walked together as far as the front staircase, and then Stella stopped. The others stopped with her.

"You realize I can't go with you," Stella said.

"Oh, Stella," Angela complained. "Why are you always such a spoilsport?"

"I realize I'm being no fun," Stella said apologetically. "But really, this has ceased to be a diversion for me. It's grown very serious indeed and I really can't see myself talking to someone directly about such an embarrassing outburst."

"For once, I'm with Stella," Nan put in. "I don't think I want to do this. And I wish you wouldn't, either," she added.

"Oh, Nan . . . Stella . . ." Angela said plaintively. "We're supposed to be a team."

"Forget it," Nan said abruptly. "I've got a bad, bad feeling about this, girls. I don't think I want to know the answers. The look on that man's face was . . . Well, I just don't want to know."

"But that's exactly why we ought to find out about it," Caledonia urged. "You know it's really important, for him to get so worked up."

Nan just shook her head and pinched her lips together tightly. "Whatever it is, he doesn't want us prying around. And Marian doesn't. So I'm not going to."

Stella nodded wordlessly and put her hand on the banister, indicating that she was on her way to her room, if no one had anything more to add. She hesitated, but Caledonia only shrugged.

"All right for you, then," Angela said, tossing her head in that Scarlett O'Hara imitation she brought off so well—without even knowing it. "All right. We'll do it alone. Without either of you. Come on, Caledonia."

Caledonia grinned, patted Nan on the shoulder, and surged up the stairs behind Angela. Stella, a few steps ahead, did not even look back at the two, huffing and puffing up behind her. At the head of the stairs, she turned right toward her own apartment and disappeared around the corner of the hall.

The Littlebrooks' apartment was off to the left, once you came out of the main staircase, and it lay on the front of the building, the street side. Perhaps to compensate because those rooms were noisier, with the constant traffic going by, they had also been made slightly larger, with bigger windows. So they were cool and airy in the almost perpetual summer weather that favored that part of Southern California. The Santa Ana winds that blew hot air from inland in a reversal of the normal wind-flow patterns could be a bother, of course, but they came only rarely during the year. There was no ocean or garden view from these windows, but there was the fun and excitement of the occasional fender bender at the traffic light to enliven the day; these residents had a ringside seat.

As a matter of fact, the argument raged perpetually at Camden about who had the best rooms. Those without sufficient hearing to be bothered by traffic claimed the front was the most stimulating; crumpled metal and broken glass and irate motorists made for

THE J. ALFRED PRUFROCK MURDERS   183

more exciting viewing than either TV or the rose garden. Those on the garden side, overlooking the sea, swore by the view they caught almost daily of schools of porpoise patrolling the kelp beds and rolling along, one might say with deliberate mischief, among the surfers. Those in the building gloated that on the rare rainy or chilly days, they did not have to risk catching cold by walking outside; those in the cottages gloated over their extra space and their kitchenettes . . . It was a debate that would never end and could never be won.

Marian and Len had a two-room suite halfway down the hall, their door marked with a wreath decorated with little china ornaments—small reproductions of Hummel figurines. Knocking on the Littlebrooks' door set the wreath swinging and the china ornaments rattling on their mounts. And for a long time, it was also ineffectual. Nobody answered the knock, and neither Angela nor Caledonia could hear any sound within.

"Maybe they're not home?" Angela said.

"Let's knock again," Caledonia suggested.

She did—and Angela leaned closer to the door to listen, just as, to her chagrin, it swung open. If Marian had made any noise crossing the carpet to reach the door, it was below the level her visitors could pick up with ears that had served for more than seven decades.

"What is it?" Marian began. "Oh, it's you. I'm sorry Angela . . . Caledonia . . . Forgive me." But she didn't move aside or invite them in.

"Marian . . ." Caledonia began her pre-agreed excuse, edging forward a little as she did so, the very size of her presence forcing Marian to edge backward, conceding about two inches of leeway in the entry. "We—uh—we wanted to talk about this month's shuffle board teams."

"Oh—but not now, surely," Marian said. "I mean, can't it wait till tomorrow?"

"We need to get it posted this weekend," Caledonia insisted, easing her weight forward on her toes so that she leaned close to Marian, whose weight rocked back without her meaning to give ground again. As Marian moved backward, Caledonia shuffled both feet forward again, another inch gained.

"Well, what about it then?" Marian asked, without much warmth.

Caledonia leaned forward again, sharply, as though to speak, and again Marian rocked backward, losing another precious half-inch. "I was wondering if you and Len would agree to split up and each work with one of the weaker players, this time? You're both so good, and you always win."

Marian swung aside in a self-deprecating motion, and Caledonia's foot came forward so that as Marian turned fully forward again, toward them, she had to back up once more, just a tiny three inches, to avoid bumping her guest. "But we like playing together. We always have . . ."

"Well, it's discouraging to some of the new people, I think, to have to play such a good, experienced team that always wins. And then there are a few other names on this list . . ." Caledonia swung a piece of paper, her list, up in a wide gesture, and Marian jerked backward to avoid getting the list squarely across her nose. At the same time, Caledonia slid forward again. She now stood eight inches inside the door frame. ("Used to watch door-to-door salesmen work that trick," she explained to Angela later.)

"Well," Marian said rather grudgingly, "come on in, since you're here. It'll save you a trip later." She waved them to a chair (for Angela) and the love seat (for Caledonia).

Seated, the visitors looked around. The door to the other room was closed tightly. "Len isn't here?" Angela asked.

"He's resting," Marian said uneasily. And then, biting her lips, she said, "About that—what happened before supper tonight—"

"My dear, please. Think nothing of it. We all have our bad moments; it's not worth mentioning," Caledonia said. Angela glared, afraid that Marian might take Caledonia's suggestion to heart. But once started, the need for her to explain was strong, and Marian plunged forward. She pulled a small chair near to them, and almost fell into it, as she went on talking—quickly—breathlessly.

"It's . . . I don't know if you've noticed that Len is—he's failing. I'm not sure . . . The doctors seem to think it has to do with hardening of the arteries; he's had a few small strokes—and apparently, they'll keep on happening. There's some forgetting already—some confusion—especially when he's tired or upset. Sometimes he doesn't seem to know any more quite where he is."

Caledonia nodded and put her large hand out to take one of Marian's. "We all let go, sooner or later, in one way or another. I'm so sorry."

Marian's eyes filled with tears. "I want him to have dignity. I don't want him to feel confused and helpless. I don't want him to get lost walking to the dining room, like Mr. Renfrew last year . . . I don't want him not to know me, like Dr. Church doesn't know Nan . . . I don't want him wandering into the lobby without his clothes, like Mrs. Fanshaw did . . ."

"Dear Marian . . . believe me . . . nobody thinks the less of him because of it. Everyone understands. It happens. You're just lucky you two are here, where people do understand and where he can be taken care of."

Marian nodded. "Oh, I know . . . I know . . . But it seems especially cruel for him. He was so—oh, I don't know—so mentally sharp. Like the crease on fresh-pressed trousers. Like well-polished boots . . . And now it's like—like cloth all covered with lint. You can't quite see the outlines any more . . . You're not quite sure what's going on under there. Well, you never knew him at his best, of course. When he was young."

"He's still handsome right now," Angela said soothingly. "He's amazing for his age . . . How old is he?"

"Older than you think—he'll be seventy this year. I know he doesn't look even fifty. Now I look my age all right . . ."

"Oh, Marian," Angela said.

"No, it's all right. I never was a beauty, and I always knew it. But I wish you could have seen him—especially in uniform. There's something about a man in military uniform anyway . . ."

"What branch of service . . ."

"I was a nurse, you see. He was brought in wounded in the last days of the war in Europe." Caledonia and Angela both knew Marian was talking about World War II—that was, after all, *the* war. "He was one of my patients. And he was such a gorgeous man, even if you couldn't see his face through all the bandages . . . and he was so ferocious about being helpless. Men make bad patients, except when they're too sick to talk or move at all, of course—and he was one of the very worst."

She laughed as she remembered. "One day, the orderlies brought the food in late, and it was something awful like Spam. Looking back, I don't suppose Spam was so bad, really . . . but we must have had Spam every meal for at least three weeks. Supplies were a problem toward the end of the war. Of course it couldn't be helped . . . but sometimes you forget, especially if you're one of the pampered darlings and an officer, and you're spoiled into thinking you'll never have anything but the best.

"Well, this orderly brought the trays into the room—and before he could even get to Len's bed, Len reared up—swathed in bandages and at that time pretending he couldn't speak a word of English—and started swearing. You could tell he was swearing, even if you couldn't speak German. I could, a little—that's why one of my duties was helping with the wounded prisoners in the officers' ward . . ."

Angela didn't dare breathe too loudly for fear she'd give away her excitement. She only glanced at Caledonia, who was listening with her mouth slightly ajar, her eyes riveted on Marian.

"Len leaned forward and grabbed the plate off the tray . . . only a tin plate, of course, but it had heft, with all that food on it . . . And he threw it at the orderly, yelling the most awful curses all the while. The orderly ducked, and I got that plate right across the bosom of my uniform. Spam, gravy, what passed for mashed potatoes ... It clung for a minute and then dripped off to the floor ... And Len said, in English, 'Oh, Sister,'—they call nurses 'Sister' you know—he said, 'Sister, forgive me. I meant that decoration for the chest of the attendant.' I was so stunned at the Spam-and-gravy trimming, I didn't even realize about the language ..."

"He spoke English?" Caledonia prompted.

Marian nodded. "He'd learned it in their equivalent of grade school and kept right on to college with it. A lot of Europeans learned English, and as an officer he was encouraged to be able to speak a foreign language well. After all, they thought they'd need English-speaking officers when they conquered England. He gets his accent and that ritzy vocabulary from his early teachers, who were apparently all Oxford men."

"Marian," Angela said, "why haven't you ever told anyone Len was German? I suppose he's an American citizen now, isn't he?"

"Yes," Marian said, sighing. "Of course. It was easy. We just got married—and eventually we could arrange for him to come here with me."

"Well"—Angela pressed the point—"there's nothing really so unusual about that. I've met three or four Germans, ex-soldiers, who came here after the war and became Americans. You didn't have to be so secretive."

"But he was an officer," Marian began.

"So were both our husbands," Angela said, gesturing to Caledonia, "and Len doesn't hold it against us. So why would we hold it against him?"

Marian shook her head. "I'd better tell you all of it, I suppose." She looked squarely at the two of them, first at Angela, bright-eyed and interested, then at Caledonia, sympathy as obvious on her large face as a black funeral band worn on a bare arm.

Marian stood up, walked away from them to the window, and

said, very softly, looking studiously away, out into the street, "I'm not sure you would be able to forgive Len. You see, he wasn't just an officer. He was an officer in the Waffen SS."

"Oh, Lord!" Caledonia said. "The SS?"

Angela's mouth was open. She snapped it shut with an effort. "But they were . . . Len is such a nice person."

"Marian," Caledonia asked, "how on earth could you get hooked up with an SS officer?"

Marian sighed again and turned back to face them. "Look at me," she said. "I'm not a pretty woman and I never was. All the way through high school I never even had a date. My brother took me to the prom and I was so embarrassed, I stayed in the ladies' room most of the evening while he stood around and talked to his friends. I've always known I was plain. No, worse than plain. Downright homely. And I decided, after I graduated from nursing school, that since I'd probably never marry, I'd make myself the best nurse in the world. That I'd make a fine career in nursing— go right to the top.

"When the war came, I volunteered for the Army nurses. And I was doing really well . . . I was a major by the time we went into Germany. Then this group of German prisoners came to us . . . all wounded. We had to take care of them, of course, till they could be taken to prison camp.

"And there was Len. He'd been badly burned—but I saw his picture—the orderlies took the things out of their pockets, you know, when they took their uniforms off them. He'd been so handsome. And he was always so nice to me . . .

"I knew all about the SS and the terrible things some of them did, but all the same, we got friendly, Len and I. Especially after I found out he spoke English and we were able to talk. The surgeons did wonders reconstructing his face; we took good care of our prisoners, at least the ones I saw. So he had plastic surgery before they sent him along to a prison camp hospital, and that's a slow business. We had a lot of time to get to know each other really well. I had time to fall in love."

Angela sighed deeply, and Caledonia was sitting absolutely still and attentive. "Well, go on," she said. "And he fell in love with you . . ."

Marian smiled sadly. "I didn't know you were such a romantic, Caledonia. Of course he didn't love me. But he was fond of me, I think. And he liked me. And of course he was using me to get special privileges while he was in the hospital. I think he already had thoughts of maybe living in the United States . . ."

"Oh, surely not," Angela said.

Marian shook her head. "I'm not a fool. What you're talking about, Caledonia, could only happen in a story. And Len was spoiled all his life. He was one of the beautiful people, one of the people everything came easy to . . . before the war. And before he was burned. Why on earth would he fall in love with me?"

"But—but you married him," Angela said.

"Of course I did. I thought he was the only chance I'd ever have. Besides, I thought he was the most beautiful man I'd ever seen, at least when those surgeons got done grafting the skin and reconstructing the face and giving him new teeth, he was. And like I told you—I was in love with him. So when he was transferred to a camp, out of the hospital, I kept track of him. And as soon as all the fighting was over, and they started processing prisoners for release, I got in touch." She smiled again.

"I don't want to disappoint you completely, girls. Now that *was* romantic. We walked through the summer woods . . . We went boating together on a little river . . . Had picnics alone under the stars . . . I've never been so happy. He courted me like they do in the movies—holding hands, bringing me flowers, thoughtful and kind—and when he asked me to marry him so we could be together in America, I said yes."

"Wasn't there a lot of difficulty bringing home a 'male war

bride'?" Caledonia asked. "I remember that movie with Ann Sheridan and Cary Grant . . . he was a French officer—an ally— not a German—and the red tape was terrible. At least, in the movie."

Marian shook her head. "I knew better than to try to get him, a German and a former officer in the SS, into this country, even though he was married to an American citizen. So I found a man who made false papers. And even that took weeks. I didn't know where to start. It's not so easy to be a successful criminal in a foreign country.

"But eventually I found the man. It took two thousand dollars American money—and that was a lot, in those days—a lot for an Army nurse, anyway. But Len got papers as a Dutch citizen. After that it got a lot easier. We were married. I was shipped home in October of 1945, and he was given transport two months later."

"Littlebrook isn't a German name," Angela said suddenly. "I don't think it's Dutch, either."

"Try 'Kleinwasser,'" Marian said. "And that's not his real name, either. But it's what we told everyone for a long time while we were still in Germany . . . I wanted Wilhelm Jaeger to disappear so completely that nobody'd ever trace him. So I got him to change his name as soon as he got out of that prison. He did everything I wanted him to. He suggested the name of a neighbor from years ago . . . 'Leonhardt Kleinwasser.' And when we got to America, we translated that to English."

"Marian . . ." Angela's little face was tight with sympathy. "Are you telling us that you married Len knowing he didn't love you"—Marian nodded—"and just kind of hoping for the best"— Marian nodded again—"and that he treated you nicely while you were courting but that he's never loved you? And you lived with him all these years, and . . ."

"Oh, no, I didn't say that." Marian was smiling again. "It's hard to say when it happened. But he came to love me—or I think he does. He acts as though he does. We were always good friends, remember, and that can substitute for a lot. And now—Well, now he needs me. It took a long time but I can honestly say that now I'm everything in the world to him." Her face glowed. "It's wonderful to be needed like that."

"Well, fine," Caledonia said. "I'm glad. But what about his background? How could you get around all that?"

Marian shrugged. "You do crazy things if you're in love. Certain things cease to matter . . . And besides, Caledonia, you've known Len now for years. Do you think he could ever have worked at a concentration camp? Or murdered people in the streets? He worked with files and records—in an SS office. Even they had to have some office workers, you know. He explained that they tried to use their own people; they didn't trust outsiders much. He may have worn that black uniform . . ."

"The Black Knight!" Angela said suddenly. "Of course. From Sweetie's list." She glanced at Caledonia, who nodded gravely. "Marian, were you and Len paying blackmail to Sweetie?"

Marian bit her lip, "Oh, God. Yes. I was so afraid she'd tell people here. About Len. They'd have put us out of Camden. And that would only be the beginning. But he's been through a lot, and he's—he's been so good to me. Such a good husband."

She looked at her hands, twisting together. "Angela, where we lived—in Charlotte, North Carolina, for years—he worked as a hospital volunteer with mental patients. He was in the Big Brothers organization. He worked with the Little League and Meals on Wheels. And after we found out we couldn't have our own children, he worked with all those projects that get Christmas toys for needy children. He did everything he could, to make up for the SS . . .

"And then she found out. Sweetie told me that one day, she saw a picture in one of those damned books of hers . . . a really handsome man in a German uniform. It didn't look anything like Len, especially the way he looks now, with his new face and all. But she told us it sort of sparked an idea. She had already been thinking about Len as a puzzle because of other things—for instance, there's his accent . . . "

"Everyone here supposes he's British," Angela said.

"Well, she did too. At first. And she kept on about what part of England did he come from? Finally he said—he felt he had to say—that he'd never seen England. His accent came from his English-educated tutors. And then, you know, once in a while, he still has a trace of German pronunciation . . ."

"I've never heard it," Caledonia assured her. "At least, not till tonight . . ."

"Well, that's the thing," Marian said. "As he's gotten a little more—you know—forgetful, easily confused . . . just once in a while it shows. Like he'll put in a *v* in for a *w* . . . or he'll stick in an *f* where a *v* should be . . . Nobody notices half the time."

"Nobody *hears* half the time," Caledonia said. "There's hardly a good pair of ears left. Paulette could hear. I think Tootsie's hearing's nearly normal. But the rest of us . . ."

"Well, Sweetie picked up on it one day. That and—well, he still carried himself in that stiff, military way—he walks like a German officer in the movies. I always hated to see him walking, from across the room. It was so obvious to me."

"Honestly," Angela said. "It wasn't to us. Oh, I guess I thought 'military.' But I never thought of the German army."

"Well, whatever the combination was, it made Sweetie curious as hell. And she zeroed in on him. First she flattered him and played on his vanity till he thought of her as a real friend."

Marian gave a small, unhappy smile. "It's amazing, you know, how vulnerable handsome men are—because they have enormous ego, really. People have played up to them all their lives—and they take it for granted. So they got to be real buddies, Len and Sweetie. I'd find them, over and over, with their heads together having a nice chat—" She twisted her hands again in agonized memory.

"Didn't that concern you?" Angela said.

"Oh, God, I was sick with worry."

"But he'd never have told her he was an SS man. I don't care how much she flattered him. Surely he wouldn't," Caledonia said. "He'd kept the secret all these years . . ."

"Of course he didn't tell her," Marian said. "Not at first, at least. He just—he talked. A lot. About his childhood, about his college days . . . I suppose it was such a pleasure to find someone he could reminisce to. It had been so long since he'd dared let down . . . She worked and worked and worked and she got one tiny little bit at a time, till there was enough to put the puzzle together. And she did. We were out in the garden—I remember so well—and she said to him 'But Len, you're practically telling me you were a Nazi!'

"He tried to work away from the conversation, but she kept after him and kept after him—laughing about it—laughing at his evasions—and all of a sudden he lost his temper. He said, 'Ja, all right! I was a German soldier. I was in the SS. And I've paid for it. Now leave me alone.' He walked away.

"Then that poisonous little woman turned to me and she actually smiled as though we were the best of friends. She said, 'Well, I do think he should keep right on paying for something that awful, you know . . . I'm sure you wouldn't want to be put out of Camden because of the dreadful things your husband may have done in the past . . . Of course I'm sure he's sorry for his war crimes . . . So why don't we say—oh, a token amount—just $35 a month, for now. To me—in cash, please—on the first, please.'

"She used to come to dinner wearing a necklace she'd bought. It looked a lot like a German war decoration—the *Eisenkreuz*—the iron cross."

"I think I saw it—on her dressing table," Angela said.

Marian bit her lip again. "She'd put that necklace on and she'd hold that cross up so it caught the light, and she'd say, 'I wore this just for you, Len. I knew you'd like it!' She loved to watch us tense up and . . ."

Caledonia shook her head. "I expect that was part of the reward, to her—the fun she got out of everybody's unhappiness."

"Everybody?" Marian was puzzled.

"Oh dear, I forgot you didn't know." Angela leaned forward and touched her shoulder, very gently. "Marian, you weren't the only ones she was taking money from. There were lots and lots of others. Just a little money from each person, you see. But a little from a lot of different people adds up."

"I see. I wondered why she didn't ask us for more. Oh, she did ask last year for a 'cost of living increase'—that was her term for it—to $50 a month. Just after she told me she supposed Len could be sent back to Germany, because he was an illegal alien. It was obvious, once you knew his background, that he'd changed his name to get into the country. *Alien.* Why, we've been here forty years. I'd almost forgotten he was anything but an American. I think he had forgotten."

"Marian . . . Marian, where are you?" It was Len, calling from the bedroom.

"Coming dear. I'm only here in the living room," Marian said, standing to move toward the closed door.

"Wait," Caledonia said, urgently. "There's more we want to ask."

"I can't," Marian said. "I'm sorry. He needs me. He'll fret if I don't come . . . Look, can you come back tomorrow? I need to talk to someone about . . . well, about Paulette . . . How she heard Sweetie talking to us and wanted a share—"

"Marian—go on. Go on! What about her?" Angela asked.

"Well, after Sweetie died, Paulette told us she was 'taking over the paper route.' That's what she said . . . She was 'taking over the paper route' and we could pay our 'subscriptions' direct to her from that time on. She said she'd heard us talking one day and now she knew everything Sweetie knew. She even boasted that her hearing was so good that she was able to eavesdrop, and we never even guessed. She seems to have made a habit of listening to other people's conversations around here—for amusement. And this time she got more than amusement out of it."

Angela nodded sympathetically. "I forget from time to time to lower my voice, myself. Because around here it really doesn't matter. Most of the time, nobody could overhear if they wanted to. Except for the staff. And Paulette . . . and maybe Tootsie, though I'm really not sure . . ."

"It must have been a shock when she told you," Caledonia said, ignoring Angela.

"Oh God! I just couldn't believe it. It was all starting over—and I'd been so glad, when I heard Sweetie was dead. I'm surprised Paulette didn't go and get that damned necklace to wear, too," she said harshly, moving toward the bedroom door.

"I'm right here, dear," she called. "I won't be a minute . . ." She turned back to them. "Please go now. He was all upset tonight and I want him calm, so he can get to sleep. We can talk more tomorrow. In fact . . . it's a good feeling to talk about it— especially to someone who doesn't want money from us." She gestured toward the hall door, and Caledonia nodded to Angela. They both rose and moved as though to leave.

"I'll tell you one thing right now, though," Marian said, as she closed the bedroom door. "Len and I don't drink much—but we each had a little cherry brandy this morning to celebrate when he found Paulette's dead body. We thought we'd be free, at last, for the first time in years. He needs that. He needs to feel he's not responsible for our financial straits . . . that our troubles aren't all his fault . . . He needs to have a little time to . . . to flicker out in peace and calm . . . He's paid his dues, more than once, thanks to those two. Now—Tomorrow, all right?"

She swung the bedroom door open exactly as Caledonia

opened the hall door, and the two departing guests heard Len's voice, "You were a long time, honey. Who was visiting?"

"Just Caledonia and Angela. We'll talk about it in the morning, okay?"

The visitors closed the door softly behind them as they left.

CHAPTER 13

C ALEDONIA INSISTED that Angela join her in her cottage for ". . . a little toddy. We both need it, girl. *I* need it, to be perfectly frank."

Angela didn't seem to mind. She was silent as they walked along. Once safely curled into Caledonia's armchair, sipping a tiny Chambord, Angela sighed, "Caledonia, I feel so awful. All the time I've been calling her ugly . . . I tell you, tonight . . . Why, she looked almost pretty."

Caledonia smiled and took a huge swallow from her cut crystal brandy snifter. "That she was, girl. You're learning. Late in life, it's true. But we'll make a human being out of you yet. Well . . . I suppose I should round up the others and fill them in." She palmed the white Princess phone. Everyone else was content to use Camden's antiquated, plain black handsets, but Caledonia had said they were unattractive, she had the money to indulge herself, and why not? Her extension in the bedroom was, incongruously, housed in a plastic image of Garfield; it didn't go with her opulent Chinese Chippendale, but it amused her—and it stayed right beside her bed, no matter how many times Angela shook her head and said, "Tacky, tacky, tacky."

"Get me Mrs. Church," Caledonia told the switchboard. There was a long wait while she savored another mouthful of brandy.

"Ah, that's really what I needed . . . something to counteract the— What did you say?" Caledonia turned her head away, as though looking into space, rather than at Angela, could make the voice on the phone clearer to her. 'Oh, I see . . . Any idea where she's gone?"

Another long wait, and then she said, "Sorry to hear that."

Another pause, then, "Oh, dear. I *am* sorry. Thanks for telling me. Well, at least Stella's with her. Yes, I'll get in touch myself later." She put the phone to rest softly and shook her head.

"What is it?"

"They've called in the doctor for Doc Church. Nan's over with him now. Beanie went with her."

"Oh, dear," Angela said, but she felt neither surprise nor anguish. Death was a frequent visitor there—and often came gently.

"Clara said she was so busy she couldn't talk—but of course she did. Doc Church was having trouble breathing earlier. Now they seem to think he's slipping away."

"Maybe we should go over there."

"Ah, we'd probably just be in the way. Besides, Beanie's there and who knows? Doc Church may get better after all—you remember he was like this about six weeks ago—"

"It seems like a year."

"Yes, it does, doesn't it? Before all the trouble with . . . you know, back when we all thought Sweetie was sweet."

"And that Paulette was just pretty and silly and man-crazy." Angela shook her head. "I didn't care much for Sweetie, it's true. But I sort of liked Paulette. Weren't you surprised about the blackmail?"

Caledonia nodded and took another swig of the brandy. *"Was I.* Two of them alike—both as mean as"—she paused, searching for the right comparison—"as someone who'd steal from a blind news vendor. Both of them taking advantage of people who couldn't fight back . . . You know I never mind getting the better of someone—but always in a fair fight. There isn't anything fair about blackmail. Of course it won't surprise Nan. She never did like Paulette at all."

"Did you know about Sweetie's being fired from her job in Duluth?" Angela asked.

"Of course not. I thought she just plain retired. You know, it really sounds as though our Sweetie was in the blackmail business even back in Duluth. Do you suppose she threatened her county councilman with exposure and he called her bluff and fired her?"

"I wouldn't be surprised. Our policeman can find out."

"He probably knows already," Caledonia said. "He seems to be quite good at his job."

"Oh, lord," Angela put her liqueur glass down suddenly. "Do you realize what this means? It means that Paulette was probably pushed down those stairs after all. I said it was probably an accident, but that would be . . ."

"Right. Never trust coincidence." Caledonia put her glass down. "Listen, I don't want to tattle—and especially not on Marian, with her problems. But maybe we should tell the Lieutenant."

Angela looked indignant. "Let him sweat information out for himself, I say. He's never been really frank with us, and besides, Marian has been through enough . . . and Len—well, he's tried to make amends. Poor man isn't likely to live out the year anyway."

Caledonia shook her head. "I don't like to think of Marian trying to get by without him."

"I managed," Angela said. "You managed. We do what we have to do."

"I only meant that it will be particularly hard for Marian. Our husbands were independent men. They had lives of their own. So we developed as individuals, if you see what I mean." Angela disagreed—at least, thinking back to how lost she'd been after her Douglas died, but she didn't interrupt.

"If I read Marian right," Caledonia went on, "she and Len made their own world, just the two of them, except for whatever they did for a living—and Len's charity work. I bet they didn't make many friends. They must have lived in fear most of the time, thinking somebody would find out . . .'"

"And somebody did." Angela said.

"And now he's wholly dependent on her," Caledonia went on. "He needs her now as much as she ever needed him. But that's going to come right around, do you see my point? His needing her becomes what she lives for—her whole reason for living. And that's dangerous. Because when he goes, so does her whole life. I certainly wouldn't want to be responsible for that."

"So we agree," Angela said. "No mentioning the Littlebrooks to the police. We like them—we like *her* anyhow, and—"

"I can't feel anything at all about *him,* you know? Isn't that odd? I was as horrified by Germany and the Nazis as anybody else. But even though I'm shocked, I can't be angry at him. Poor old Len, with his false teeth—"

"I should have guessed," Angela muttered.

"—And his grafted skin. No wonder he hasn't got wrinkles. He's seventy, but his face is only forty-five."

"I used to think he was handsome."

"Well, he still is," Caledonia said. "Those surgeons did a bang-up job, all right. I'd never have guessed that face was manmade."

"Oh, I suppose he's handsome. But thinking of him," Angela said, "I just think 'Poor old Len.' *She's* the one I keep remembering and worrying about and feeling sorry for."

"The Mud Fence, you mean?" Caledonia asked wickedly.

"Don't." Angela closed her eyes. "Don't remind me I said that."

"Well, anyhow . . . We don't have to talk about them, but I think we do have to say something to Martinez. He's got to know Paulette was killed on purpose. I wonder if he's still here at this hour of the night?" She pulled the little phone to her and picked it up again. "Clara? Listen, Clara, is that detective here tonight?—Well, listen, would you find him for me, please?—What?—Oh, no rush . . . it's not urgent at all. Just, when you find him, tell him I'd like to speak to him. Okay? Yes, thank you."

She turned to Angela. "All right, that's done. Clara will ask him to phone down here. And we're going to tell him that Paulette was in on the blackmail deal. All right?"

Angela nodded a bit apprehensively. "He'll want to know how we found out, won't he?"

"Well, we just won't tell him, that's all," Caledonia said, jutting out her chin. "Here—let me get you another one of those."

"Why is Clara on the desk tonight?" Angela asked. "It should be Jimmy Taylor."

"Oh, he's probably got an exam—or a girlfriend. I hope Clara volunteered for the extra duty and Torgeson didn't just stick her with it when Jimmy didn't show up." She carried Angela's little glass to the bar, filled it with the last of the Chambord, and poured herself another snifter of brandy. She had just put the brandy bottle firmly but regretfully into the cupboard and was shifting the contents to fit the brandy into the back, when there was a knock on the cottage door. "Answer that, will you?" she told Angela, while she fished among the bottles.

Angela pattered across the room, swung the door open and caught her breath.

"Good evening, Mrs. Benbow," Martinez said, with that little bow. "The woman at the desk . . . your Clara . . . told me you ladies wanted to see me?"

"Oh, dear," Angela said, "we didn't want to *see* you. I mean, Caledonia was going to tell you something on the phone, that's all."

"Am I unwelcome just now?" Martinez remained silky polite, but there was an edge of insistence in his tone.

"Oh, no, not at all, Lieutenant," Caledonia said. "Please come in. It's just—we were having a little after-dinner drink. I hope you'll join us?"

Martinez glanced at his watch. "Why, thank you, Ma'am. I think I can safely say it's after working hours, and I can officially declare myself to be off duty. Otherwise . . ." He eased into the room and seated himself in the first chair he came to, a pleasant little antique upholstered in rose velvet. "You're having liqueur? I'll join you with anything handy. Ah, I see you have B & B . . . That'll do fine for me."

Caledonia poured it saying, "Sure you wouldn't prefer brandy?"

"Positive. This is welcome. Thank you. And now, ladies?" He half-toasted them, sipped and looked at them with inquiry.

Angela and Caledonia exchanged glances, and Angela said, "Uh—well—uh. Lieutenant, how did you get here so fast? We only just left the message."

"I was standing around the corner from the desk talking to someone. Clara couldn't see me, but I heard her mention my name. So I just put my head around the corner as she was hanging up the phone, she relayed the message, I walked down the path immediately . . . and here I am." He flashed that winning smile of his. "Magical, isn't it? Now back to the point—"

"Well, this is really Caledonia's story. But earlier you said you were trying to find out what killed Paulette Piper . . . and we ran across some information . . ."

Martinez smiled. "I heard that you were defending the theory of accidental death, in the lobby tonight before dinner."

"Yes," Angela said. "But now we know better."

"Well," Caledonia interrupted. "at least we think we do. If she *wasn't* murdered, it if *was* an accident, it was an incredible coincidence! And I don't believe in those much."

"Neither do I," Martinez said, nodding. "This is excellent, thank you," he added, sipping at the B & B. "Now, suppose you tell me how you came to this conclusion."

"Well, it's a little complicated."

Martinez' smile never wavered. "I'd be surprised if it wasn't. Go on with the story. I'll do my best to follow."

"We found out tonight that Paulette had tried to take over from Sweetie. As a blackmailer."

The Lieutenant raised his eyebrows but said nothing. Caledonia went on. "You see, Paulette was terribly proud she had good ears, while most of us are slightly hard of hearing . . . some more, some less, but usually there's at least a degree of loss at our age. She had no loss, and she was always showing off a little."

Martinez's face showed no expression. He merely sat back in the chair and waited for Caledonia to continue.

"Well, I guess you could say it was poetic justice in a way. Her good ears got her the information (she heard Sweetie putting out one of her ultimatums), and those good ears got her killed—at least, that's what we think. Because she tried to take over when Sweetie was dead, on the basis on information she'd overheard."

"Very interesting. Now the other question—who told you this? Unless of course she was trying to blackmail one of you or your— Wait a minute. Where are the other two ladies?"

"Other two? Oh, you mean Stella and Nan," Caledonia said. "Well—I suppose Stella's in bed by now."

"Lieutenant," Angela put in, "Caledonia and I went up to ask questions after supper. Nan and Stella didn't come—they weren't happy about asking personal questions. But we—we still wanted to be helpful to you, you see?"

"And your curiosity was driving you, of course."

Angela shrugged. "Anyway, when we got back downstairs, we phoned Nan and discovered she's over at our little hospital across the street. It's her husband. You know how sick he is . . . getting weaker every day. He's had pneumonia before, but he pulled through. Tonight, he's bad off again. It's serious enough that they've called the doctor."

"He may not live, Lieutenant," Caledonia added.

"You're not going over there to be with her?" he asked.

"She really doesn't need a whole troop of us, Lieutenant. Stella was there for a while, and that should be enough. Things here work a bit differently from outside anyway. If this was anywhere but a retirement center, friends and family would all show up and stand by to run errands and take care of details. In here we're used to death and dying. Oh, we're sorry about it, but all the details are taken care of by the professionals. In the outside world, someone's death is the occasion for a gathering. All the visiting and the talking and the comforting . . . all the food and all the flowers . . . it's like you're holding a big open house or something. Here we usually wait for a signal from the widow or the widower as to how much help she or he wants. I think Nan will want us with her, in time. But when she does, she'll let us know."

"You think Dr. Church is dying this time, then?"

"Probably. He's so very weak . . . and getting weaker every day. It was just a matter of—well, weeks probably—after he had pneumonia in September."

"That's beside the point right now," Angela said impatiently. "About the murder—we really thought you ought to know Paulette's death wasn't an accident."

Martinez turned to her and smiled. "Well, thank you very much for your news—as far as it goes. You're also going to share with me the source of this information, aren't you?"

Angela tried playing the coquette; dimpling and looking sideways were almost automatic with her when she wanted to be let off the hook. "Now, Lieutenant, you wouldn't want us to betray a confidence, would you?"

"Yes. I would. Absolutely."

"If it were a matter of honor?"

"Even so, Ma'am. What kind of honor does a murderer have anyway, in your opinion?"

"Oh, these people—I mean, the source of our information didn't commit the murder. That's why we'd rather not say anything. You'd only want to know why they were being blackmailed, and it was the kind of thing the police shouldn't know. I mean, it would only make trouble for these—for our informant."

Martinez did not point out that things the police might find interesting almost inevitably meant trouble for somebody. He merely continued, "Yes, but how do you know these—your informant *didn't* push Mrs. Piper downstairs? Look at it logically." He stood and began to pace like a lecturer in a college class, gesturing with his little glass to make his points.

"Suppose you're right, and Mrs. Piper was killed by someone who resented and feared her blackmail. We know of only one suspect . . . only one person she was blackmailing. And that's your 'source'—the person whose secret Mrs. Piper heard discussed aloud by Sweetie."

Angela's eyes were puzzled. "That *sounds* logical," she said. "But it *feels* wrong."

"*Feels* wrong?"

"You don't know the people—the person—involved. We do. Caledonia and I agreed that if we told you who gave us the information, you'd figure out their secret—and if you did that, the very thing they paid blackmail to keep from happening would have happened. Do you follow?"

Martinez nodded. "Believe it or not, I do. It's a police matter you're keeping secret, right? Ladies, ladies. How many times am I going to have to lecture you? This is not only a dangerous business—now you're committing a crime."

"We are not," Angela said.

"You are. Don't terms like 'tampering with evidence' and 'accessory after the fact' mean anything to you?"

"We're only trying to protect our friends," Angela protested.

"They don't deserve to have more trouble," Caledonia said.

"And if trouble has to come, at least we don't want to be responsible for it."

"All right, ladies. You don't want to talk? Then just sit and listen to a little detective work in action. You've already told me pretty much what I need to know. From all the "we" and "they" I'm hearing, I'd take it the party you're shielding is not a single person, but a couple. That narrows the field considerably. Camden boasts only a few couples.

"Second point—you talked about 'going upstairs' after dinner . . . to talk to your couple, I suppose. And there are only four couples who live on the second floor.

"Third"—he ticked the points off on raised fingers—"I heard rumors about an explosion of emotion during a pre-dinner discussion tonight. Someone told me Len Littlebrook started yelling and carrying on and had to be taken upstairs by his wife. So my dazzling bit of deduction ends with the conclusion that the people you're trying to shield are Len and Marian Littlebrook. Tell me— am I right?"

Caledonia was looking deeply into her brandy glass, like a gypsy trying to see the future in a crystal made of amber liquid. Angela was staring at Martinez with the rapt and dismayed expression of a bird who looked up from its nap and finds itself eye to eye with a hungry cat.

"And tell me," Martinez said, a slight smile of satisfaction playing on his lips, "would it be Mr. Littlebrook's background as an ex-Nazi and a soldier in Germany in World War II that is the dark secret you're trying to hide for your friends' sake?"

Caledonia stared at the lieutenant with a wide-eyed expression. "How did you find *that* out?"

Angela was simply muttering, "Oh dear, oh dear, oh dear . . ."

"Well?" Caledonia challenged belligerently.

"What exactly do you think I do, between the time you see me having lunch and now, when I join you for a drink? What do you think I did this afternoon, for example?" They didn't answer and he went on, "I was doing my homework, that's what I was doing. To you, being a detective may mean breaking into locked apartments and looking through private papers and stealing purses . . ."

"I never . . ." Angela protested. "I told you how I got that purse. And what's more, I gave it right to you."

Martinez ignored her. "To me, being a detective is mostly asking questions of people who don't much want to answer them, and when that doesn't turn anything up, looking into books, into public records and into archives. The best detectives in the world are dull men who read everything, listen to everything and remember all they've seen and heard.

"And I am a detective, as well as a policeman. I have listened—and watched—and asked questions. With some very good help I've got information from public records and from private papers. And things have been putting themselves together for me here"—he tapped the side of his head—"ever since the day I first stepped inside Camden. Patterns have formed . . .

"Those books in Miss Gilfillan's shelves weren't just accidental acquisitions, for instance. She was a librarian. She could borrow most books she wanted casually. The ones she kept were special to her for some reason. And when the idea of blackmail first seemed a possibility, we looked at those books more carefully. Mrs. Benbow, what were some of the titles?"

"I don't really remember," Angela said meekly—apologetically.

"Well," Martinez said, "one of them was about the Nazis and the war crimes trials. She'd read it, so we read it. And in the margin, by the picture of a German officer, there was an indentation on the paper where she'd scribbled a note. She'd erased it, but we could still make out what it said. It said 'Len?'

"Well, of course the man in the picture couldn't have been Littlebrook—too old for one thing. But something about him—that bearing, that stiff-backed, on parade look . . . I noticed Littlebrook's military bearing the first time I saw him. I could certainly imagine Littlebrook in a similar pose . . .

"I'm not sure how your Miss Gilfillan found out the details about him. I did it the old-fashioned way—through research. At the time, we hadn't finished the background searches on you yet—"

"On us!" Caledonia sounded outraged.

"Of course. On every one of the residents. But I hurried up the process on him. It wasn't really hard to confirm his naturalization, once we figured out the name change—and from there to look back to his visa when he entered the country—and from there back to his marriage to an American. There was a paper trail in the public records anybody could have followed, if they'd gone to the trouble.

"But when we tried to reach back before that wedding— nothing. Now a lot of old German records were destroyed in the war. But it's amazing how many times you hear about missing records, and come to find out there's a good reason to be glad they're missing. Has either of you visited Germany since the war? To hear Germans talk today, you'd think the Nazi party had only about ten members. Nobody was in it themselves—none of their friends were in it—

"Now, I don't know exactly what your friend Littlebrook did for a living during the war, but it had to be something unpleasant and probably criminal, in the sense of war crimes. I'll find out eventually. But don't you two ladies think you are fooling me or hiding information from me. All you're doing is slowing me down a little. So why not tell me now and save us a day or two?"

"We didn't mean them to suffer any more," Caledonia said. "They've been through so much. And he's, well, whatever he was, he's not only been a good man, but a good citizen in all these years since the war. But now . . . now he's a dying man—in mind and in body, I think. And she . . . she loves him—"

"Mrs. Wingate," Martinez said. "Please. Information first, sales pitch later."

"Angela?" Caledonia asked. Angela shrugged and sighed. "Okay," Caledonia said. "I guess we might as well, then. He was an SS officer. He worked in an office, though; he wasn't out doing all those awful things . . ."

Martinez shook his head. "Mrs. Benbow, privates worked in the office, corporals worked in the office, sergeants worked in the office. I don't think officers did. At least, not unless they were the bosses. But never mind."

"She fell in love when he was a prisoner of the Americans and in the hospital. He had to have plastic surgery, so his face is all different. She got him a new name and new papers to go with the new face, and they married. He got into America as a Dutch citizen. But now he's an American."

"Mrs. Wingate, he applied for citizenship giving false information. He can be deported for that alone."

"Please," Caledonia said, "you're not going to deport him, are you? He's old and sick . . . but it would simply kill Marian, after all these years, whatever it might do to him."

Martinez shook his head. "My immediate concern is a murder. Who killed your Miss Gilfillan. And then who killed Mrs. Piper, if she *was* killed. I am not, at the moment, thinking about doing the immigration authorities' job. We can deal with all of that later. First, tell me why you're so sure Mr. Littlebrook didn't kill one or both of those women."

"He couldn't," Caledonia said. "He's not . . . well, he's gotten, you know, kind of removed. Marian really leads him around. It's a wonder he thought to go and get help when he found Paulette lying at the bottom of the stairs."

"How about his wife, though?" Martinez prompted. "She's very protective of him. She might have committed the murder to protect him."

"But she didn't even know Paulette was dead," Angela said. "She said they drank a toast when Len came and told her."

"No proof. No proof at all," Martinez said. "Well, at least I have someone to suspect, now—and a motive. There were a lot of suspects for Miss Gilfillan's death. And probably eventually we'll have a lot for Mrs. Piper's. It's comforting to have some place to start, anyhow."

"Suspects? You have a lot of suspects for Sweetie's death?" Angela's eyes were bright. "People here?"

Martinez had his solemn expression back in place. "Yes, here at Camden."

"Who? Oh, I promise I won't breathe a word . . ."

"Mrs. Benbow, you don't really expect me to tell you, do you?"

"Well, you did say we were going to share information . . ."

"Information. Not speculation. Will it help you if I tell you that you aren't a suspect?"

"Am I then?" Caledonia asked.

"No, Ma'am. And now . . . if you have nothing further to tell me, I certainly have nothing more I'm anxious to tell you. I'll be saying good evening . . . of course with special thanks for the information you did share." He put his glass down. "I think I'll check across the street to see how Mrs. Church's husband is faring. If there is news, may I phone you, provided it's not too late?"

"Why, thank you, Lieutenant," Caledonia said, hoisting herself up so she could make the token move toward the door that would pass for showing him out. "We'd appreciate it. I am a night person, even if Angela retires early. Please call this cottage if you have news. That's very thoughtful."

When he had gone, Angela and Caledonia just looked at each other for a moment. "Well, that's really something," Angela said. "He knew it all already. And we had to work so hard to find out."

"Yes, and I bet he even knows things that we don't know yet," Caledonia added. "Well," she said, sighing. "Time to take a hot bath and watch some television, I guess. I'll let you know if I hear about Nan."

"All right. I'll just go on to my own room, then." Angela yawned. "Too much excitement for one day, I'd say. Good night." She plodded home, and was asleep two minutes after she lay down in her bed.

CHAPTER 14

DOC CHURCH died in the night. One minute he was lying there, unconscious, unaware, his worn face relaxed and calm. He drew a rasping breath, and wheezed it out. Drew another, wheezed it out. And then—he did not draw the next. And he was gone.

Nan had sat beside him, holding his hand and talking softly to him, as the nurses came and went. Their doctor had been called early in the evening and came at once. He examined the old man briefly—stroked the pale forehead and smoothed back the wispy white hair; then he turned away to exchange a few quiet words with Nan, folded his stethoscope back into his bag and left as quietly as he had come.

Nan remained at her vigil long after Stella had reluctantly returned to her cottage. She whispered soothing words and reached out, now and then, gently to touch the blank, relaxed face, to pat the motionless shoulder. The old man slept. Perhaps he felt her fingers flutter against his cheek; perhaps he heard her words. There was no way to tell. And sometime after midnight he died.

Martinez had come in near the end, looking at Nan holding her husband's flaccid hand, listened to her crooning comfort. He said a few words and then turned on his heel and drove home for the night.

"You just left her there?" Swanson asked the next day as they swung off the freeway at the Camden turn.

"She wasn't going anywhere."

"But he died . . ."

". . . And she went home to bed. I wasn't going to ask her questions while she was telling him she loved him and how wonderful he was and . . . just in general, saying thanks for all those years—and goodbye."

Shorty shook his head. "Man, that's—that's so sad. I'm used to people dying. I don't like it, but I'm used to it. We see enough of it, on the force. But they don't just sort of fade out like that, do they?"

"It's different from our usual, all right," Martinez said. Suddenly he waved his hand to the right. "Park there. It's red, but *we* don't have to worry about tickets." Shorty parked their car in a loading zone near Camden's lobby doors, and they walked in to breakfast.

Caledonia Wingate and Angela Benbow were at their table sipping juice and coffee; neither Nan nor Stella had joined them yet. Martinez came to them. "I see from your expressions you've heard the news about Doc Church," he said.

Caledonia nodded. "They put a notice out on the desk so we could read it on our way through the lobby. Listen," she said in an accusing tone, "I thought you were going to call me last night."

"It happened some time after midnight. I'd finally gone home myself, and I assumed you would be asleep. They phoned me from the nursing facility to tell me—I told them to. But I didn't see any reason to disturb your sleep as well as mine."

Caledonia hadn't absorbed enough coffee yet to be either pleasant or grateful. "Mmmmff," was all she said.

"I do have an inquiry you can help me with this morning, ladies. I'm interested in how people spend their leisure time here. What do you do with your spare time?"

Angela was puzzled. "You mean like—bridge? And exercise class?" Caledonia groaned.

"Yes," Martinez said. "What hobbies do you have? What do people do who have all day? I've never had time on my hands, myself . . ."

Angela thought a moment. "Some of the residents play shuffle-board. I don't. A few like to garden, but I think the staff gardeners aren't too thrilled with our help. We visit a lot—talk, I mean."

"Gossip, you mean," Caledonia put in.

Angela ignored her. "Sometimes there are group projects like— well, like working for the bazaar, of course."

"How do you mean," Martinez asked. "Crafts?"

"Well, crafts—art work—needlework."

"My grandmother used to knit, I remember." Martinez smiled. "Everyone in the family got two afghans and a couple of sweaters. Does either of you knit, by chance?"

"Gawd, no," Caledonia muttered, dipping her head down to her coffee cup. "I despise artsy-craftsy activities. I'd rather be horse-whipped than *use* a tea-cozy, never mind make one."

"I do fancy needlework, and I crochet a little," Angela said quickly, as though trying to compensate for Caledonia's bluntness. "Mary Moffet does crewel work sometimes. And of course Stella knits. Oh, and Nan does, too. Well, wait now—maybe she doesn't any more. At least, I haven't seen her with knitting in her hand for quite a while." She was clearly not terribly interested in the subject, but trying to be helpful.

Martinez just kept smiling. "Speaking of Mrs. Church, do you expect her to join you this morning?" he asked them both.

"Probably not today—or the rest of the week," Angela said. "Residents usually stay by themselves a little while, after a death."

"Naturally, and perfectly understandable. Let's see, the Churches' cottage is the third in line, isn't it?" Martinez asked.

Angela nodded. "On your left as you go down toward the sea from the main building."

"Thank you, ladies." Martinez rejoined Shorty at the guest table, drank one cup of coffee and set off down the path.

"I wonder what he wants with Nan?" Caledonia muttered into her third cup of coffee.

"Paying his respects perhaps," Angela said. "You've almost finished nearly the whole pot of coffee. Are you feeling more human now?"

"Starting to."

"Well then, what's on the agenda for today?"

"Oh, well, I really hadn't thought. Martinez kind of took the wind out of my sails last night. He knows everything we know, I think."

"Now, Caledonia, you don't know that's true. We didn't discuss everything we'd found out."

"Well, he knew about Marian and Len."

"Some of it. Not all of it. I think we still know more about them than he does. And we've found out a few things before he has. There's some satisfaction in being first. Also we've found out things about other people as well—about Grogan—about Torgeson—"

"He probably knows all about them, too," Caledonia said. "We haven't done a damn thing to help solve this thing. We've broken glass and we've broken the law, we've crawled through windows, we've pried into desks and closets . . . and we got nothing that man probably doesn't have by simply asking questions. Asking questions and reading, he said."

"I was interested in what he said about her books. Sweetie's books. Did you catch that?"

"Yes. Or rather, no. I heard it"—Caledonia tipped the pot to drain a fourth, and obviously last, cup of coffee—"but I'm not sure what you're getting at about it." She shook the last drops from the pot.

"He said a librarian doesn't keep books around for no reason. She would just borrow from a library any books she only wanted to read once. If she kept a book, it had to be for a reason."

"Well?"

"Well, I think we should go back, today, and take another look through that library."

"Go *back*." Caledonia gave an incredulous look. "You've got to be joking, Angela."

"No, no, I'm very serious. Listen, there's got to be something important about those books—something I didn't see the first time."

Caledonia groaned. "How do you propose to get in this time? Kick a hole in the wall? They put a board over the window we broke. Besides, it's broad daylight. Somebody just might notice you crawling through that other window, even if we broke a pane and unlocked it for you."

Angela shook her head, a smug smile on her face. "You haven't looked today, that's all. I did, while I took my morning stroll through the garden. They seem to have taken the padlock off the door. I guess they have everything they want from the place, or something. We get in by just opening the door and walking in, I suppose."

"Not so fast. People ordinarily lock doors around here . . . to keep the absentminded ones from walking into someone else's room and taking anything that appeals to them. You and I were lucky that first time we went to Sweetie's, that's all. The place'll be locked."

"And the nurses hang the master key on the pegboard just inside their office, too, Mrs. Know-It-All."

"Gosh," Caledonia sighed. "God really did intend for you to be a thief, Angela. I know the nurses have a master key—so they can get in to give medication when we're ill. But I never even thought of it. And come to that, how come *you* didn't think of that key before, the first time we went down there?"

"Well, we decided so fast . . . and we weren't up here. We were down at your place—practically next door to Sweetie's cottage. So we just walked straight over. Besides, I'm just getting into the 'mind-set,' as some psychiatrist called it on the Phil Donahue Show a few weeks back. He said if you act like a successful businessman long enough, you start to think like a successful businessman. I guess if you act like a burglar, you start to think like a burglar, that's all."

When they finished a light breakfast (Angela had one slice of toast, Caledonia just a stack of pancakes), they walked out of the lobby and down to the nurses' office.

"Tell them you're sick," Angela suggested.

"No way," Caledonia said. "This was your idea—*you* tell them you're sick. And furthermore, those keys hang on a nail up behind the door. I know exactly where they are. I'm not sure you could even reach them. But I know I can. So I'll do the taking—you be the diversion."

"All right," Angela said. "I'm the invalid, then. Let's see. Mild indigestion, I guess . . . that's the safest. It won't hurt me if they give me an antacid tablet I don't really need." And she scowled horribly, hoping she was suggesting response to abdominal pain, and moaned softly as she began to limp, bending over to clutch at her waist.

"Indigestion is one thing . . ." Caledonia said, pinching Angela's arm. "A cow mourning for her lost calf is another. And lighten up on the Groucho Marx crouch, too. Just look faintly pained . . . that'll do it. Think solemn thoughts . . ." They turned into the nurses' office.

Mary Washington, one of the black nurses, was on duty. "Hello, ladies," she said cheerfully. "How can I help you?"

"I was in at breakfast," Angela said, in a strained voice, "and I got this awful pain—OUCH!" Caledonia had punched her on the shoulder. "I mean," she said, revising her vocal tones upward from agony to mild discomfort, "it was bad at first, but it got much better. I would really like you to check me out, though."

"Sure thing," Mary said. "You just sit down over here and roll up a sleeve so I can get your blood pressure." She slipped an inflatable cuff around Angela's arm and began to work the bulb-pump. "Let's see about this pressure now . . ."

Five minutes later, informed that it was probably just a little gas and that she was as healthy as a horse, Angela let Caledonia help her out of the office and down the hall, back toward the main lobby, "Did you get 'em?" Angela asked.

"You betcha," Caledonia said, opening her huge palm to display four keys on a ring. Together, grinning with self-satisfaction, they sailed down the path to the cottage containing Sweetie's apartment.

"I hated to fool Mary that way," Angela said. "She's the nicest nurse we've got."

"In a good cause, my dear—in a good cause," Caledonia said, smirking. "Wait—should we get Beanie to join us?"

"Stella? Oh, Caledonia, you know how it upset her last time we talked about breaking into Sweetie's place. She'd probably just slow us down arguing against the project. Anyway, look—we're right here."

They hesitated a moment on the little front porch. From the next-door apartment, a quavery baritone was singing a barely recognizable version of "Oh, Susannah!" Mr. Grogan was home—and making up for lost time with the bottle.

"*Oh, it rained so hard, the night I left, the weather* . . . DAMN! What about that weather? Oh, I remember—*the weather was so dry—hy* . . . *The sun so hot* . . .—come to think of it, I'm a bit dry myself.—You don't say, Mr. Grogan. Well, won't a bonny chap like yourself have another little drink? Just to break the drought, you see.—Mighty handsome of you sir, mighty handsome. Don't mind if I do.—Now let's see, where was I again?—*Oh the sun so hot, I froze myself . . . Susannah, don't you cry-hy!*"

Caledonia shook her head. "They should have kept him over at the hospital for another few days at least."

Angela frowned. "We shall have to take that man in hand, Caledonia. That can be our next project. Something to keep the four of us busy, when we've got this murder business disposed of. He's really out of control."

"Well, at any rate, we don't have to worry about his hearing us in Sweetie's. We could fire a cannon and he'd ignore it. Hold it . . . look at the roses or something—there's Mary Moffet coming up the walk . . ."

With an aplomb that would have been beyond her a week earlier, Angela reached out and held up a bright pink bud. "These Princess Elizabeths need more spray," she said loudly. "We really must tell the gardener . . . Oh, hello there, Mary" she said brightly.

Mrs. Moffet, twittering along with tiny steps, was momentarily stopped dead in her tracks by Angela's unusual friendliness. "Hello, Angela . . . Hello, Caledonia . . . Haven't got time to visit—Emma Grant is driving me to the dentist. No cavity—it's just cleaning time . . ."

Angela and Caledonia waved, wordlessly, grinning like a pair of mute baboons, and watched her disappear through the lobby door, then turned as one, back to the door, while Caledonia fumbled with the keys.

"Hurry up, hurry up," Angela said.

"I'm hurrying as fast as I can. I don't know which key is which—ah, here we are." The door swung open and the ladies shot through and shut the door behind them. Grogan's fourth rendition of the refrain from "Oh, Susannah" masked any sound they made.

"Oh, dear, they're packing her up." Angela was dismayed.

Cardboard grocery store cartons stood all around the room, half of them full.

"Well, maybe so, but they may not have taken the books away yet."

"Right . . . Look, there are half of them still on the shelf—there, behind the cartons. I guess the box would . . ." Angela pointed to the carton directly in front of the bookcase. "Yes, some of the books are already packed." Angela started to go down on her knees . . . and then, at a twinge in the one, gasped slightly and folded herself along a different line, to sit on the floor, instead of kneeling.

"Mmmm," Caledonia said, glancing at the titles. "Novels and old favorites. I don't see any reason to think these are clues to blackmail."

"How about this." Angela picked up the book on the Nuremberg trials. "This may be where Sweetie found the picture that started her in on Len."

"That one's been thoroughly looked over by now, I expect. We can afford to ignore it. I think it would be too much to suppose that Camden had more than one ex-Nazi among the residents."

"Maybe there's something here . . ." Angela pulled over a stack of phone books, college annuals, and mail order catalogues. "I'll start on this bunch. I didn't bother with them the first time I looked at the books. I don't think I even saw them, really."

Caledonia levered herself with some difficulty to the floor beside the box. "Well-well-well, this is odd."

"What's odd?"

"Angela, did you take a look at this phone book first time around?" Caledonia said, reaching to pull a heavy volume from the stack. It was the book with the needlepoint cover that said PHONE BOOK.

"No, I just told you. I was in a hurry, and I didn't think there'd be anything interesting in a phone book."

"Didn't it strike you as odd that she'd keep an L.A. book here? At least I suppose it's L.A.'s—this certainly isn't the thin Camden village directory." She had flipped the fancy cover open. "Oh-ho. So that's it. *Those Wonderful B Movies*—and listen to the subtitle—*Including the First Complete History of Porn Flicks.* How about that."

"Inside a phone book cover?" Angela said.

"Yes. Interesting, isn't it? She was hiding it—but not much. Like she wanted it around—handy but not on display." She started to turn the pages.

For a while, neither spoke. Then Caledonia laughed. "Here's a ghastly picture of Dick Powell with lipstick on—in *Page Miss Glory*—I bet you don't remember that one."

"I bet I do," Angela said. "Marion Davies, right?"

"Right. Terrible, wasn't it? But I thought it was pretty good, back then." Another minute passed and Caledonia chuckled again. "Oh, my . . . One of those pictures where Sherlock Holmes moved from Victorian England to the 1940s to fight the war . . . *Sherlock Holmes and the Secret Weapon*—that was a real stinker."

"Do you remember that picture with Lassie as a war dog, in the K-9 corps or something? What was that thing called . . ."

Caledonia flipped to the index, then forward again to a new page. "Here it is—*Courage of Lassie*—my sakes. Did you know Elizabeth Taylor was in that thing?" She sighed and flipped a few more pages. "Oh, this takes me back. Dick Foran and Rod Cameron and Jon Hall and Gail Patrick and Maria Montez and Gale Sondergaard and Dennis O'Keefe . . . They're most of them dead now. It doesn't really seem possible. I see them practically every day—or rather, every night. Well, let's keep going. Are you finding anything?"

"Not a thing. I thought I might recognize somebody in these college annuals. But if any of the residents are in these pictures, they've changed so much I don't know them." For a while, they read on in silence. Then—

"Oh, good grief!" Caledonia said.

"What is it?" Angela craned her neck, but to her surprise Caledonia jerked the book back, pressing its open pages against her ample bosom.

"Oh, no you don't," Caledonia said. "You just go on with your own book."

"What is it?"

"The section on pornography," Caledonia said, grinning. "I think you're too young to see this, Angela. Or maybe just too well brought up, since actually, neither of us is too young for anything, I'm afraid. The point is, I think you've probably never seen anything like this. This one picture . . ." She released the book slightly to peek again. "Oh, heavens, what a tangle. I didn't think people could get into positions like that."

"Well, I certainly wouldn't be shocked, if that's what you mean."

"Yes you would. Ever seen a real porn flick?" Caledonia asked.

"I don't think so. I really don't know."

"Then you haven't. Believe me, Angela, if you'd seen one—at least, one of the low-class, no-holds-barred kind—you'd remember you'd seen it. Now girl, go back to your own work. I don't want you having nightmares . . ." She brought the book down and turned a page. "My gosh!"

"Well, what is it? What are they doing in those pictures?"

"You know perfectly well what they're doing. The only difference between these actors and perfectly ordinary people is the inventiveness. There's this girl from the circus, upside down on a trapeze . . ."

"Caledonia!"

"Oh, I'm just teasing you, Angela. It's really pretty dull stuff—especially these still pictures. Pretty much just sleazy and cheap. In fact," she turned another page, shaking her head. Turned another . . . and another . . . "Each page is pretty much like the last. The only difference is each one has a different person in it. Believe me, it's just one sex scene after another, and all almost the same . . . Hey, wait a minute!"

"What now?" Angela said. "Another girl on a trapeze?"

"Huh-uh." Caledonia was staring at a picture with great intensity. She put her huge finger in one page to hold her place, while with the other hand she leafed ahead. "Let me see if there's another of . . . Yes, here. Same one in this one. Yes, I'm sure of it. Angela, my eyes aren't as good as they were. Look at these pictures and see if you recognize anybody."

She held the book out—"Keep my place there . . ."

Angela put a hand into the opening and looked at the picture that lay open under Caledonia's pointing finger. "I don't see . . ."

"Angela, the girl and the sailor—second couple from the left—they're dancing . . . I think."

"I don't know what you want me to see. It's just a girl and a sailor, that's all. They aren't even doing . . . you know—what the rest of them are doing." She waved her hand at the photo, in which eight couples in a night club setting were busy comporting themselves as no ladies and gentlemen would, in public. "These two are just dancing. Except . . ." She peered closer. "Oh, my! Oh, dear!—He does have his hand in a sort of strange place . . . But no, I don't see anything even faintly familiar about them."

"You don't recognize her?"

Angela squinted even closer. "No. But then from the back that way—Maybe this other . . ." She turned the pages to the place she held open . . . and squinted again.

This time she gazed at a man and woman posed in a satin-sheeted bed. The camera was placed at a low angle, so that the woman was obscured by the bed and by the body of the man. Above him, however, mirrors on the ceiling caught the action from another angle and the woman's face was clearly visible. A young woman with a soft face and blonde hair spread out on the pillow . . . her smile making deep dimples in her chin and up around the corners of her mouth . . . she looked about twelve years old.

"It's Nan!" Angela gasped. She read the legend under the picture. "It says 'Dotty White, also called "Snow" White for her look of childish innocence, strikes her most famous pose.' Caledonia, it can't be Nan! Are there other pictures of the same woman in here?" She began to turn the remaining pages, hunting . . . "Oh dear. Oh dear!"

She gestured to yet another picture and read aloud, *"Emily Dingle's Defiance—'Snow' White, in her role as a detective, investigates the scene of a crime, while the chief of police investigates her . . . the last known film of 'The Queen of Porn.' Production values were excellent in this film—the first of the slick, big-budget trend that marked post-war releases."*

Caledonia nodded. "She told us once she played a detective. And she said she retired in the 1940s."

"She hasn't changed," Angela whispered. "I mean, her face looks almost the same. I knew her right away."

"It's no wonder Sweetie recognized her."

"You don't know that, Caledonia," Angela said. "You don't know that."

"Yes, I do. The name 'Snow White' was on the blackmail list, wasn't it?"

"Yes, but—"

"Didn't Nan object as soon as she found out we wanted to look into Sweetie's private life? Didn't she run in the opposite direction, and we had to go in here alone the first time?"

"And she knew how the furniture used to be," Angela remembered suddenly. "When I came through the window, that second time, and fell onto the couch, she said 'The couch didn't used to be there,' or something like that. Sweetie never had guests in—she said her place was too small. So how did Nan know that?"

"Unless," Caledonia said, "she'd been in here and had seen for herself."

Angela sighed. "I guess we'll have to ask her about it . . ."

"Now?" Caledonia said. "Of all times . . . Maybe we ought to wait."

Angela shook her head. "I want her to know the book is here. But maybe the Lieutenant hasn't seen it yet."

"Even if he had time to look all the way through it, he might not have recognized her. The only way we knew it was Nan was the face. It would have to be someone who knew her well, I think, to recognize her. I mean, even if she doesn't have wrinkles like the rest of us do . . ."

"Layers of fat," Angela said. "Fat people don't wrinkle as much."

"Yes, well, unless Martinez looked through the book himself—"

"Or that assistant Swanson did—"

"Yes, or that assistant. It's possible nobody even made the connection. Martinez said he had other people doing his research, didn't he?"

"Well, okay, but I think Nan at least ought to know and be ready, if he asks her any questions."

Caledonia stood up with difficulty. "Damn . . . it's a long way down to and up from that floor. Listen, girl, I'm taking this book."

"Isn't that against the law? I mean, it's evidence."

"We've broken laws left and right, as it is, and I don't want to leave it here. In case the police *didn't* see."

"Oh. Right. Let's get out of here. Oh, and Caledonia—please—let's not tell Stella. If breaking into Sweetie's shocked her, how would she feel about . . . about Nan and those movies?"

Caledonia nodded her concurrence, and for once she had not a single word to add.

By mutual agreement, Caledonia took the book home with her to her apartment. The two met again over lunch, but did not mention their discovery. Perhaps they would not have discussed it anyway, but Stella's presence inhibited them so much that conversation was confined almost entirely to "Pass the salt," and "Care for another roll?" None of the three seemed to have much appetite.

Stella did not, of course, volunteer conversation easily. But as they folded their napkins to leave the table, she managed to fill them in on Nan's calm acceptance of her husband's death during the night. "I think she was so ready for it, she had thought it out in advance. What she'd say . . . what she'd do . . ." The other two nodded.

"Well, it's been expected a long time," Caledonia said. Angela only nodded agreement. Mercifully, Stella was not inclined to question what was for Angela unusual silence. "What I'd have said if she'd asked me what the trouble was, I don't know," she said to Caledonia as they watched Stella heading up the stairs toward her own room.

"Beanie's not usually curious about what other people feel," Caledonia said. "That's one of the nice things about her. She can be a restful companion, if you don't feel communicative. Lucky for us, right?"

Back in her own room, Angela curled up for a nap, feeling very tired. But she couldn't sleep. An image of Nan as she was now, white-haired and grandmotherly, kept dancing through her mind, coupled with the image of a young sailor . . .

After about an hour, much to her own surprise, she donned slacks and tennis shoes and went for a walk on the beach. But the sun was scalding and the sand leaked into her shoes, and she gave up the effort, feeling hot and prickly, her throat aching as though she were going to cry.

By supper time, Angela had still not worked up an appetite, and Caledonia picked at her food; again, neither of them had much to say. Stella looked curious, but as they expected, she was far too well bred to ask curious questions unless they volunteered information, and they didn't volunteer.

"Have a little drink after dinner?" Caledonia invited, when Stella had left the table, headed for her own rooms and an evening topped off by *Night Court* followed by *L.A. Law.*

"No, I don't think so," Angela said flatly. "Thank you, though. Goodnight." And she wandered off to her own room, where she watched re-runs of *Wheel of Fortune* and *Family Feud* until it was time for bed. Unlike Caledonia, Angela was distinctly not a night person.

Of course she couldn't sleep. The harder she tried, the less sleepy she felt.

You heard about insomnia from one resident or another almost every day in dining room conversation, or in the gossip sessions before lunch and supper: "I had a dreadful night—never closed my eyes a wink," or "Did you see the late late show last night on TV? I wasn't sleepy anyway so I watched it—it was Charles Laughton in *Ruggles of Red Gap*—I had forgotten Mary Boland was in that, and Leila Hyams—"

As a rule, Angela was unsympathetic. Most nights she slept like a log and thought, rather vocally, that if you didn't sleep well yourself, you just weren't trying.

On those few nights when she couldn't sleep, Angela usually read a book or played the TV—very softly, of course. The chances were her neighbors were too deaf to hear even the commercials, played at full volume. But if one hoped for some consideration in return, one tried to be considerate, or so she said if the subject came up. Tonight she tried to turn to Johnny Carson, but was disappointed to find it was a rebroadcast of a show that had aired a year before. She always hated listening to the dated jokes.

Picking up the remote control, she moved ahead through the progression of channels and found an old western, but it was nearly done—half-way through the final battle with the Indians; the station jumped—and she had the roller derby; another jump—to two stations showing professional wrestling; then it was a talk show in Spanish—which Angela not only did not speak, but which reminded her too strongly of Lieutenant Martinez. She smiled thinking of his even white teeth, his thin aristocratic nose . . . No harm, after all, in thinking about a handsome man—but thoughts of Martinez reminded her of the murder and the blackmail and . . . Nan.

The memory tugged at the edge of her consciousness like a persistent ache. She shuddered . . . and closed her mind's eye by determinedly concentrating on the television. She flipped the channels again, and settled for an Abbot and Costello comedy that had replaced the western. But "Pocomoco . . . slowly I turned . . . " was not enough to nudge her into forgetfulness.

She thumbed the OFF button on the remote control, and the TV eye contracted inward and closed on itself. With a sigh, she selected a light coat from her closet and drew it on over her robe and gown.

She hesitated as she eased her outer door open and peered down the hall toward the lobby. She listened a moment, straining her ears. There seemed to be no one else out there—but with bad hearing, one couldn't be sure. If anyone sees me, she thought, they'll think I'm sneaking, edging along this way, peeking through the cracks. She rebuked herself and yanked the door wide open, reflexively feeling for her key clip, fastened on the edge of her robe pocket, as she did so.

Down the steps, and into the dark chasm of the lobby she went, shuffling softly across the marble floor, preparing a silly excuse to offer the night clerk for her midnight wandering. But nobody seemed to be on duty at the desk. Whoever had tonight's desk-shift was answering a call—from one of the residents perhaps. Or a call of nature. Either way, there was nobody to take over on the desk if the night clerk stepped out. And so there was no one in the lobby. Angela slid gratefully past the rectangle of light and out into the garden. She hesitated on the patio till her eyes grew accustomed to the dark, then eased forward down the path. Six paces to the two little steps . . . yes, there they were . . .

She padded on down the path—hesitating at Caledonia's cottage, but thinking better of stopping. The lights were out. How can she sleep tonight? Angela wondered. And she moved on . . . stopping a second time in front of Nan's.

Nan's lights were on. Angela sat down on one of the benches beside the walk and stared at the lights and at the cottage a long time. Finally, with infinite reluctance, she went up onto the porch and knocked softly at the door.

CHAPTER 15

NAN ANSWERED the knock within moments . . . almost as though she'd expected someone to come calling. "Oh, Angela. Come in. Come in."

"I didn't want to disturb you," Angela said. "We heard about Doc and we're so sorry."

"Of course. I know you are—and thanks. But it's been coming for a long time, and we've known it would be sometime soon. Can I get you something, Angela?"

Angela muttered something about not wanting to be trouble . . .

"I was just getting myself some warm milk," Nan said, sighing. "It's no bother."

Angela's stomach quivered. "Oh, no warm milk, thanks," she said quickly. "Maybe a soft drink? Something without caffeine if you have it?"

Nan smiled briefly. "I forgot you hate to drink milk. Actually, I don't know why *I* was going to have milk. I used to heat some up for Doc, once in a while. To help him sleep. And I was thinking of him, just now, so . . . You know, I don't really like it much myself. I'll join you in the soft drink."

She slid smoothly into the kitchen, her feet moving in tiny, even steps, so that she seemed to glide on rollers. Angela listened to caps hiss-pop off the bottles . . . ice cubes clunk into glasses . . .

"Here you are," Nan said, returning with a glass of fizzy brown soda. "New brand . . . thought I'd try it. Tell me what you think . . ."

Angela sipped. "It's fine."

"You really think so?"

"Oh, yes. Certainly. Fine."

They sat quietly and sipped without saying anything. Finally Nan spoke, "I appreciate your coming over, Angela. I don't especially want to be by myself just now. In fact, I think I'll come in to meals—maybe starting tomorrow."

"Of course. It's the best thing, I think."

"Well, this wasn't a shock to me, you know. More like—relief. Doc left me months ago. There was just a shell lying in that bed. He wouldn't want to live like that, if he could know . . . He'd have been glad to get it over with."

"But all the same . . ."

"Yes, I know. All the same . . ."

There was another long pause, and finally Angela could stand it no more. "Nan, I know this isn't the time . . . But I've got to tell you. We found the book. Caledonia and I."

"The book? What book?"

"A book about old movies. I—We found you in the book, Nan."

"Oh. I see. At Sweetie's, right?"

"Yes." Angela gulped. "Snow White, right?"

Nan nodded calmly. "That's right. Dotty 'Snow' White." She sighed. "Sweetie said she was going to tell Doc about the films I did, you see. I couldn't stand for that to happen. So I paid up, like everybody else did. Except of course I didn't know then that there was anybody else paying her. But it didn't matter whether there was or wasn't anyone else. I had to keep her from telling Doc."

"He never knew about those movies? How on earth—"

"Oh, I told him I was in films when I first met him. I tried to impress him—told him I played lead parts. But since he never saw me in a movie—and I wouldn't discuss the movies I made—he assumed I was telling fibs . . . That I was maybe a bit player or an extra, not a featured player or a star. I—I let him think that.

"Then one time, right after Doc and I were engaged, he asked if he could come on the set and see me work. I knew I'd pushed my luck too far. I told him I was walking out on the picture and quitting the studio. He wanted to know why. I told him the first thing that came into my head. I said it was because they wanted me to do a nude scene. He said 'Great. I'd hate for anyone else to look at you the way I do.' And I knew right then he couldn't have stood to hear the truth . . . So I promised myself he'd never know. I guess I thought I could keep it secret forever.

"I let myself get fat on purpose, you know . . . Best disguise in the world. It changes your face—"

"It didn't change yours much," Angela said. "I knew you right away. Oh, I'm sorry . . . I—"

Nan shook her head. "It's okay, Angela. But I figured, even if it didn't change me—women are better than men at recognizing other women, because they look at the faces, and most men don't. Anyway, not in the kind of movie I was doing. But women don't usually see porn flicks. And even if men did remember my face from a film—they don't ogle real life fat ladies, anyhow. I told myself nobody would ever recognize me.

"I didn't even worry much when two fellows did that book and found some old still shots—or maybe made prints from clips from the film. I don't know which. I saw a copy when it first came out, seven years ago, but I just didn't worry about it. And then, worse luck, Sweetie got hold of it."

"Oh, Nan . . . How awful for you."

"She said she got suspicious because I never talked about my film career—wouldn't tell my stage name. She started hunting through pictorial histories of the movies, looking for me. Like a hunter stalking a deer. It was my bad luck this particular book came out just then. The review in the paper raved about how complete it was—so she found it and read it from cover to cover and recognized me. She even bought a copy of her own."

"Why did she want to have it for herself? No, don't tell me. I know. She'd bring it out whenever you were at her place, wouldn't she? And show it to you and comment on the pictures of you . . ."

"Exactly. But how did you know?"

"Because that's the kind of thing she did to Marian and Len, too. Oh, I forgot—you don't know about that yet. Well, we'll tell you all about it later. Right now, let's talk about you. Oh, Nan . . ."

Nan smiled wanly. "I'm surprised you're still speaking to me. Maybe you won't, out in public."

Angela swallowed hard. "Maybe I wouldn't have, a while ago. But Nan, you're my friend. Whatever you've done."

"That's nice to hear. I'm sorry to have to put it to the test this way . . ."

"Are you sure Doc never knew?"

"Of course I'm sure. He couldn't have kept that secret. He wouldn't have."

"But it wouldn't have hurt anything if she did tell him, now. I mean, he's—he was—like being asleep, I thought. For weeks."

Nan shook her head again. "Nobody knows how much they hear and understand. Just because they can't answer doesn't mean they don't hear . . . and know what's going on, too. I just couldn't take that chance."

"So you paid her blackmail."

"Oh, I paid. And paid, and paid, and paid . . . Our savings are almost gone, between her asking for her 'donations' and Doc being in the health facility. We didn't have all that much to start with, you see. Porn stars don't get Social Security, you know, and dentists are self-employed—no pensions or annuities or health insurance for him."

Angela shook her head, clearly distressed but not knowing what to say.

"It's all right, Angela. Don't get all weepy on me. I'm glad you still think of me as a friend, that's all. Does Caledonia know?"

"Yes. We found the book together. We—we didn't tell anybody, Nan. Not even Stella . . ." Nan nodded. She seemed to understand the unspoken thought behind the statement. "And Nan . . . we stole the book so the police wouldn't find it."

Nan smiled again. "Too late, Angela. Martinez came to see me last night at the hospital. He didn't say anything then except 'Good evening.' I wondered what he wanted. Mr. Tactful. He said he didn't want to intrude while Doc was—anyway, he came by the cottage this morning. Chatted about this and that—the weather . . . the bazaar . . . my hobbies. Finally, he told me."

"He was curious about all of us and tried to find out background information, but when he tried to find out about me, he hit a blank wall at first. So he had someone look up old-time theatrical agents till he found one who did know about me— about the kind of films I did, my stage name, my nickname. Then he looked up that book in a library . . . He read the old gossip columns . . . They used to run items about me once in a while. Why, he even knows the name of almost every film I did— showed me a list. That's something even I don't remember."

"Nan, I'm so sorry . . . Not just about Doc. About Sweetie—and all the trouble you've had. And I'm sorry you had to . . . to do work like that. Those movies."

"Don't be. I was never ashamed of it in the old days . . . not for a minute. You and I really come from opposite sides of the tracks, Angela. Doing sex films for a big salary was success to me, compared to what I came out of—shantytown and a drunken father. It was only later—when Doc and I were married, and then when we got here—that it became so important to bury my past. I . . . Well, I wanted to be like all of you. Really respectable.

"I never meant to fool you about who I was or what I was, you know. I wasn't trying to fool Doc. But he wouldn't have understood—and I thought none of you would, either. You're all such innocents." She sighed.

"I looked like an innocent myself, in the films . . . That was part of why they paid me so much. And now—well, nobody thinks of a little, fat, white-haired lady with dimples on her chin as being wicked. So at least the image was easy to keep up. And being with all of you—I kind of forgot about my own past. You and the others here are so . . . so sheltered. None of you knows a blessed thing about real life. I've seen things you haven't even thought of." She sat back in her chair and closed her eyes.

"Oh, Angela," she said faintly, sighing again. "I'm so terribly tired. I've worked so hard—it's been such a struggle. It was hard enough just to hide my past from Doc, in the early days. Then, just when I really started to relax—to think it was all over with— he got sick. That's all I thought about for a long time. Then Sweetie—and Pauline—started that blackmail—well, there were times, I tell you, I just wanted to give up. But I couldn't let down for an instant. I had to find a way to keep fighting. For Doc. But now—well, I can't really think of any reason to go on scrapping and clawing. Doc can't be hurt any more. And for myself—well, if you don't want me to stay here at Camden, I'd understand."

On impulse, Angela reached out and put an arm around Nan's plump shoulders. She had never done that before . . . never been one to hug or to waste kisses on other women. She was faintly embarrassed, and drew her arm away almost at once. "I—I'm sorry, Nan. About everything, you know? I keep saying that, don't I? But I don't know what else to say. I better go now. Let you rest."

"Wait—Angela, I need to say 'I'm sorry' too. About your door. About scaring you that way."

"My door?"

"Yes. That was me trying to get in that night. I was frantic to get at Sweetie's purse—to see if there was anything at all that would give me away . . . maybe a list—like the one you found. Funny, I never even thought of looking in that Kleenex box when I was going through her apartment."

"You?"

"Yes, that was me too. I went over as soon as I had the chance—after she died. She was so sure of herself, she hadn't even locked her door. And nobody had thought to lock it for her—afterward. I just walked right in."

"We found it open ourselves the day we searched."

"A lot of good it did me. I didn't find a thing. I felt bad about being so careless, throwing things around—but I was in a panic. I was so afraid someone would find me. All I could think about was—had she left notes about me? Something to give me away?"

"Why didn't you take the book away?"

"Well, I'm not sure it ever crossed my mind to take it. I was just concentrating on finding a piece of paper. Besides—out of sight, out of mind—she kept it tucked inside one of those fancy phone book covers, you know. I didn't see it, so I didn't think of it. Maybe because I was trying to hurry so much. I don't know. Later, when you took that purse of hers—I guess I went a little crazy. I had to know if there was something in it. I tried to pick your lock with an embroidery scissors . . . and a crochet hook . . .

"I couldn't, of course. I don't know what on earth ever made me think I could. I didn't realize it would wake you and frighten you. Your hearing is better than I thought." Nan grinned—and then caught her breath and yawned deeply. "I *am* tired."

"You'll feel more like yourself in a day or two," Angela said. "And about breakfast . . . don't come if you don't feel up to it. Wait till lunchtime, at least."

"Thanks, Angela. I might wait, at that." Nan sighed again. "Look, I won't see you out. I'll just sit here a while . . ."

Angela walked back up to the main building as quickly as she could without running. The shadows seemed darker than ever, the whispers of leaves against the building more ominous. She was glad to reach the warmth and comfort of her own little suite again and draw the door shut after her.

The next morning at breakfast, Nan and Stella were both among the missing, but then so was Caledonia. Angela ate a hasty breakfast alone, then phoned Caledonia (at the earliest hour a Wingate would think of as civilized) to tell her about the evening's excursion . . . and about Nan's confidences, which Angela poured out almost word for word. "I didn't really expect her to come in for breakfast, of course," Angela told Caledonia. "She's not a late sleeper, like you are, but she's got a lot of mourning to do before she faces the world, no matter how bravely she talks."

Caledonia agreed. "I don't doubt she's feeling beat, too. Who could blame her if she slept late for the next week. All she's been through—and then having to pay blackmail. I wish I'd known. I'd have made Sweetie behave herself . . . Boy oh boy, I'd have . . . I'd have done . . . I don't know . . . but I'd have done *something*."

Later at lunch, to which she did manage to appear, Caledonia was calmer. "I hate Nan's having had to go through that alone," she told Angela over a chicken mushroom crepe. "I wish she'd told us. It's easier, sometimes, if someone else knows. You don't feel so—I don't know—desperate."

"What about that book of movies?" Angela asked. "There's no point in hiding it, if Martinez already knows. Do you think we should take it back?"

"I returned it," Caledonia assured her. "I'd forgotten to take the master keys back. I just slid the book into that packing box down at Sweetie's, and then I hustled back to the nurses' office, and walked in to see them all upside down, hunting. There was such a flap going on, with everybody searching in drawers, in wastebaskets. So I just walked to a far corner, sat down, and pretended to pick the keys up from an in-basket that was filled with file folders. 'If you're looking for a set of keys,' I said, 'here's one—under these papers.' They were so pleased to find them—and so busy yelling at each other for not searching thoroughly—nobody even asked me what I wanted. I just got up and walked out again."

Angela laughed with delight. But her laugh was cut short, for as she looked up, Stella was entering the room. It was unlike her to be late, but then nothing was going quite as planned lately, Angela thought to herself. "Now not a word about Nan," she whispered quickly to Caledonia. "Oh, hello Stella," she said aloud. "You'll love the little crepes today."

Stella nodded in silent acknowledgement and waded into her appetizer—a delightful apricot-avocado mousse, which she ate with what for her might even pass for gusto. Conversation lapsed as forks were plied and mouths were used primarily for chewing.

None of the ladies noticed Martinez as he approached, not till he was next to the table, bowing politely. "Good afternoon, ladies. Have you heard from Mrs. Church today?"

"Oh yes, yes . . . She seems . . . She says she'll start coming up to meals at once," Angela said.

"We're encouraging her to," Caledonia added. "We do with all the new widows. It's probably good for them to get back to normal activities as soon as possible. But some can—some can't. I'm betting she can. She's taken a lot, and I think she can manage this."

"I'm glad to hear it. I think—Mrs. Benbow, what is that pinned to your belt?"

Angela moved her hand downward and touched her keys on their little jeweled "clothespin."

"Those are my room keys, Lieutenant. It's a handy way to hold onto them if you don't have pockets . . . And even if you do, it saves making the pockets bulge. I carry the clip all the time."

"May I see it, please?"

"Yes, certainly . . ." Amused at the lieutenant's interest, Angela undid the little clip and passed it over to him. "Caledonia gave us each one—let's see, it must have been four or five years ago—at Christmas. I didn't want to wear mine at first . . ."

Caledonia raised her eyebrows. "Why, Angela. You said you loved it."

Angela laughed deprecatingly. "I thought people would see it and think I was getting forgetful . . . likely to leave my keys lying by my plate at lunch or . . . Well, when the other girls all started to wear theirs all the time, I realized it wasn't conspicuous—and it is handy, that's certain."

"Other girls?" Martinez asked. "Who else has them?"

"Oh, Nan and Stella . . ." Stella smiled and nodded. "And of course Caledonia. And Marian and Tootsie and Sweetie . . . Lieutenant, we used to like Sweetie. I mean, Mrs. Wingate did. I never did."

"Yes, we found a clip like this attached to Miss Gilfillan's key. It was lying on a table in her living room." Martinez returned to his point—pointing to her gold clip. "Does everybody around this place have one of these?"

"Oh, I don't think so," Caledonia said. "I saw them in one of those catalogues and sent away for them. The older we get, the more catalogue shopping we do, Lieutenant . . . we let our fingers do the walking."

"Well, then anyone here could have bought one."

"No, not necessarily. A lot of the other girls don't have the money I do. I shop in some pretty high-priced catalogues . . . Gumps, and Nieman-Marcus, and Willoughby and Taylor. These little clips are imitated by other places, but not with real stones, like these."

"Real stones?" Angela said. "Caledonia! I didn't know this was a *real* amethyst."

"Well, of course it is. All the stones are genuine. I wanted to give you girls something nice."

"Mrs. Wingate, do you remember who you gave this one to?"

Martinez asked as he reached into his pocket and pulled out another clip. It was an exact duplicate of Angela's except that it was set with a milky-looking, blue gray stone with brownish markings. The little clasp was twisted and there was no key attached.

"I suppose that's a real moss agate, then?" Angela asked.

"A real moss agate," Caledonia affirmed. "Let's see . . . It's so long ago, I can hardly remember. It seems to me that Sweetie had a garnet. I think Marian had a moonstone. Of course I know that mine is a carnelian. That must be—I think that might be Nan's. Where did you find it?"

"Ladies, perhaps we'd better talk somewhere else. If you're through with lunch, would you join me in the second-floor sewing room?"

Napkins were folded hastily and the three left quickly, almost on Martinez' heels, pretending they didn't notice that every pair of eyes in the dining room was fastened on them before they'd got halfway to the door . . .

Martinez' face was grave a few minutes later as he held chairs for them. "Ladies, I'll want you to talk to your friend, Mrs. Church, on my behalf." He held up the damaged key clip. "We found this little clip on a top step where Mrs. Piper fell. She clutched at everything she could, as she fell down those stairs. And we think she got hold of this . . . And that it belonged to some person who met her there by the stairs. The key and the ring that holds it on the clip had been wrenched off. Of course before today, I didn't realize anyone could tell me who it belonged to."

Angela's eyes were round and Caledonia reached a hand toward him, apprehensively, in appeal. "Now, Lieutenant, I said I wasn't really sure it was Nan's. It might be—I just don't remember."

"There are other things, too," Martinez said. "Mrs. Church knits. You told me so yesterday. Not very many woman here do, though that surprises me. I think I had a stereotype about all old women sitting and knitting, begging your pardon, Mrs. Austin," he added as he noticed that Stella had pursed her lips in apparent annoyance. "Sorry about that. I only meant—"

"What difference does it make if Nan does knit?" Angela asked, defensively.

"Your Sweetie Gilfillan was stabbed several times—as though someone were in a rage—with something long and thin. And one suggestion was a knitting needle. We found a pair of steel knitting needles in the trash over behind your health facility building— right across the street. One of the needles had blood on it that matched the deceased's. I asked Mrs. Church about her knitting yesterday, and she said she'd quit knitting years ago. But you said, 'She knits,' in the present tense. So I assumed she still did—or had until recently."

"Oh, God!" Caledonia said. "You're telling us that Nan Church killed Sweetie and Paulette both, aren't you?"

"That's my belief, yes."

"That isn't possible," Angela declared. "Nan's . . . Well, you don't know her, Lieutenant. She's tough-minded and capable— but she's so kind. Now *I* might kill someone—ask anyone around here."

"Angela," Caledonia objected, "you're being hard on yourself."

"Oh, I know what they say about me behind my back." She tossed her head. "It really doesn't bother me. But the point is, nobody would believe that of Nan. They like her because she's so jolly—so good-natured—so nice. I don't think there's anybody here who dislikes her."

"Mrs. Benbow," Martinez said patiently, "you don't have to be an unpopular person or have a hard heart to murder someone. All you have to have is something so important to you that you'd do anything, hurt anybody, sacrifice anything to defend it. Now think. Did Mrs. Church have that streak of protectiveness in her?"

Angela bit her lip and didn't answer.

"Mrs. Wingate," he turned to Caledonia, sitting unhappy and silent. "Once you told me old people would kill to protect the quality of life in those few years they had left, and think the risk a small price to pay. Think about Mrs. Church and her life. Would she have killed to protect herself?" Caledonia turned her head away. "How about to protect her husband?"

"It's not fair," Angela interrupted. "She's fought so hard to keep him going and to keep him happy ... And now he's dead and she could be free and on her own. Maybe be happy again some time—and now it's all going to be spoiled. Sweetie deserved to die ... so did Paulette ... and Nan deserves the chance to be happy."

"Wait," Stella interrupted, with unaccustomed vigor. "Are you saying that Nan was being blackmailed, too? *Nan!*"

"Oh dear, I forgot—you don't know anything about all this, do you, Stella? I'm sorry. I'll explain it all later," Angela said in a rush. "But Lieutenant, please—this is important. Can't you leave Nan alone now?"

Martinez shook his head. "That's very loyal of you, Ma'am. But you're talking nonsense and you know it. There are other ways to settle matters besides resorting to murder. Why didn't Mrs. Church come to us? We could have taken care of things discreetly. But she took care of matters herself—and by killing two people. She may be as nice as you say she is ... as nice as she seems ... but killing a fellow human being is a self-centered, shortsighted, vicious solution to a problem." The three women sat silent and stared at him. "Unless, of course, it's some sort of accident. If someone killed in sudden, uncontrollable rage over some good reason that would be murder, but in the second or third degree. What they call mitigating circumstances. But still murder. Still a crime." Caledonia looked at the floor. Angela into the handkerchief with which she was drying tears. Stella bit her lips and twisted her hands tightly together till the knuckles were bloodless and white.

"I've asked you here," he went on, "for a very unorthodox purpose. I want you to go to Mrs. Church and tell her that I know she killed those two women. I want you to tell her I'll be down to discuss it with her shortly . . . Let's say in a couple hours. I'm hoping you'll convince her to do the right thing."

Angela was puzzled. "If you disapprove so strongly of what she did, why—"

"Disapprove?" Martinez said. "That's putting it mildly."

Caledonia nodded her head. "You're a thoroughgoing romantic, aren't you, Lieutenant? That's it, isn't it? And—you like her too, don't you?"

Martinez looked solemnly at Caledonia. "Think what you like. But please talk to her."

Caledonia surged to her feet, her sunset-colored caftan fluttering around her. "Come on, girls." She pulled at Angela's hand and beckoned to Stella. "Let's go do what the man asks us to."

"But—But—" Angela was protesting, even as Caledonia dragged her off through the door toward the elevator.

"Don't you get it?" Caledonia asked her as the old machine creaked and swayed and jolted and groaned its way to the lobby. "It's like all those old movies. He's giving her an out."

"An out?"

"Don't be an idiot, Angela. Sorry—I said I wasn't going to put you down any more, was I? No, listen—think about it. He's giving her a chance to run away. Of course"—she stopped a moment—"I'm sure she's got sleeping pills in her medicine chest . . ." She shook her head. "No, he couldn't be thinking that. Well, whatever he's thinking, she wouldn't have to go on trial. She wouldn't have to tell everything . . . about the murders, about those wretched films . . ."

"Films?" Stella asked.

"Oh, Stella—later, *please*," Angela said. The elevator stopped with a little jounce and the door slid open. Three other residents jostled in for the upward trip, and Angela resumed her silence till she and her companions had made their way across the lobby and out the garden door.

When they were safely outside, out of earshot, Stella stopped in her tracks. "Now let me understand this. The lieutenant believes that Nan killed both Sweetie and Paulette. And yet you believe he wants her to get away?"

"Well," Caledonia explained, "I think he wants to give her a choice. That's all. I think he hates the thought of arresting her. I think for all his sermonizing, our lieutenant secretly sympathizes with disposing of Sweetie."

"Caledonia," Angela said, "I don't think I can stand this. I really don't. Why on earth did we get mixed up in all this to begin with? It was fun at first . . . I never liked Sweetie much, and I didn't really care who killed her, as long as it wasn't something that was going to hurt me. And now—it does hurt me."

"Yes, it hurts."

"But you—Caledonia, how on earth can we tell her we know?"

"Nothing about this is easy. But—listen—How much money have you got?"

"Here? This minute? None."

"No, I mean in your apartment. In cash."

"I think . . . about $100 . . . no, $150."

"You can get it later. I've got nearly $500. I just cashed a check. How about you, Stella?"

"Well, perhaps two or three hundred—but I don't think—I mean, we'd be aiding and abetting a criminal."

"Stella, this is *Nan* we're talking about," Caledonia said. "The point is, we have to help. We're going to warn her. And we're going to help her pack her bag, give her our cash, and get her out of here . . . right now. And I don't want to hear any arguments. She'll be on her way by the time Martinez comes to check on her."

"Oh, dear," Angela said. "He'll be *so* upset."

"Angela, dear, read my lips. I'm going to tell you again. I think our young lieutenant just wants her gone. He doesn't want her dragged through this. If you ask me, he's on our side, yours and mine—and Nan's. Come on."

"I'm not at all sure we should—" Stella began. Caledonia glared mightily, and Stella subsided with a weak, "But on the other hand, I suppose . . ."

They labored down the path, up onto the porch of Nan's cottage, and Caledonia knocked on the door . . . and they waited.

"Come on . . . come on . . ." Caledonia muttered.

"Hurry . . ." Angela whispered. "Hurry!"

Caledonia knocked again. And again they waited. "Do you hear anything inside?" Caledonia asked. "Your ears are a little better than mine."

"Not a sound," Angela said. "Nan . . ." She called aloud, putting her mouth up next to the crack in the door. "Nan."

"Try the window. We've got to hurry."

Angela went to the big picture window. Venetian blinds were drawn and she couldn't see in, but she rapped sharply on the glass. "Nan, let us in . . ."

Caledonia tried the knob. The door stayed shut.

"All right . . . let's go up to the office," she suggested.

At the desk, she grabbed Clara's hand, as the clerk swung past carrying a jumbled pile of mail. "Clara," Caledonia said, "has Mrs. Church picked up her mail today?"

"Nothing much for her," Clara said. "Two catalogues—a Joan Cook and one from Miles Kimball. They've got such good—"

"Clara, she hasn't been to meals and we're worried."

"Oh, my. Just a minute." Clara shifted gears without hesitation, following the automatic procedure by which Camden checked on its residents whenever they had not been to a meal or were thought to be ill. First, she went to the switchboard and rang the apartment. After a short pause, when there was no answer, she laid down the headset, and headed for the inner office.

"I'm going to find Mr. Torgeson, ladies," she said over her

shoulder, her cheerful expression firmly in place, as it always was when she sensed potential problems.

In only a moment, Torgeson swung out of the side door, looked around the corner at the desk, and beckoned the three women to follow him. "Come with me, ladies, if you will. This may need a woman's touch. The poor lady, in her time of loss . . ."

At Nan's door he fiddled with a large set of keys, selecting a master and inserting it, and snapped the lock open. The living room was untenanted.

"Nan," Caledonia called.

"Nan," Angela echoed.

"Nan," Stella murmured.

"Mrs. Church," Torgeson filled in the bass part.

In procession, the four moved through the little hall, Caledonia in the lead, Torgeson next, Angela and Stella side by side, bringing up the rear, to the tiny bedroom. "Nan, are you still . . . Oh, dear," Caledonia said in a muffled voice. "I think . . . I think . . ." She moved in and bent over the bed.

"What is it?" Angela asked, craning her neck.

Nan lay motionless across the bed, still dressed in the clothing she had worn the night before.

"She's dead," Caledonia said. "Like she sat down, and just fell over backward there. Peaceful and serene . . . and just plain dead."

CHAPTER 16

"**A**RE YOU *sure* it was suicide, Lieutenant?" Caledonia asked.

Martinez sat in the Wingate living room, perched on the rose velvet chair, holding a small sherry. Angela was curled into a sad little knot on the couch, snuffling occasionally and mopping tears. The double funeral for the Churches had been hard on her supply of handkerchiefs.

Caledonia overflowed an easy chair, her black crepe caftan standing out in the dainty pastel surroundings like an ink blot dropped onto lightly tinted note paper. Stella, wearing a black crepe afternoon frock with a collar of handmade Belgian lace, sat stiffly in a straight chair near the door, her feet tucked demurely together beneath her; she was knitting, of course. Angela, peering up through a very damp handkerchief, found herself wondering, irrelevantly, if that charcoal gray garment was the same piece of work Stella had been patiently constructing now for several weeks—and who it was for. "Probably a relative," she thought. "Family's all Stella would take that much trouble for. How she can work at a time like this . . ." But to be fair, Angela noticed, rebuking herself for her flash of petty annoyance, today Stella frequently stopped her steady, clicking cadence to go back and count her stitches again, and for her that was a sure sign of inner turmoil.

"She took the whole bottle of sleeping pills, Mrs. Wingate," Martinez was saying in response to Caledonia's question. "It couldn't have been an accident. And she left a note—in her own handwriting, you'll remember." He took out a small notebook and cleared his throat as he read, *"Forgive me for the things I've had to do. You know why. Angela can explain. I've lived my life for Doc and now he's gone, and I'm so tired. You've been good friends and I've loved you.'"*

Caledonia nodded solemnly. "I guess it's clear enough."

"She really died of a broken heart," Angela said. "That's what it was. Oh dear . . ." She buried her face in her tiny handkerchief.

"Possibly so, Ma'am," Martinez said. "She'd lost the one thing she lived for, her husband. He was the center of her universe. The killings were for his sake, of course. She probably thought no more about them than—well, than she did about making the decision to move in here, into this sheltered environment, for her husband's sake. Everything she did was for him."

"In a way," Angela said, "she even got fat for his sake. To help keep the secret she thought would hurt him so much."

Martinez nodded. "And when he was gone, there wasn't anything left to go on living for. She just sort of—gave out."

Angela nodded. "She said she was tired . . . very tired . . . that last night I talked to her. She wasn't tense and upset—just tired and very, very sad. She didn't even mind talking about—you know—those movies. She said she'd never told anybody before, but she just chatted away—like she was talking about the weather."

"It's not really surprising," said Martinez, ever the philosopher. "There's a strange truth that's responsible for easily half our successful cases. People want to talk about themselves, about what they've done. Some people see their crimes as accomplishments and they want to brag—to get recognition. But even when they know perfectly well that talking about a crime will mean arrest and conviction, a lot of people can't seem to stop themselves. And everyone wants to explain *why* they did it. There's this universal urge to be understood."

"Don't you have rules about that?" Caledonia asked.

"The Miranda Rulings . . . Yes. We're supposed to be sure they know that talking about themselves can be dangerous. It's ironic, but sometimes it's all we can do to keep them quiet long enough to read them their rights."

Stella shook her head, her eyes on the dark gray yarn moving through her fingers. "I never understood the urge to confess. It doesn't make sense to me."

"Well, you ladies were also lucky, of course. You got to people in weak moments—Grogan, hurt and in the hospital; Marian Littlebrook, terrified by her husband's emotional explosion; Nan Church, worn out with worry about her husband, then suffering the terrible psychological letdown of his death. In each case, the mood was right . . . and you were there to be on the receiving end of perfectly human impulses to talk about things that shouldn't have been talked about. You've stumbled onto the secret behind a lot of successful police work."

"I'm not sure that it doesn't have something to do with our age," Angela said.

"Your age? You mean people trust you and talk to you because you're older . . ."

"Certainly not," she snapped. "I meant because *they* were older. The people we talked to. You may have noticed that older people love to talk about themselves. And hardly anybody wants to listen. It's a treat to get someone who wants to hear what they have to say. If you lived here, believe me you'd know; these people take full advantage of any chance to talk about themselves—and most of them overdo it."

"You could be right," Martinez said. "Perhaps I ought to bear that in mind when I'm questioning older witnesses."

"Nan really did it? She killed both of them? There's no mistake?" Caledonia said. "I still can't believe it."

"Oh yes, Mrs. Wingate. Believe it. She did it. Everything fit together, finally. The weapon she used, for instance. And the fact that she stopped knitting; she'd thrown her needles away, you see. And the timing on that morning Mrs. Piper was pushed down the stairs. Mrs. Church would never have joined the joggers ordinarily, not at her weight and with her heart condition. But you tell me she said she'd been out jogging—and on a damp, gray morning at that. Didn't you think at the time that was a ridiculous excuse for her being late to breakfast?"

"No," Angela said meekly. "I believed it. I thought she was just sort of responding to Mrs. Piper's invitation for someone to meet her and go jogging."

"She was. That invitation was apparently a pretty strong hint . . . I think the Piper woman may have approached Mrs. Church earlier suggesting the meeting and hinting at the blackmail. After all, it had worked well with the Littlebrooks. They started paying up. By saying she'd go jogging, Mrs. Piper was telling her next victim when and where to meet her. In the upper hallway to the door to the kitchen stairs—the ones the joggers always used—in the early morning, about jogging time.

"I'm not sure Mrs. Church set out for that appointment with any intention of paying. But on the other hand, I really don't think she set out with the intention of killing Mrs. Piper, either. It's possible that Mrs. Church just struck out at her—pushed her in a sudden burst of temper. After all, she couldn't count on Mrs. Piper's falling down the stairs, let alone her dying in the fall. That's a pretty uncertain method of murder, if you're planning to kill someone."

"What about Sweetie?" Caledonia asked.

"Well, from the number of wounds inflicted on Ms. Gilfillan . . . and from the choice of weapons—something right there at hand, but hardly something designed as a weapon—it's possible that Mrs. Church just lost her temper then, as well.

"The fact is, I'm not sure she ever planned to kill anyone. She was under a lot of pressure. Her bank account was almost down to zero and Medicare didn't cover her husband's care in the nursing facility . . . Anyway, she simply couldn't afford to go on paying blackmail. But I think that kind of pressure could make her explode with rage more easily than it could turn her into a calculating murderer."

"How could Sweetie do that to her," Angela said softly.

"To all of them," Caledonia added furiously.

Martinez shrugged. There were some questions for which even he had no answers.

Caledonia gritted her teeth. "I say—and you can tell me I'm out of line if you want to—I say there are times law and order should defer to individual human needs."

"No, Mrs. Wingate," Martinez said. "That would be anarchy. There's always a way to operate within the law—people just won't take the time to use it. They hesitate to talk to the police or the district attorney—they keep trying to shortcut the process. That's what murder really is—a shortcut—and never justifiable. Never."

"But Lieutenant," Stella said, entering the conversation once more, "surely you don't believe that applies to Nan. Why, you asked us yourself to contact her and tell her."

"You gave her two hours' lead time so she could run away," Caledonia said.

"No, ladies, You're mistaken. I would never have done that."

"But Lieutenant," Angela said, "you sent us down . . . You told us . . ."

"I send you to Mrs. Church," Martinez said in a firm voice, "thinking you might get the truth from her. Certainly she'd talk to you more easily than to me. It was in the back of my mind that you might even persuade her to make a full confession to me. You see, I had no real evidence—nothing the district attorney would have been happy about taking into court. Nothing I'd like to make an arrest on."

Stella's clicking needles flew faster. "I thought you were being *sympathetic,*" Stella said. "I thought you understood the desperation . . . But you were just thinking about whether or not you could go to court."

"I'm sorry to disillusion you, Ma'am." Martinez said. He said it sadly, with regret, Angela thought.

Stella seemed unimpressed. Her mouth drew tighter, the yarn fairly flew from the ball concealed in her tapestry bag, and her needles stuttered along with a sound like someone tapping urgently against a window pane. Caledonia turned to look at her friend and smiled. "Stella, you have the world's most expressive knitting needles. The click get louder when you're agitated, softer when you're at rest. Listen to them rattle now, Angela . . ."

Angela smiled as well, in spite of herself, her soggy Kleenex momentarily set aside. "Oh, Stella, now we can tell you're more annoyed than ever! That metallic click-clickety-click is . . . Stella, when did you change knitting needles?"

The clicking stopped for a moment, then began again, as fast as ever. "I don't believe I did," Stella said. "These are the ones I've always used."

"No they're not," Angela said. "Last week you had plastic ones. Bright pink. I couldn't help but notice them—you don't usually have anything bright-colored."

Stella shrugged and looked back down at her work. "Angela, you've made me miss my count." She stopped and began patiently counting the stitches already hanging from the right-hand needle. "Ten, twelve, fourteen, sixteen . . ."

"May I give you another sherry, Lieutenant?" Caledonia asked, flowing upward from her chair and rolling across the room, moving the decanter from one glass to another. "Angela?"

"Yes, please," Angela said, absently accepting the sherry and sipping it slowly as she searched her memory. Then she sat bolt upright and carefully set the glass aside. "Lieutenant," she began, "wasn't the stone set in that key clip you found by Paulette's body—wasn't that a moss agate?"

"Yes. You said it was Mrs. Church's."

"No . . . *not* Mrs. Church's," Angela said suddenly. "Yours, Stella. It was *yours.*"

"Now you've made me lose count again," Stella said crossly, shifting the right-hand needle so she could begin all over. "Two—four—six—"

"Well, wasn't it yours?" Angela said. "Stella, *you* killed Sweetie and Paulette, didn't you? You stabbed Sweetie with your steel knitting needles. Then you threw them away and used plastic needles till you could slip out and buy more . . ."

Stella patiently laid her knitting into her lap. "Angela, metal needles feel better in my hands, that's all. I tried the plastic, but they didn't slip through the yarn right. Not the way I'm used to. That's all."

"But you bought new needles." Angela darted over to Stella and tipped the pair of needles up from her lap so the other two could see the shiny knobs at the top. "Look at that steel gleam. Here by the ocean, metal dulls and corrodes fast. People have to wash their cars every week, just from the salt and sand in the air. Only new metal shines that way."

Stella managed a small smile. "Exactly. I *did* throw the old ones away—because they were corroded. Those rough spots in the metal can pick at delicate yarn."

"But how do you explain the key clip?" Angela pressed on. "That agate was yours, Stella."

"Nonsense," Stella said, digging down into her knitting bag and retrieving a key attached to a little clip. "Here's mine." She held up a clip set with a large onyx.

"What is all this?" Martinez said, suddenly less sure of himself. "Mrs. Wingate, I thought you identified the key clip we found as belonging to Nan Church."

"I thought it did," Mrs. Wingate said, worriedly. "But I can't really remember—maybe it didn't, after all."

"Oh, Cal, don't you remember the system?" Angela said. "You told me about it at the time . . ."

"Oh! Yes, of course!" Light dawned on the Wingate brow. "It was easily five years ago, you see . . . but I *do* remember. Lieutenant, I had a system for choosing which clip went to which person. Each stone had the same first letter as the initial of the girl I gave it to. Angela—amethyst . . . Tootsie—turquoise . . . Marian—moonstone . . . Mine was C—a carnelian. You see?"

"But that's not right," Stella interrupted. "You certainly never told *us* that."

"She told *me*," Angela insisted. "*I* knew it."

"But not all the stones fit our initials. I mean, how about that garnet she gave Sweetie!"

"It was a G!" Angela said. She began to stride about the room, lecturing like a high school debater. "G for garnet, G for Gilfillan. Find me a way that M for moss or A for agate fits either 'Nan' or 'Church.'"

"A for agate and A for Anne," Stella said. "'Nan' is merely a vulgar nickname for 'Anne,' isn't it? Don't you remember that King Henry VIII called Anne Boleyn 'Nan'? I seem . . . It seems to me . . ." She was frowning in an effort to concentrate, but her voice seemed vague and her sentence trailed off thinly.

"Oh, Stella," Angela said, "what nonsense. You *know* Nan's real name is 'Nancy'—not 'Anne'."

"I remember now!" Caledonia turned to Martinez, who was watching unblinkingly, poised on the edge of his chair. "I remember—I had a terrible time with N and C—so I got her mother-of-pearl."

"M?" said Martinez.

"N!" Angela said triumphantly, "N for nacre—N for Nan. Do you see?"

"But mine is an onyx," Stella said, holding it aloft. Her voice was tight and high, her lips thinned with tension.

"No, it can't have been," Angela said. "That makes no sense at all. You must have bought that for yourself, to replace the one that was torn away when Paulette fell. But you got yourself the wrong kind of stone. Because you didn't know about the initials."

"I remember, too. I thought of giving her a sapphire," Caledonia murmured irrelevantly. "S for Stella. But the others were only semi-precious stones, and it seemed out of proportion. So I gave her . . ."

"The moss agate!" Angela finished for her in a rush. "A for agate, A for Austin!"

"No!" Stella stood up and began to back up in tiny steps, but her shoulders touched the wall and she had to stop moving back. Her hands, straining like claws, gripped her knitting as though it were a life vest thrown to a woman overboard. "No. You're wrong. Nan did it—she killed them both. You told me about her dreadful life. She had so much to hide. What reason would *I* have to kill a blackmailer? My family tree is there for anyone to see—my family background is a matter of record. I have lived my life in a way to make them proud of me—there's nothing . . . nothing . . . Everybody knows who *I* am and what *I* stand for. There's been no hint of scandal in my family for generations." Her words were spilling over each other and tears were rolling down her narrow, pinched face.

"Did she threaten you?" Martinez said gently. He got to his feet and moved to stand facing her. "Did she say she'd found something that would create a scandal? Hurt your reputation? Your family's good name?"

Stella was weeping freely, making no attempt to put a handkerchief to her flowing eyes, holding the knitting up with both hands, between herself and Martinez, like a protective shield. "Oh, you *do* understand. You *do* see. She said . . . Sweetie said she'd found out I was . . . was adopted. You see, I'm not a Chambers by blood. That's my family, you know. The Chambers of Albany. But she found out . . ."

"That's not so terrible, Mrs. Austin," Martinez said gently. "A lot of people are adopted. What did it matter if the Chambers weren't your real mother and father?"

"But she *was*. She *was* my real mother," Stella said. Her quavering voice had dropped to a whisper. "Don't tell. Please don't tell. I wasn't . . . that is, my mother had . . . she'd married my father after I was on the way. And he wasn't even my father. You see? It was some boy she knew. So I'm not really a Chambers at all. I'm not . . ." The tears coursed freely again and her voice choked on the words, "I'm not legitimate."

"Oh, Beanie," Caledonia said, sighing. "How could you have thought that would matter to us?"

Stella did not seem to hear her. Her eyes were still fixed on Martinez's sympathetic face. "Nobody else ever knew. Nobody— not ever. Only Mummy and Daddy. They told me never to tell. From the time I was a little, little girl . . . And I promised. I promised nobody would ever know . . . I had to keep my promise, do you see? I promised, and I had to keep my promise."

"If it was you who stabbed Sweetie, then it was you who met Paulette and pushed her down the stairs," Angela murmured from behind Martinez, who had now moved close to Stella, face to face. He could have touched her, but he did not. They looked almost like old friends saying a lingering goodbye.

Stella nodded again. "You were right about it all," she said, looking pleadingly at Martinez, tears still running bright on her withered cheeks. "You said it all happened by accident, and you were right, Lieutenant, I *didn't* mean to. Just as you said. It just— happened. I was so angry . . . so angry . . . Not the first time. The first time I was just—stunned. She talked to me that first time in the garden. She said she had gone through public records, that the dates of my parent's marriage and my birth were all wrong—too close. She said she found adoption records . . . she said she could prove Mummy had lied on my birth certificate. Because Daddy adopted me legally, you see. And if I really was his child, he wouldn't have had to do that. But Mummy had put his name on the birth certificate . . ."

"Mrs. Austin, there could be dozens of reasons why a child's real father might put through a legal adoption. It needn't have meant . . ."

"Oh, but people would have guessed," she corrected him urgently. "And even if they hadn't guessed . . . it would have been too embarrassing. Too embarrassing. She said she'd see me out on Beach Lane the next morning—to set up terms. *Terms.* She wanted me to pay blackmail."

"Why didn't you just pay her? The others did," Angela asked. "She'd have kept the secret then. Why kill her?"

"But *she* knew," Stella explained, lecturing, as if to a stubborn child. "I told you. I promised Mummy and Daddy that *nobody* would ever find out. *Nobody.* I met her at the top of the steps to the beach. She asked me if I'd brought money. But while we were talking . . ." Her voice dropped again. "Oh, this is so awful . . . She—she—"

"Go on, Mrs. Austin," Martinez nudged her gently with his voice.

"She laughed. She laughed at me. For caring so much. She laughed at Mummy and Daddy. I had my knitting bag with me . . . I must have reached into it. I don't remember. She thought I was getting out money and she came very close to me . . . and said 'I knew you'd pay up. You're just like all the others' and she laughed. That's when I hit her—and all of a sudden there was blood. I had hit her with the needles. They . . ."—she shuddered slightly—"they went *in,* you see. And then I knew—I knew that was the way to take care of everything. So I just went on and on . . . She fell away from me—down that hill to the beach. And I came back home here. I threw the needles away on my way back. I couldn't bear to look at them."

"I suppose you pushed Paulette the same way? In a fit of temper?" Caledonia said. Unlike Angela, who was standing now, near to and just behind Martinez, Caledonia had sunk back into her chair and was taking deep, slow breaths to compose herself.

Stella looked at Caledonia as little as she looked at Angela. Her eyes were still fixed on Martinez' coal black eyes. "It was an accident, too. It was. She was in the garden that day Sweetie told me. Who'd have thought she heard us? Oh, I was angry, all right. I *had* to stop them. Mummy would die, if anyone knew . . . and I promised her and Daddy. I couldn't let anybody tell—why, it would kill her."

"Hasn't your mother already passed away?" Martinez said gently.

Stella paused. "Yes. Of course. I meant . . . I only meant . . ." She released the knitting with one blue-veined hand and passed the fingertips gently over her eyes. "I'm a little confused. I'm not sure . . . I'm not sure what I meant. What did I say?"

Martinez reached out and put a soft hand on her arm. She flinched, but she did not pull away. "Mrs. Austin, we'd better go and see about all this. Don't be afraid. I'll take care of you." He put the tiniest bit of pressure on her elbow, turning her toward the cottage door. "Come along . . ."

"Thank you, Lieutenant, " she said. "You know, I shall be grateful to get it all cleared up at last. It's really been a terrible burden."

At the door she hesitated and turned back. Martinez waited, his hand still softly on her arm.

"Caledonia . . . Thank you for your hospitality," Stella said in a formal, dazed voice. "Angela, I never meant for Nan to take the blame, you know. But she was dead. It really didn't matter."

"Your family's dead, too," Angela said, her little spine rigid, her mouth set. "Nan's reputation matters every bit as much as their good name. You wouldn't let *them* be maligned, but you would let us think that *Nan*—"

Stella turned to Martinez. "She doesn't understand," she sighed. "Oh, dear . . ."

"Well," he soothed, "you'll tell me all about it, and I'll explain it so she does understand. Believe me."

"I believe you, Lieutenant," Stella said, and smiled fully for the first time. "I believe you." Martinez guided her out the door and up the walk toward the main building. Angela and Caledonia heard her small voice as it faded away—"I *do* believe you. Yes, I do."

There was a pause in the ensuing silence, and at last Caledonia hauled herself upward again, out of her chair. "Sit down, Angela, sit down. That was smart work, girl, and I propose to toast you . . . Join me in another sherry?"

Angela wordlessly held out her glass.

CHAPTER 17

ANGELA, CALEDONIA, and Lieutenant Martinez met again less than one week later. It was sherry time (or so Caledonia had declared it), and the shadows were beginning to edge through the garden, reaching up to caress the main building. The lowering sun sent warm gold through Caledonia's sheer drapes and painted the rose velvet on Angela's chair a soft apricot.

"Stella's mad, isn't she, Lieutenant?" Caledonia said as she poured the sherry from her exquisite cut glass decanter. "Poor, poor old Beanie. The last person in the world I'd have said was unbalanced."

"It's not for me to judge her mental condition," Martinez answered. 'But if you want a guess?" he added, in a more expansive tone.

"Of course we do," Angela said. "You're off duty now, don't forget. You can behave as though we were friends. Or rather— well, I hope we are friends. So . . ."

"I think she'll be declared unfit to stand trial," Martinez said. "That was very clever detective work, Mrs. Benbow, and I've wanted to tell you so. Your guesses were made up of little things—but by sheer intuition, you put together a pattern that made sense. It fit all the loose ends together."

263

"Like knitting them together," Caledonia said wryly.

Martinez inclined his head slightly and took a sip of his sherry.

"So what will happen now, Lieutenant?" Caledonia said. "Will Stella go to the state hospital, if the judge finds her incompetent?"

"I think so. I hope so."

"Lieutenant," Angela said. "I thought you had no sympathy for anyone who murdered."

Martinez shrugged. "I am, I fear, human. I can't govern emotion. I felt sorry for Mrs. Church even when I thought she was a killer. I feel sorry for Mrs. Austin, even though I know she murdered simply to protect her family's name.

"At any rate," he want on, "the matter will be closed, officially. The fact that Mrs. Church committed suicide needn't be made public, I think. Incidentally, her note—about the 'terrible things' she'd done—referred, obviously, not to murder but to her career in films."

"I hope you mean that nobody needs to know about those movies," Caledonia said.

"What movies, Mrs. Wingate?" Martinez said poker-faced. "I don't know what you're talking about. Excellent sherry, by the way," and he smiled. Caledonia smiled back and poured him another little glass full.

"Wait," Angela said. "What about the Littlebrooks?"

"What about them?" Martinez asked.

"Well, aren't you going to do anything about them?"

"About *what* about them, Ma'am? I have no hard evidence that they were guilty of a crime—I only know what you told me—but secondhand evidence is not admissible in court, you know. Oh, if he were younger and healthy, I might see what could be done about investigating your Mr. Littlebrook. The SS did terrible things—they were totally ruthless. You can be sure *they* would have persecuted a senile old man."

"Are you saying you forgive . . ."

"Ah now, Mrs. Benbow," Martinez said. "Forgiveness is something else again. He's not a person I would ever accept as my friend. I thank you for asking me to drop by," he added to Caledonia and put his emptied glass down on a tiny pie-crust table by his elbow.

"Lieutenant," Caledonia said, surging to her feet to see him out. "You're a very nice young man. Do you know that?"

"Why, thank you, Mrs. Wingate." He took her hand and bowed over it with a continental flair. "You're a very special lady yourself."

Angela hopped to her feet. "That's all? You're just leaving like that? There isn't any more to this whole thing?"

"No more," he said, smiling. "It's over. You seem disappointed."

"Well, Lieutenant, the whole thing was frightening . . . awful . . . and sad. But in a funny way, I enjoyed it. And I enjoyed having you here. You—you're . . ." She picked her courage up. "You're *so* much like Gilbert Roland."

"Angela!" Caledonia was amused.

"It's true," Angela said. "Exactly like Gilbert Roland."

"I've meant to ask you about that, Ma'am. You mentioned it before. Just who *is* Gilbert Roland?"

Angela's mouth popped open in dismay. "You don't know? You never heard of . . ."

"This younger generation," Caledonia said, grinning. "An actor, Lieutenant. A Spaniard, I believe . . . or a Mexican. He was very handsome and—oh, you know, virile . . . oh-so-dashing . . . right on into his sixties. Dark hair, a little moustache, a slight accent . . . and always a wide leather brace on his left forearm."

"Oh *him*. I do remember him now—from the late late movies. Honestly, do I look like him?" Martinez asked Angela, and his grin was a little foolish.

"Not really," she said. "Not when you look so conceited. Only sometimes . . . in the right light."

He grinned widely. "Serves me right. I asked for that, didn't I? Now let me tell you something about you two ladies."

"Uh-oh," Caledonia said, pretending to brace herself.

"No—it's not bad. It's . . . I'm going to miss you two." He flashed his brilliant smile at Caledonia and bowed that graceful, courtly little bow. She nodded back, gratified. Then he turned to Angela and took her hand and kissed it most gallantly. And then on an impulse, he leaned down and kissed her cheek.

Angela blushed and dimpled up at him. The angle of her head, her three-cornered smile, her sideways glance were all pure Scarlett O'Hara. "Oh, Lieutenant . . ."

"You remind me so very much of my late grandmother," he said. "A real lady. Well, goodbye . . . I hope to see you both again one day," and he hurried out.

"His *grandmother?*" Angela was outraged. "His GRAND-MOTHER! Why that young . . ."

Angela's spluttering and Caledonia's sudden burst of laughter rang in the lieutenant's ears as he moved away up the path between the rows of roses, nodding in the October sunshine.

> *"I have heard the mermaids singing, each to each . . .*
> *We have lingered in the chambers of the sea*
> *By sea-girls wreathed with seaweed red and brown*
> *Till human voices wake us, and we drown."*
>
> from "The Love Song of J. Alfred Prufrock"
> by T. S. Eliot